AMERICAN AIRLINES' SECRET WAR IN CHINA

_ AMERICAN _
AIRLINES' SECRET
WAR IN CHINA

PROJECT SEVEN ALPHA WWII

LELAND SHANLE

Pen & Sword
AVIATION

First published in 2008 and reprinted in this format in 2016 by
Pen & Sword AVIATION
An imprint of
Pen & Sword Books Ltd
47 Church Street, Barnsley
South Yorkshire
S70 2AS

ISBN 978 1 47388 771 8

A CIP catalogue record for this book
is available from the British Library

Printed and bound in England
By CPI Group (UK) Ltd, Croydon, CR0 4YY

Pen & Sword Books Ltd incorporates the Imprints of Pen & Sword Aviation,
Pen & Sword Family History, Pen & Sword Maritime, Pen & Sword Military,
Pen & Sword Discovery, Pen & Sword Politics, Pen & Sword Atlas,
Pen & Sword Archaeology, Wharncliffe Local History, Leo Cooper,
Wharncliffe True Crime, Wharncliffe Transport, Pen & Sword Select,
Pen & Sword Military Classics, The Praetorian Press, Claymore Press,
Remember When, Seaforth Publishing and Frontline Publishing

For a complete list of Pen & Sword titles please contact
PEN & SWORD BOOKS LIMITED
47 Church Street, Barnsley, South Yorkshire, S70 2AS, England
E-mail: enquiries@pen-and-sword.co.uk
Website: www.pen-and-sword.co.uk

Contents

Dedication

To the Seven Alpha men of American Airlines

This book is dedicated to all the men and women of aviation, past, present and future; the airline trail blazers of the twenties and thirties, my grandfather William among them; the aviators who flew through the war torn skies over the past 100 years, my uncles Bob, Bill and Larry among them; and the fallen aviators, my uncle Larry among them. To the aviators catapulting from carriers, circling for hours on a tanker track, hovering over a hostile mountain peak; or shooting a localizer approach to a mountain-encircled airport, after flying all night; and of course, to the men and women on the ground who keep them in the air. The past and present is meaningless without a future; to the next generation of aviators, my children among them.

But mostly, this book is dedicated to my family, whom I literally dragged around the world in my pursuit of aviation: Leland, David, Kaitlyn, William – and especially Laura, the love of my life.

Chapter 1

Project Seven Alpha
19 June 1984

The Hawaiian sun had begun to set over the Pacific, casting long shadows across Honolulu International Airport. An American Airlines captain sat in the cockpit of his DC-10 Luxury Liner and watched as the sun started its journey below the horizon. On any other day in his life, this would have been a non-event. Not that he hadn't enjoyed, even reveled in the many passings of the sun he had witnessed. Sometimes he thought he could remember each one individually. He had always marveled how magical it was that a twice-daily event could hold such mystery, such diversity, as it unfolded so many times and in so many ways, right in front of him.

He had seen most of his sunrises and sunsets from the cockpits of aircraft. He had watched many from the ground, but to him, to truly experience a rise or set of the sun, you had to be in the air. You had to be a part of it. This sunset, he mused, was not only an announcement to the world that the day was done; it was a very private message to him that the biggest part of his life – his professional life – was coming to an end.

The best part of his life had been his family, but to say that flying had not been the most consuming part of his life would not be honest. When the sun rose again he would be sixty years old, the FAA's mandatory retirement age. *"Sixty!"* thought the captain. *"How can that be? My mind, my essence is unchanged – how can I be sixty?"*

He would watch the sun set, then rise, one more time as a professional line pilot, a wide body captain for American Airlines.

He'd still have his old Stearman biplane, the plane he'd learned to fly at the age of seventeen; it would be fun to putt around in it, but it would never be the same. No, like the day he had retired from the reserves as a naval aviator, this chapter in his life would be complete tomorrow when he landed in Dallas.

He contemplated all this as he watched a seagull effortlessly floating on the updraft created by the heat coming off the concrete tarmac. His meditative state was broken by the entry of the first officer and flight engineer into the cockpit. He turned and looked at the young flight engineer. He looked fifteen but was actually nineteen. *"I feel like him, not some sixty year old man"*, the captain thought.

He smiled, watching the FE slump into his seat. The younger man reached into his kit bag and instead of pulling out a manual or checklist, produced a small headset and what appeared to be a tape recorder. The FE slipped on the headphones and began to tap his fingers on his panel. The captain was smiling and watching the youngster when he noticed in his periphery that the first officer was holding something out to him.

The FO was 41 years old, handsome, of average height with blond hair and blue eyes. He wore his hair in military style, close-cropped, with a hint of grey around the temples. This was a milestone flight for him as well; it would be his last as a first officer. He would go to upgrade training for captain after this flight.

The captain turned and took what he assumed was the aircraft logbook. He slipped on his reading glasses, a humiliation to which he had succumbed ten years earlier. It was not the log book.

"What's this?" he asked the FO.

"Captain, your lovely bride thought you might like this," responded the FO.

On his lap sat a black leather scrapbook, stamped with the gold wings of a naval aviator and the silver wings of an American Airlines captain. Under the wings, in silver letters, also stamped into the leather, were the words, "An Aviator's Life." The captain quickly scanned a few pages of photos showing the aircraft and people he had known intimately; they always seemed to be intertwined. He stopped on an 8 x 10 of a motley-looking bunch standing in front of a DC-3, after an obviously hard night of drinking and carousing. Tears welled in his eyes.

Suddenly, the FO craned his head around and snapped to the FE: "What the hell is that noise, Wrench?"

The captain quickly wiped his eyes as he smirked to himself. Wrench was either an affectionate or derogatory term for flight engineer, depending on the inflection when delivered. It stemmed from the days when FEs were also mechanics. The FO was too young to have flown with a true wrench; they were all long gone. FEs in general would be gone soon too, as the industry moved back to two-man crews. The more things changed, the more they stayed the same – how true in the airlines.

The noise that seemed to truly disturb the first officer was a combination of the FE singing and the overshoot from the headset.

"What is that?" the FO demanded again.

"What?" responded the FE as he slid off the headset.

"That noise," countered the FO, pointing at the headset.

"It's 'Pulling Mussels from a Shell' by The Squeeze," retorted the FE with righteous indignation.

"It's what?" said the FO, shaking his head.

The captain slid out of his seat and patted the FE on the shoulder.

"Don't pay much attention to the first officer," he said. "His father said the same thing about rock and roll."

"Hey that's not fair," protested the FO.

"Oh, yes it is, my young first officer, because I'm the captain and I say so."

The Captain winked at the FE as he moved toward the cockpit door.

"I'll get the exterior pre-flight inspection tonight, Mr Engineer."

"Cool – thanks, Gramps," the FE said, smiling smugly at the FO while returning the headset to its previous position.

"That's Captain to you, numb-nuts!" snapped the FO with more than a hint of irritation.

The FE shrugged and cranked up the volume to his new Walkman.

"Aren't these Japanese toys the coolest?"

"Yeah, the coolest," said the Captain, pulling the cockpit door closed behind him.

The Captain stood on the tarmac and let the warm Pacific trade winds envelope him. Such a glorious day, he thought. How could it come to such a disastrous conclusion? Put to pasture. How could he ever fit into a normal life? *Normal.* He had to laugh; he didn't know normal. Normal to him had meant catapulting off the pitching deck of an aircraft carrier in search of other men – men he would have to kill before they killed him. Normal had meant weaving his way through the mountains encircling Mexico City, at night, with an engine on fire. No, he did not know normal. Even his working day wasn't normal. He was starting his day at sunset, and it would end at sunrise. He had never tasted normalcy and felt fortunate that he had not. *Thank God.* Just the thought of it made him feel sick.

He turned away from the sunset and faced his aircraft. What an incredible machine: the Douglas Corporation Model 10, series 30. Normal people called it a jumbo jet. What an insult. This "jumbo," lightly loaded, could climb out like a scalded dog, 30 degrees nose up, still accelerating, powered by three engines and producing a combined 156,000 pounds of thrust. In denial of its size, it handled like a dream, light and responsive on the controls. In the colors of American Airlines, brushed aluminum with red, white, and blue stripes, it was beautiful – certainly no jumbo.

Pilots called it a wide body. A wide body was the top of the commercial pilot pyramid. It was what the professional line pilots of all airlines aimed for. In a job where your hourly rate was factored by the weight of the aircraft you flew, it was where the greatest financial reward was as well.

"Paid by the pound," he often told his wife. "The same as if I was pickin' cotton."

She always responded that a cotton picker didn't spend half of every month on the road, nor did any of the cotton picker's co-workers die on the job.

To him, it wasn't about the money. He liked it and had no

intention of giving any back, but the money was not what made his blood run. It was the adventure of flying, going somewhere – Paris, England, Hawaii. It was the pleasure of sitting in Piccadilly, enjoying a cold beer – or a daiquiri on the beach, watching the moon rise over the Pacific. Now it was all coming to an end.

The brushed aluminum fuselage began to glisten in the evening sun, giving it a liquid appearance. He watched the red sun's reflection move down the fuselage. When it got to the midpoint, his mind flashed back to a different time, in this same place – a time when a red sun on an airplane meant something quite different. It meant war.

He gazed across to the Hickam Air Force Base side of the field. Even from here, he could see bullet holes in the façade of the old buildings. He looked toward Ford Island and Battleship Row, where he knew the USS *Arizona* lay on the bottom of Pearl Harbor, still leaking fuel oil, her crew entombed for eternity.

He looked back to the red sun on the fuselage and remembered the intense hatred that had burned in him, demanding retribution. He was surprised how easily the feeling returned, like an old friend – comfortable, familiar. *Vengeance!* It had been so long; literally a lifetime. Yet, the intensity of emotion had surged into him like the ocean into the sinking *Arizona*.

It was back, as if it was 1944 again, and he was still hunting the Imperial Japanese Navy in his F-6F Hellcat. The hunting had been good. He knew what the good Book said, but vengeance had been his – over and over again, and none had ever been enough. He had been an absolute killing machine, revenge his motivation, hatred his sustenance.

Then the war was over. For everyone it seemed, except him.

He closed his eyes and breathed in the trade wind. His old friend, hatred, slipped away, though in his mind's eye he still saw the flames. To him, fire had always and would always mean war. There had been so much of it: a black greasy smear slowly being consumed by orange as he hammered .50 caliber rounds into a doomed Japanese aircraft; on the water as ships burned, spreading fuel like molten pools of blood, consuming the crew as they desperately tried to swim away. The islands seemed to be perpetually on fire, flames of war fanned by a divine wind.

AMERICAN AIRLINES FLAGSHIP DC-3

Chapter 2

War
7 December 1941

Flames wrapped around the nacelle attaching the Pratt and Whitney R-1830 Wasp engine to the wing of an American Airlines DC-3. Due to the speed of the aircraft, the fire was flat against the aluminum skin, burning brightly like a welder's torch.

The Captain leaned forward so he could look past his young first officer's head. The FO was sitting sideways in his seat to lean over and tune the ADF* radio, which was located behind the captain's seat. He had heard enough reports on the sneak attack at Pearl Harbor. He tapped his toes to Glen Miller and sweetened up the reception.

Captain Dane "J.T." Dobbs of American Airlines poked his first officer on the knee and nodded out the side windscreen toward the right engine.

"Holy shit, number two's on fire!" the FO yelled over the din of flight.

He sat bolt upright, pressing his face against the side windscreen. Whirling around to face the captain, he was stunned to find him calmly winding the clock.

"Captain, what are you doing?" His voice betrayed his panic.

"I'm winding the clock." J.T. smiled calmly at the FO, who looked like he was passing a kidney stone. "Okay, my young first officer, what do ya say we put out that blow torch?"

"Absolutely," replied the FO, trying to regain his composure.

* Automatic Direction Finder

J.T. reached up, gripped the number two engine throttle and methodically began calling out the emergency procedure for an engine fire in flight.

"Throttle affected engine idle."

The young FO was still rattled; his attention was drawn out to the fire still burning in the right engine. Normally, the experienced J.T. would have just done the emergency procedures by himself, but a lesson was needed. He had to keep this kid in the fight – the FO had to learn to become an aviator, not just a pilot.

Captain: "Confirm I have the correct throttle," he said, louder than before.

The FO's attention was pulled back into the cockpit.

"What? Oh yeah," he said. "You got the right one – pull it!"

"Fuel mixture affected engine idle cut off."

The FO was half in, half out of the game. J.T. pulled him back again.

"Junior, confirm!"

FO: "Confirmed, confirmed!"

Captain: "Fuel selector off."

FO: "Fuel selector confirmed off."

The familiarity of the memorized emergency procedures calmed the first officer. He was back in the game. The first three steps of the checklist cut the fuel to the burning engine. The intensity of the flames decreased 60 percent with the stopped flow of high octane AVGAS. However, the fire did not go out. The heat had cracked the engine case, and now it was being fed by hot oil escaping from the crankcase.

Captain: "Propeller engine number two, feather."

FO: "Prop number two, feathered."

By feathering the propeller, the blades were turned sideways in the air stream, greatly reducing the drag and allowing the DC-3 to fly on one engine. Feathering also kept the propeller from rotating, thus freezing the engine and stopping the pumping of oil that fed the fire.

Captain: "Firewall shutoff valve engine number two, off."

FO: "Number two firewall shutoff valve, off."

The crew had shut off the fuel supply to the number two engine, preventing the flames from spreading or growing. They had configured the aircraft to fly. Now it was time to fight the remaining fire.

Captain: "Cowl flap engine number two, closed."

FO: "Cowl flap number two, closed."

Captain: "CO2 selector switch number two."

FO: "CO2 selected to number two."

Captain: "CO2 discharge handle, pull."

FO: " CO2 handle, pulled."

Carbon dioxide discharged into the engine nacelle. With the cowl flaps closed, air flow through the nacelle was cut off, allowing the invisible gas to smother the oil fire. The FO was again glued to his side windscreen.

"It's out! It's out!" shouted the young first officer. "Shit hot, skipper, the fire's out!"

Captain: "Engine fire checklist, complete."

FO: "Roger that, complete."

"Okay hot shot," said J.T., "run the checklist again. Make sure we didn't miss anything. Also, pull out the single engine approach checklist. I'm going to call the company in El Paso and tell them we're headed their way."

"Roger that, skipper."

The FO cheerfully set about his duties as if nothing had happened. His experienced captain smiled.

With the number two engine shut down and the fire out, the cockpit returned to a normal cadence. J.T. trimmed the DC-3 and began a slow descent; the aircraft would be unable to maintain its current altitude with an engine shut down.

The ADF airways followed valleys and mountain passes for just this reason. The airways were a system of radio beacons that sent out a continuous signal on a specific frequency. Air crews tuned in the frequency on the ADF radio. The presentation in the cockpit was a round dial with a simple needle, which always pointed to the radio station. It was attached by a pin and hovered over a compass card that was slaved to magnetic north. As the aircraft turned, the heading on the compass card would also turn, always showing the aircraft's heading in relation to north.

The needle always pointed to the radio station, giving the

crew a known bearing. No wind? Merely line up the needle and the compass heading with the nose as you go down the airway. To correct for wind, estimate the amount of drift with the plotter side of the MB4A computer, a circular slide ruler used to convert aviation-related numbers. The crew would put a heading correction into the estimated wind to hold the needle on the proper course. The ground rule was that the head of the needle or pointer fell, and the tail rose, if you offset either from your base course.

To hold the exact course, constant monitoring and corrections to headings were necessary. Along with maintaining the specific bearing on the charts, the minimum en route altitudes also had to be maintained – not only to avoid terrain but to ensure reception of the radio stations. The needle always pointed to the station. So, when closing on a station, they flew the head of the needle. When they passed the station, marked by the needle passing off either wing tip, they switched to flying the tail of it. Once the halfway point was estimated, they switched frequency to the next station. Exact location could be determined by triangulation, which used more than one station. The ADF routes were new, set up to allow flight into bad weather and at night. Pilots quickly realized they could also tune in commercial radio stations with their new toy when they didn't need it for navigation.

Today, they could fly visually. It was a beautiful day, and Captain Dobbs was not going to let an engine fire spoil it. He leveled the American Airlines DC-3 out at its single engine, drift-down altitude. He set the single engine cruise power setting and scanned his remaining engine's gauges. The cylinder head temperature was a little high, so he cracked the engine cowl flaps, just a bit, to allow airflow through the air-cooled cylinder heads. That done, he turned his attention to the day and its incredible beauty.

Guadalupe Peak was passing to their north. Because the silver AA bird was headed east, the peak was on J.T.'s side of the plane. He soaked in the pure joy of mechanized flight, of being able to see so many of nature's wonders in a single day – in a single life. He really did pity the rest of humanity. *Earthlings.*

Effortlessly, subconsciously, J.T. manipulated the controls with almost imperceptible smoothness – even under the current *in extremis* situation.

The FO nudged him out of his reverie with a question.

"Skipper, do you want me to find us an emergency divert field?"

"Nah, we'll be all right, Jon. El Paso is one of our stations – we'll head there. No use stranding ourselves in the desert."

The new FO said nothing. Jon Gaus was a tall, lanky Missouri boy with wide shoulders and a young man's waist; his uniform hung on him as if it were still on a rack. He had brown hair, green eyes – he was an average Joe.

J.T. could tell that young Jon was not particularly happy with his decision, but to J.T. it wasn't a big deal. Flying, to him, was about calculated risk. Granted, there was a lot to manage, but to a man like J.T. that was a huge part of the reward of aviation. Right now, the risk of landing at an unfamiliar field in unknown condition, without facilities, far exceeded the risk of continuing on to El Paso. He had flown mail for years in the twenties and thirties. To him, this was a non-event. However, he could tell that his first officer did not share his ease of mind. He leaned over to the right side of the cockpit.

"Hey Jon, don't sweat it." J.T. winked. "I've got thousands of hours running mail in single-engined aircraft. I never had an incident."

Of course, that reassuring statement depended on one's interpretation. J.T. had, in fact, dead-sticked aircraft back to earth with failed engines quite a few times in the early, heady days of airmail. Back in those days, pilots planned their own routes and created their own approaches. While you could never eliminate the risk, you could manage it to an acceptable level. Having a plan was the best way to start.

Admittedly, J.T.'s acceptance level had changed over the years as the technology and experience of the fledgling industry grew. What had not changed was that he always left himself an out, an option, another chance to survive.

He had no intention of "going west" – dying – like so many of his friends. The thought of auguring in and becoming biological garbage mixed into the metallic wreckage of an aircraft held no glory for him. He held life too dearly to sacrifice it due to a careless or flawed decision. In the duality that was his existence, he lusted for the excitement of life far too much to ever walk away from the risk and reward of flight.

To J.T., the true aviators felt this same calling. There were many pilots, but not all of them were aviators. A pilot might fly an airplane to make a buck; an aviator flew it as a way of life. Managing the risk safely, to him, would always be a byproduct of professionalism. If you kept your shit together under duress, you would survive to fly another day.

If nothing else, Captain Dane "J.T." Dobbs of Soddy-Daisy, Tennessee was a survivor. He had grown up on a small farm, dreaming of adventure. World War I provided it. He had survived the Great War, flying as a fighter pilot with Eddie Rickenbacker in the 94th Aero Squadron, the Hat in the Ring. Then barnstorming, mail, finally landing with American Airlines in the very beginning.

He had never flown as a copilot. In fact, for most of his flying years, he was alone in open cockpits. It wasn't arrogance or nonchalance that young Jon saw across the cockpit. It was confidence, self assurance, and a healthy dose of experience. With all that he had seen and done in twenty-three years of flying, an engine fire when he had another engine that worked, was truly insignificant.

He would leave himself an out, as always. He would go the long way to El Paso, valley to valley just in case. If the good engine let go, he'd find a place to land. He glanced at his young copilot and smiled. He'd learn. *Learn, quit or die.* Which he chose would be up to him.

The true blessing, so far on this trip, was not that the fire went out or that the number one engine continued to purr smoothly. The true blessing was that none of the passengers had noticed.

"You want a direct heading, skipper?" Jon asked.

"Nah, we're going valley to valley."

"That will add a lot of time, Captain!"

The experienced captain glanced over at his squirming first

officer with a tad of irritation. He was done with explaining his every decision.

"Without a doubt, Jon."

Their single engine landing had been routine at El Paso Airport. The wind was calm, the normally dust-blown El Paso afternoon quite pleasant. J.T. had got the passengers settled down in the old wooden terminal and called the company for a rescue aircraft. Now he was relaxing, tipped against the terminal in a rickety ladder-back chair. Jon stood between him and the DC-3, glancing over his shoulder at the burned-out engine. He fidgeted a while, then finally spoke.

"Captain, sorry I, ah, got a little out of trim back there."

J.T. pushed his hat back and righted the chair.

"You did fine, Jonny."

"Yeah, sure. I was a babbling idiot."

J.T. held up his hand. "You'll learn."

Jon turned and looked again at the charred engine nacelle.

"Well, I hope so, skipper." He eased back around to face J.T. "You gotta tell me one thing…the clock."

J.T. stood up. "The clock?"

"Yeah, the damn clock, I mean we're a flying blow torch and you're winding the clock!"

Captain Dobbs of American Airlines allowed a smirk.

"First, do no harm," he said.

Jon looked confused. "What?"

"Hippocratic oath. Look, when things start getting a little out of trim, the last thing you want to do is make it worse."

Jon looked up. "Wind the clock?"

J.T. nodded. "Beats shutting down the wrong engine."

They watched a shiny DC-3 in AA colors on approach.

"Why didn't we land?" asked Jon.

"Don't compound one emergency by turning it into two, Jon."

"I don't follow, boss."

J.T. nodded toward the passengers, who had begun filing out of the terminal at the sound of the approaching aircraft. Among them were an elderly couple and a young mother with her infant.

"How long do you think they would have lasted at an uninhabited divert field if it took a while to find us?" asked J.T. "It was an option, but only a last one. We went down the valleys just in case."

The arriving DC-3 taxied to the tarmac, revved its left engine and pivoted on the right main mount brake, swinging the tail toward the terminal door and shutting down both engines as it came to a halt.

Captain Charles Henry Brennan Jr. was first out the door. He was the same age as J.T., average in every way except for his cutting blue eyes. His young first officer, Trey, slid out next: blond, taller and thinner than Charles Henry, but with the same cutting eyes. He was, in fact, Charles Henry Brennan the Third – Trey for short. His father ambled up to J.T.

"How'd the new guy do?"

"Oh, I was wetting all over myself," said J.T. "It's a good thing he was on board."

Charles Henry turned toward the burned-out engine.

"Yeah, sure," he said. "Let's go."

Standing under the damaged engine was a fireplug of a man in his late thirties or early forties. He wore a perfect crew cut and held a stub of a cigar clenched tightly between his teeth.

"You burn up another one of my engines, Cappy?" he snarled.

"'Fraid so, Chief," J.T. replied with a shrug.

Charles Henry nodded to the rescue bird, and the four pilots slunk away as the chief began to spit out epithets in several languages.

"J.T., you hear about Pearl?" asked Charles Henry.

"Yeah, a couple of hours ago on the ADF."

"It's gonna be a shit storm."

"Without a doubt," said J.T. "You'd better get David into an American Airlines cockpit soon, or he'll get drafted."

"He doesn't want to fly. That's fine with me – one less thing to worry about. We'll send him to college; make him an accountant or something."

"Shit, Charles Henry – that's like a death sentence!"

"For you and me, but as Laura likes to point out, not everyone likes hurtling through the heavens like a madman."

J.T. shook his head. "I pity them."

The two young FOs were close in trail of the captains, engaged in their own conversation. Jon shook his head.

"Pissing himself my butt, Trey. He just sat there – "

Trey cut him off.

"Yeah, I know – winding the damn clock."

As they climbed into the DC-3, Charles Henry turned to J.T.

"You want it?" he asked.

J.T. nodded and turned to the youngsters.

"Come on, there, Jon. We're driving."

They moved toward the cockpit as the passengers struggled awkwardly into their seats. Once there, they ran an abbreviated checklist and started both engines. Jon called the company to get the route clearance as J.T. taxied the aircraft toward the active runway, making the slight S-turns necessary to see where he was going. The DC-3 was a tail-dragger. That meant the tail literally dragged on the ground, sitting atop a little tail wheel. This caused the nose to sit high in the air. The configuration was good for landing on grass, dirt or rough fields in general, which many of the fields of the day were, but it reduced over-the-nose visibility.

Jon got clearance for takeoff as they rounded the corner onto the runway. J.T. continued rolling and pushed the props to full pitch and the throttles to takeoff power. He fine-tuned the power to forty-two inches of manifold pressure and nodded to Jon.

"Okay, you got it," he said. "Take us to Dallas."

Jon looked sideways at J.T., nodded and took the controls.

"I got it," he replied.

The DC-3 rose effortlessly into the air. Jon eased into a right-hand 15-degree angle of bank and headed east as the sun set in the west.

"You got good hands, junior," quipped J.T.

A SECTION OF SPAD S.XIIIs OVER FRANCE

Chapter 3

Flashback
24 September 1918

Dawn patrol over the trenches of France. A lone section of SPAD model S.XIII fighters of the 94th Aero Squadron floated lazily at 18,000 feet. The two aircraft had been airborne for an hour and a half; they were nearing the end of their patrol. The mid-morning sun shone brightly on the mirror image biplane fighters. Each had a mottled, green camouflage paint scheme. Added to the green were vertical red, white, and blue stripes on the tail, signifying that it was from an American squadron.

The SPADs had twenty-seven foot wingspans and were 20 feet long. The two wings of the SPAD were close together compared with other fighters of the day. A stout, flat-faced fuselage held the single, 200 horsepower, Hispano-Suiza 8B engine, which was mated to a six-foot long wooden propeller. Two-thirds of the way down the tapering fuselage, Uncle Sam's red, white, and blue top hat was painted with a black ring around it. It signified the squadron motto: Hat in the Ring.

As the fuselage narrowed to a point, a highly swept vertical tail rose from it at a 30-degree angle. The horizontal tail, or stabilizer, was thin and compact like the wings. A tail skid, a simple piece of curved wood that kept the tail from coming into contact with the ground, completed the assembly. The fighter sat on a fixed undercarriage of two wheels that were attached under the pilot but swept forward, putting the wheels just aft of the propeller. Armed with two 7.7 millimeter, Vickers synchronized machine guns, the SPAD had deadly fire power.

The compact fighter looked deceptively solid. In fact, it was constructed, like all the fighters of the day, of a wooden frame covered with doped, or glued, cloth. It was all held together with wood struts and metal bracing wires.

There were two schools of thought in fighter aircraft design. One held that maneuverability was the key to success in the air. The other held that speed was the key to survival. The SPAD S.XIII was built for speed.

Clad in leather flight gear head to toe, the lead pilot turned to face his wingman. He wore a tight, leather helmet and heavy, glass goggles. Around his neck was a flowing white silk scarf. His face was the only exposed area of his body, and it held a large grin. He pointed to his eyes, then held up four fingers signaling that he had four enemy aircraft in sight. Then he patted himself on the back, signaling: "Follow me."

First Lieutenant J.T. Dobbs slowly rolled left, away from his wingman, until he was inverted, or upside down. He influenced the nose by easing the control stick back toward his lap, but mostly he let the heavy engine pull the aircraft toward the earth and the enemy. Second Lieutenant Charles Henry Brennan Jr. matched the lead aircraft's maneuver exactly, flying his own with smooth precision. The pair pounced in perfect formation upon their prey.

Below them, an unsuspecting division of German fighters continued on their course. The four aircraft were Fokker DR-1 (V 5) tri-wing fighters. Smaller than their American foes, the black Fokkers cruised along, blissfully unaware that they were being stalked.

The Fokker's top wing was 4 feet shorter than the SPAD's; each sequential wing was a little shorter than the one above it. A fourth small wing was between the fixed wheels under the bottom, main wing. Their wings were also staggered, meaning the top, longest wing was furthest forward. It was attached by two thick end struts at the tips, and two V-struts attached at the fuselage. Approximately six inches further aft, and attached at the top of the squared off fuselage, was the middle wing. The third main wing was attached to the bottom of the fuselage and to the middle wing at the tip, utilizing the same thick wooden strut as the top wing. There were no external bracing wires.

The fuselage was rounded at the forward engine nacelle, then squared-off aft of the cockpit. It tapered down as it moved aft and was 2 feet shorter than a SPAD. A large, triangular, horizontal tail joined the flat, upper surface of the fuselage. Its vertical tail was a rounded surface that looked like the top part of a club in the suit of clubs from a deck of playing cards. The entire stabilizer moved, instead of incorporating a rudder. Its surface was painted white with a black Maltese cross in the center. There were white squares with the same crosses on the fuselage and wings; the rest of the aircraft was painted black.

An eight-foot propeller, powered by a 110-horsepower, Oberursal UR II rotary engine, provided thrust. The engine actually spun on its mount, allowing a fixed half-cowl to control the temperature. The half-enclosed cowl on the flat, front surface had two small cooling holes onto which the ground crew had painted eyes and brows. From a straight-on pass, the DR-1 had a menacing face, like a medieval mask. Above the face were two 7.92 millimeter, LMG 08/15 machine guns. The DR-1 was built to maneuver.

The section of SPADs fell out of the sun toward the black Fokkers, executing a maneuver called a split S. The maneuver involved reversing their course by doing a vertical half-circle. Base course for the SPADs had started on a northern heading, the DR-1s had passed below them going south. Halfway through their circle, pointed straight at the earth, the SPADs, at full power, reached redline speed. First Lieutenant Dobbs was feeling four times the force of gravity as he pulled his nose through the bottom of the maneuver, thus changing his course to match the southern heading of the DR-1s. He could have pulled more g but wanted to ease it enough to arrive behind and slightly below the Germans, who were still 500 feet below his attacking flight.

Effectively using the sun for cover, the Americans converted to the seven o'clock position. As they emerged from the glare of the sun behind the DR-1s, they unmasked. The Germans saw them and reacted instantaneously from their tactical formation. The overall leader of the division pulled up into a steep climb. The section leader, slightly offset to the right and aft of the lead, began a climbing, right-hand turn. Each of the wingmen was on the outside of his respective lead. Neither followed their lead. Instead, they each did a max performance evasive turn, level with the horizon.

Inexperienced fighter pilots did not like to fight in the vertical; it was unnatural. The rough and unbalanced manner in which they handled their aircraft left no doubt that they were new. Rookie fighter pilots often showed up in theater with less than fifteen hours total flight time as a pilot. Thus, they would be easy prey and could wait.

The two experienced DR-1 pilots did exactly what they should have done normally. Lieutenant Dobbs jumped the division leader on the left; Lieutenant Brennan took the section leader on the right.

The Fokker DR-1 was the best climbing fighter in theater. Its three main wings and one semi-wing created an incredible amount of lift. Unfortunately, with it came a lot of induced drag, a byproduct of generating lift. The practical result was that while the DR-1 could out-climb and out-turn any other fighter, it was slow by comparison. An added problem was that the underpowered UR II engine did not accelerate the aircraft well, so that once it got slow – unless it nosed over – it stayed slow.

The vertical counter normally would have been the correct one. In this case, however, the DR-1 pilots had not seen the split S maneuver due to the angle of the sun. In the descending vertical move, the SPAD pilots had used gravity to accelerate. They had traded altitude for airspeed.

Seeing the SPADs for the first time below them, the Germans assumed they had climbed to engage and consequently were slow. Their counter-tactic would be to out-climb the Americans, thus neutralizing the threat. Once they gained adequate separation, they would then roll in on the SPADs from their altitude advantage. The superior turning ability of the DR-1 would allow them to quickly turn the table on their adversary.

But unknown to them, the SPADs had a 38 knot speed advantage over the DR-1s. They used the kinetic energy to climb with the DR-1s, trading the airspeed back for altitude. Looking over his shoulder, the shocked division leader realized his fatal mistake and, reacting out of survival instinct, put on a maximum performance left turn. It didn't work – he was slow now. At 75 knots, the aircraft shuddered but didn't turn well. Dobbs had his SPAD at its maneuvering speed of 105 knots. He anticipated the German's turn and pulled his nose to where he knew the DR-1 was going as he armed the twin Vickers synchronized machine guns. The SPAD was at 100 feet and closing. At 80 feet, he opened fire. The heavy, 7.7 millimeter rounds were cam-synchronized to pass between the spinning propellers. This caused them to shoot at a reduced rate of fire, but the solid weight of each bullet more than made up for the rate loss.

The twin Vickers were lethal to both the fragile aircraft and the pilot. At 80 feet, Dobbs did not miss. Every round seemed to impact the DR-1 or disappear into its fuselage. The German desperately pulled into a nose-low break turn, trying to use gravity to regain life-giving airspeed. Dobbs matched the move while continuing to hammer 7.7 millimeter rounds into the engine and cockpit. Closing to 50 feet, Dobbs eased his engine throttle to idle. He was now saddled up, in the slang of fighter pilots, pumping the throttle to maintain his position.

He was scoring multiple hits; oil was streaming from the cowl down the side of the German aircraft. In the DR-1, the pilot sat high, his upper body was completely exposed – not that the fabric would even slow a bullet down. It was psychological; he had lost his edge, terrified by his sudden vulnerability. The German began to panic, aggressively jerking his control stick back and forth in an attempt to escape certain death. His Fokker writhed as if in pain, but thanks to the short duration of the inputs, he never left Dobbs' gun sight. Suddenly, the German went limp and was blown aft by the force of the 80-knot wind, his left arm flailing in the slipstream. Black, streaming oil was now mixing with crimson blood. Dobbs continued to fire.

Mercifully, the engine finally exploded, engulfing the cowl in orange flame, and the aircraft began a death spiral to the earth below. Behind it trailed a long, black funeral plume.

Dobbs did not linger after his kill. Down to 80 knots, he was now vulnerable. He snap-rolled and inverted again, pulling into another split S from 16,000 feet to get his airspeed back. He was heads up, looking for the third Fokker. He glanced over to see his own wingman finish off the section lead. With his SPAD's nose pointed straight down and his throttle pushed all the way forward, he quickly had his airspeed back. With a tally-ho on the third DR-1, now in front of him and 300 feet lower, he pulled hard through the bottom of the split S in pursuit of his quarry.

Obviously, the inexperienced DR-1 pilot had lost sight of the fight. He was rocking his wings back and forth looking for his lead. Dobbs closed the distance rapidly. The terminal rookie saw him coming and began a futile attempt to dive away. A 30-knot advantage in top speed allowed the SPAD to continue to close. The young German glanced behind him, horrified to see the SPAD closing in for the kill. Its wheels seemed to transform into fangs as it got closer – he was frozen with fear.

Because the DR-1 was not maneuvering, Dobbs opened up at 200 feet with his twin Vickers. A single round from a short, three-second burst ripped through the soft flesh of the rookie's neck, creating a puff of pink as it exited, finding the fuel tank located in front of him. Instantaneously, the entire DR-1 was consumed by flame. Dobbs pulled off and watched the fireball fall to the earth. The intensity of it captivated him. The pyre that had once been an aircraft and a man plummeted to the earth below, shedding flaming parts.

Still rolled in a left, 30-degree angle of bank turn, the hair suddenly stood on the back of Dobbs' neck. "What am I doing?" he thought. "I'm in the middle of a fight – where's that fourth DR?"

The thought had not completed formulating in his mind when he first felt, then saw with his periphery, the fourth Fokker DR-1 slash through his top right wing. Looking behind him as Lieutenant Brennan gave chase, the fourth DR-1 pilot never saw the lead SPAD.

The midair collision was spectacular; both aircraft disintegrated. Dobbs' right remaining lower wing, now unsupported by braces, collapsed and separated from the aircraft, initiating a violent spin to the farmland below. Dobbs was hopelessly trapped on board. He fought for control even though he knew it was futile. The spinning ground grew closer and closer…

8 December, 1941

J.T. jerked awake, eyes stinging from the salt in his sweat. Mouth dry, his heart pounded as if he were having a heart attack. Blinking, he focused his eyes and met the soft brown gaze of his Kate. In the early morning light, she was so innocent and beautiful that it hurt to look at her after what he had just relived.

Kate raised herself on one elbow. Before she could speak, J.T. spun his feet out of bed and walked out of the room. Fifteen minutes later, she found him on the back porch watching the sunrise.

"It's been a while since you've had one of those," she said, handing him a steaming cup of coffee.

J.T. nodded and sipped the hot coffee. She had turned the radio on. The news talked of the attacks on Pearl Harbor, the Philippine Islands, virtually all over the Orient.

Kate took his arm.

"You worried about this?"

J.T. nodded. "This is going to be big, Kate."

Her head lowered.

"Bigger than the last war, bigger than yours?" Kate looked up at him, worry in her brown eyes.

"It's the whole damn world this time, not just Europe." He shrugged. "It will be plenty big, for all of us."

"Does Charles Henry share your concern?"

J.T. looked into her eyes with foreboding.

"He's got four more concerns than I do."

A half mile away, Charles Henry and Trey sat on another porch, watching the same sunrise.

"Are you going to have to worry about this, Dad?" asked Trey.

The same newscast was playing in the background.

"Probably not." Charles Henry paused, feeling suddenly sick to his stomach, and turned to his oldest son. "But you will."

He tossed his coffee into the yard and walked inside, leaving Trey in stunned silence.

Chapter 4

The White House
8 December 1941

Franklin Delano Roosevelt sat in his high-backed, wooden wheelchair, intently studying an intelligence report. Behind him, and on every wall, were charts from around the world, detailing all the military theaters. They depicted the Japanese attacks of the previous day and were being updated hourly. The advance of the red ink was daunting. C.R. Smith, president of American Airlines, sat nervously, smoothing the brim of his fedora. He was trying to avert his eyes from the highly classified maps, but could not.

The magnitude of the Japanese attacks was staggering. Smith was no military strategist, but he could read a map. What he saw was an Allied force reeling from a flood of red ink; red ink that represented the forces of Imperial Japan.

Suddenly, FDR looked up and spoke.

"C.R., thank you for flying down from New York on such short notice," he said. "I need your help – actually, the country needs your help."

C.R. stiffened.

"Anything I can do, or my airline can do, you've got, Mr. President."

"Fine, fine, C.R.," said the President. "I knew we could count on you. Listen, I don't need to tell you we are in quite a pickle here."

He motioned to the Pacific charts.

"What few assets we have are slated for Europe and Northern Africa. We absolutely must hold Great Britain, or all of Europe is lost. To do that we are shipping everything we can to England and applying pressure to the Axis' southern flank in North Africa, while the Russians fight it out on the Eastern front. The navy will have to hold the Pacific until we can spool up. The problem that needs immediate attention is in western China and Burma."

FDR pointed to the chart with his cigarette holder.

"Most of Eastern China is lost to the Japs. Now, what we need is to give the Emperor a second front to worry about."

C.R. wiped his brow with a white handkerchief.

"Yes sir," he stammered, overwhelmed.

FDR put his cigarette holder into a large, glass ashtray and crossed his hands on a chart on top of his desk.

"Well, old Hirohito is marching through Indochina like Grant took Richmond. The Brits won't last long in Singapore. I'm afraid the Philippines are lost; it's just a matter of time. We are not in a position to reinforce them before the inevitable. So we are shifting our efforts – here."

FDR pointed to Burma and western China on the map under his hands.

"We must keep the Japanese engaged here, and the Germans in North Africa. Once Malaya and Singapore fall, the Japs will turn their efforts to Burma. They will make a full court press for Rangoon to cut the Burma Road. It is the last ground supply route to Chiang Kai-shek. Without our help, his China front will collapse. With China pacified, the Japanese will move on India, and then press forward to the Middle East. If the Japanese and Germans link up in the Middle East, the war could be over very quickly."

C.R. had been focusing on the Himalayan mountain chain on the map.

"Over, sir?" he said. "Is it really that bad already?"

FDR grimaced.

"Yes, C.R., it is. If Hitler and Hirohito hook up in southwest Asia, they will move on all fronts against the Soviets, who are hanging on by withdrawing into interior Russia. If the Japs attack through Siberia, and the Germans through the Caucuses, the USSR will fall.

"That will leave England, North America and Australia. We are not exactly in a position to run to each other's flanks."

C.R. studied the map.

"Well, at least we are safe here in the States," he said.

FDR cocked his head to the side.

"C.R., we have Japanese commandos on the ground in the Aleutians." FDR pointed to the island chain on the map. "They are reconnoitering for an invasion."

C.R.'s jaw dropped.

"My God, Mr President – that's Alaska!"

"Yes, it is. We have intelligence that Wake is next, then probably Midway."

FDR picked up his cigarette holder and tapped Wake on the chart, then Midway, then moved toward the Hawaiian Islands.

C.R. blurted, "Then Hawaii?"

"I'm afraid so," said the President, "unless Nimitz can stop the Imperial Japanese fleet. But I'm too much of a realist to hope for that. Pray, yes, but not hope. It is imperative that we move now, C.R., before Wake and Midway are in the hands of the Japanese."

Both men sat silent. The weight of the conversation fell over them like a lead cloak. Finally, the President spoke.

"C.R., I need – your country needs – hell, the whole damn free world needs a squadron of cargo planes in the China-Burma theater next week!"

"American Airlines, sir?" asked C.R.

"I can't think of a more appropriate airline, can you?"

"That's combat, Mr. President."

FDR nodded.

"Yes. Yes, it is."

"And the Hump, that's worse than combat!"

The President pulled a sheet of paper and a fountain pen out of the top drawer of the simple oak desk.

"Shall I issue an order of draft," he said. "For the crews?"

C.R. looked up with a twinge of insult.

"Negative, sir," he said. "That will not be necessary. I'll lead a volunteer group out myself. I have a lot of WWI veterans – they'll know what's at stake."

FDR pushed away from the desk, wheeling toward the door.

"Fine, fine, C.R.," he said. "But I need you here."

"Why, sir?"

Roosevelt stopped halfway to the door.

"Because I want you to build me an air force, a cargo carrying, troop transporting air force, the biggest one in the history of the world. Congress approved your commission today. You are now a full colonel in the U.S. Army Air Corps."

C.R. cleared his throat.

"Sir, I'm just a pilot running an airline," he said, "and not that big an airline at that."

The President flashed his famous grin.

"Nonsense, Colonel. You are a leader, and that is what we need right now – that, and time. We have precious little time, so we will have to rely on leadership."

FDR wheeled out the door, leaving C.R. Smith sitting quietly alone in the map room.

Chapter 5

The Fall of Empire
9 December 1941

The moon set over the Straits of Malacca with a foreboding hue. The blood-red tint was caused by the moonlight refracting through the air pollution that drifted up from the city of Kuala Lumpur. Colonel Harry M. Jessip of His Majesty's British Army sat stiffly upright at a makeshift desk in a musty tent. The tent stood in a defensive position in the hills northwest of Kuala Lumpur. The Colonel felt strangely serene; he had accepted what he knew to be his fate. He gazed out the open end of the dark tent at the moon as it disappeared. Its message seemed clear to him. The Imperial Japanese Army had invaded the Malayan Peninsula the day before and was moving south toward Singapore. Colonel Jessip had been tasked with stopping their advance, but he held no illusion of success. His force would be little more than a bump in the road for the Japanese as they sped toward Singapore.

An orderly stepped into the tent, holding an old kerosene lamp. The light shone brightly at the source but dissipated quickly, absorbed by the heavy darkness in the tent. He set the lamp on the colonel's desk.

"Colonel?"

"Yes, Private Jones, what is it?"

"Sir, Captain Cantrell is here as ordered."

"Very good, Private. Send him in, please."

The private answered with a brisk, "Yes, sir!" and a snap of the heels. He executed a smart about-face and marched into the darkness.

Captain Bernard D. Cantrell – the last scion of "The Cantrells" – Dukes of the Royal Court – strode confidently in. A tall, handsome man, he was perfectly kempt, not a dark hair out of place. His uniform was impeccably tailored and surprisingly fresh. His superior breeding and upbringing were obvious as he stepped into the light.

The colonel, a man of more humble upbringing, looked up with a palpable sense of discomfort. "The captain is not an unpleasant chap", he thought, "quite the contrary." Were it not for his splendid presentation, one would never suspect he was a Royal. Alas, it was always there for the Colonel, like an aura swirling about him. Along with the headaches of fielding an antique regiment, he had the added responsibility of a Royal in his command.

While it was never voiced, Colonel Jessip knew all too well the negative attention that would come his way if a Royal was to come to harm under his command. Certainly, his career would come to an abrupt end.

That concern for career had diminished to memory now, insignificant. The end to his career – and most likely his life – was close at hand, and he knew it. A man in his late fifties, Jessip had hoped to retire to his country estate, actually a cottage on ten acres, at the conclusion of this tour of duty.

He had spent his entire adult life in the service of the King. Until recently, he had planned on playing with his grandchildren, tending to his garden and returning to his passion: writing poetry. His poetry was a secret he had kept well-guarded from his troops all these years. Only his darling Harriet knew his secret.

That was all gone now, dissipating even more rapidly than the light of the kerosene lamp. He sat more stiffly than formally; the presence of Captain Cantrell always had that effect. Cantrell had noticed this change in the Colonel in his presence, which caused awkwardness in his own manner. He truly liked Colonel Jessip and thought him an outstanding leader, worthy of generalship.

The Colonel knew Singapore was lost. The Imperial Japanese Army was whisking across China and Indochina with incredible speed and stealth. Like a barely audible whisper, they would slowly draw attention, then stun – the first clap of thunder from a fast-moving squall. Their shadowy presence seemed surreal, like the return of the ancient samurai warriors. But the death and destruction wrought by this force was all too real.

The savage nature, not only of the campaigns, but also the ensuing occupation, were well known to the colonel. He had seen the intelligence reports from Nanking. He knew prisoners were regarded with disdain by the Japanese. Colonel Jessip had no misconception of his treatment should he survive. Still, he was disconnected from his and the command's ultimate fate. To him it was a given, an absolute. Any thought wasted on it was just that – wasted.

He would carry out his duties in the defense of Singapore magnificently, even in light of the obvious futility of the gesture. Colonel Jessip was intent on bloodying the Japanese nose on the morn, one that he felt would be his last.

The colonel was a student of maneuver. Bonaparte had put a new emphasis on an old principle of warfare: maneuver would allow a smaller force a decided advantage over larger, entrenched forces. Jessip knew from his studies that the British hero Wellington had been lucky at Waterloo. The Austrians had come to the rescue from Austerlitz just in time.

There would be no rescue for Singapore. In 1938, the Admiralty had spent millions of pounds fortifying the British colony. Unfortunately, all the defenses pointed out to sea. The Japanese had decided not to cooperate by dying on the seawalls of Singapore Harbor. Instead, they were landing on the northern end of the Malay peninsula. Their carrier-based fighters had already destroyed the Royal Air Force in Malaya, catching most of it on the ground. The single bright spot for the British was the Royal Navy. HMS *Prince of Wales* and HMS *Repulse* had sortied the previous day to destroy the invading flotilla.

This was how Colonel Jessip found himself along with his Regiment, on the Malayan Peninsula waiting to die. General Percival had sent him to stop the Japanese advance. If the Royal Navy could destroy their support flotilla, it may halt their advance to await supplies. If the Japanese got the entire invasion force onto the peninsula unmolested, they would be unstoppable. He had to assume that their main force had landed and was on the move south.

These thoughts floated in his consciousness but were not his current focus. What was occupying his mind were two things: his Harriet, and Cantrell. He had no intention of allowing a Royal to fall into the hands of the Japanese on his watch. He would kill the proverbial two birds with one stone. This was on his mind as he stared into the dark edges of his tent.

"Sir, you sent for me," Cantrell broke the silence.

"Yes, yes, Captain." The Colonel spoke crisply as he pulled his own impeccable, Army-issued uniform tight. "I have a mission for you, most secret – top, actually."

Cantrell snapped to attention.

"Yes, sir. I shall not fail you!"

The Colonel straightened his tie and moved from behind the desk.

"Captain," he said, "I want you to personally select twenty of the fittest and finest officers, along with eighty non-commissioned of the same caliber. No officer above the rank of captain. They must all be in top physical shape, able to endure extreme hardship for long periods of time. All must be warriors. You shall pick them personally – however, they will be made to believe all choices have come from me on a prepared list. That will allow you some cover, as it were."

Captain Cantrell relaxed his posture imperceptibly.

"Yes, sir," he said. "And the mission?"

The Colonel wiped the sweat from his brow and softened his tone.

"You will equip yourselves to move rapidly – seven days' rations; one per man, per day. Each man shall carry a hundred rounds and five grenades, no heavy weapons. The only extra burden will be four UHF radios and all excess batteries – "

Captain Cantrell interrupted.

"Sir, we have only six in the regiment."

"Yes." The Colonel shrugged. "And after tomorrow we shan't need any."

Cantrell sensed what was unfolding. He stiffened at the thought.

"And our mission…sir?"

The Colonel turned and sat back down at his desk. He knew that Cantrell would resist; after all he was a nobleman. "I must frame this delicately", he thought as he sat quietly.

Captain Cantrell broke the silence again.

"Colonel, what is our mission?"

The Colonel looked up, tired. The stiffness of formality melted away in an instant.

"You shall leave here at once," he said. "You and your men shall evade the enemy. Make no contact, regardless of the situation – "

Cantrell cut him off.

"Do you mean to say we shall run? Run away in the face of the enemy? I won't do it, I can't do it!"

Colonel Jessip slammed his open hand on his makeshift desk. The report startled Cantrell.

"Captain Cantrell," he spat out, "you will do your duty as I assign it – as I do mine. Is that clear?"

Cantrell leaned on the desk, his composure now lost.

"I will not act as a coward," he said. "And you, sir, know that I cannot!"

It was a first. He had played the royal card. Colonel Jessip used it to his advantage. He jumped up and met Cantrell's glare. All pretenses were put aside.

"And you know," he murmured, "that I cannot, will not, allow a Royal to fall into the hands of the Japanese. Oh, my friend, you will do what you are told, or on the morn when we are overrun, the Japs will find you in irons for insubordination! How would that scandal read in the *Daily Mirror*?"

Cantrell stiffened. He knew he was defeated.

"Don't worry, Captain," continued Jessip. "You shall fight, and I dare say you will rue the day, and long for the quick and glorious death tomorrow brings."

The Colonel returned to form and, in a cheerful manner, went on.

"Now that all of that is settled, back to point: again, you shall make no contact with the enemy on your tactical withdrawal. You shall slip through the enemy lines; I believe them to be quite undefined due to the speed of their advance – "

Captain Cantrell again interrupted.

"And then?"

Colonel Jessip looked up.

"Well, Captain, you shall attack and kill the Japanese, of course."

The Captain cocked his head, wondering what this cagey old war dog was up to.

"I don't understand, Colonel."

"Captain, Captain," the Colonel said with a smirk. "This isn't a 'save your ass and off to London' mission. I have served Great Britain and the Crown my entire adult life, and so shall you. It just won't be in a Jap prison camp – or a mass grave.

"No, Captain," he continued, "you shall move into the currently unoccupied areas of Burma and China. After the impending meltdown of the Far East command, you and your officers will help set up a new army, one that can fight. Oh yes, my young Captain, you will be in the bush for quite some time. Which, by the by, reminds me."

The Colonel reached into his desk drawer and took out two gold oak leafs. They glinted in the lantern light as he handed them to Cantrell. They had obviously just been polished.

"Here," he said. "These were mine. Now they are yours. Your promotion is effective immediately. Congratulations, Major."

Cantrell held the oak leaves in his hand. Staring at them, he began to stammer.

"Sir, I ... ah – "

This time, the Colonel interrupted.

"Already done. Battle field promotion; the administrative papers went out last week. Even if you disappear, all London knows is that you were promoted and sent on a highly classified mission."

"Colonel, I don't know what to say or do." Cantrell seemed dazed and off balance.

Colonel Jessip held up his hand.

"Major Cantrell, the old British Army of Empire, a barracks army of occupation, will breathe its last gasp in Singapore very soon. It is up to you, and the young tigers you train, to build the new British Army – an army of speed, an army of maneuver."

"Sir, if you believe this, why don't you move the battalion to Burma?"

The Colonel shook his head.

"No, my orders and destiny are clear. Both hold me here."

A long silence enveloped the tent. It was now Cantrell's turn to stare into the darkness and the Colonel's turn to interrupt.

"One more operational item before you go, Major."

The new Major was still lost in thought.

"Major? Major Cantrell."

He snapped to attention.

"Yes, sir?"

The Colonel cleared his throat.

"As I was saying; I want you to take the Sergeant Major. He's old but tough as old boots. You might let him assist in the selection of the non-commissioned. And I have one additional issue to resolve: the Yanks."

"The Yanks, sir?" asked Cantrell.

"Yes, Captain Russell's embassy bunch. They are obnoxious but most resourceful."

Major Cantrell allowed a smile.

"Yes, most," he said, then quickly added, "sir."

"After all," added Colonel Jessip, "this isn't their fight. Not yet, anyway. They should not have to make our last stand."

The Colonel stiffened to his original posture, smoothed out his tunic and returned to his crisp military delivery.

"Well then," he said. "That is that! Good luck, Major. You are dismissed."

Major Cantrell snapped off his best salute. The gesture was not missed by Colonel Jessip. Cantrell executed a precise about-face and marched toward the darkness. He stopped when the Colonel called his given name.

"Bernard," whispered Jessip, "a personal favor."

Cantrell turned at the edge of the darkness.

"Of course, sir. Anything I can do."

The Colonel drew a letter from his tunic's inside pocket.

"Could you see that this letter is delivered to my wife?"

As the Major took the envelope, Jessip held fast and pulled him back into the light.

"I would prefer in person."

Their eyes met for the last time, and for the first time, the Colonel reminded Cantrell of his own father. It struck him as odd that he had never realized it before. Perhaps it was the light.

"I shall take care of it, Colonel Jessip," he said. "I shall personally take care of everything. Everything."

Jessip acknowledged the subtle yet obvious meaning of Cantrell's response with a nod. He returned to his cheerful, professional voice.

"Well then, you must be off. Time is critical, eh?"

Major Cantrell came out of the Colonel's tent and stood blinded in the dark after the intense light of the Colonel's lantern. He sensed that someone was next to him, but could not recognize who it was until he spoke.

"Sir, I've taken the liberty of assembling eighty of the King's finest."

Cantrell instantly recognized the bark and cadence of Sergeant Major Menzies.

The Sergeant Major was a bull of a man. Not a brutish bull in a china shop, though. Menzies had the graceful air of a bull in the ring, a bull that even matadors would fear. He was slight, not even 5 feet 6 tall, but he was sinewy, leathery, with pure, hardened muscle. A foot shorter than some of his men, they nevertheless feared and respected the Scotsman.

Menzies had no issue with his size – in fact, he saw it as an advantage in combat. A true soldier of the British Empire, he always embraced his surroundings, learning the local fighting techniques of the Chinese, Koreans and Indians. No matter the land he was in, he studied their martial arts. Over the years, the Sergeant Major had melded what he'd learned into his own deadly style.

He had only been called out once by one of his troops. Private Edmondson had a few too many Singapore Slings one Saturday night and decided that the much smaller and older Sergeant Major needed his comeuppance. Afterwards, there were many renditions of what happened by the personnel present – many, because it had started and ended in such a flash of disciplined violence that no one could be sure of anything except the outcome: Private Edmondson was unconscious on the floor and spent the following week in the infirmary.

The Sergeant Major brought no charges against the Private. In fact, he never mentioned it again. Menzies was truly a living, breathing weapon. No one doubted that, or tested him again.

Curiously, Private Edmondson's name was on the list of eighty. Cantrell thought to himself that he should have anticipated that the Sergeant Major would be a step ahead of him.

"Outstanding, Sergeant Major," he replied, trying to regain his bearing. "We shall need to outfit them with – "

The Sergeant Major cut him off.

"Done, Major."

"And the radios?"

"Done, Major."

"Excellent, Sergeant Major. Well then, I must go over the list of officers."

As Cantrell turned to walk away, Menzies stopped him.

"Sir, if I may be so bold?"

Cantrell turned to face the diminutive Sergeant Major.

"Yes, what is it, man?"

"Well sir, what with formality being an impediment to speed and time being of the essence – "

"Sergeant Major, speak freely."

Menzies cleared his throat.

"Sir, I have prepared a list of thirty officers to expedite the process."

Even in the darkness, he could tell that the young Major's eyebrows had peaked.

"Really?"

The Sergeant Major softened his voice to a whisper.

"Sir, with all due respect," he said, "you can't see an asshole from above."

Cantrell did all he could to stifle his laugh.

"Well, Sergeant Major, I shall take that under advisement. Thank you."

The professional soldier snapped audibly to attention.

"You are quite welcome, Major."

"How is it," asked Cantrell over his shoulder as he walked

away, "seeing as it is so dark and my promotion came so abruptly, that you know of it?"

He could feel Menzies' smile.

"Well, sir, either nothing happens in this King's army that I don't know about, or I can see in the dark."

The Major thought about it for a second.

"I suspect it is both, Sergeant Major."

Back in his quarters – hovel would be a more accurate description – the new major pored over the list of officers. Menzies had not missed a single one. All of the officers on the list were top-notch war fighters. He quickly checked off twenty, noting that the Sergeant Major had even included Captain Russell.

Captain James Russell and his troops were all that was left of the United States China Marines. They had been attached to the American Embassy in Peking. As the situation became tenuous in China, the ambassador and his staff sought refuge in Singapore. They soon proceeded to the United States. After the attack on Pearl, Captain Russell had placed his unit under the command of Colonel Jessip.

Educated at the United States Naval Academy, Russell was what fellow officers called a natural. He was neither political nor petty. Respected by seniors and juniors, he was a professional – a Marine's marine.

Russell had a military manner hammered into him at the academy. While it was appropriate and proper, he lacked the polish and finesse of Cantrell. Unlike the Colonel, he was not impressed with royalty, and because of this more than any other reason, he and Cantrell had become friends.

Major Cantrell sat back and thought to himself for a moment. "Well, this will mean Russell will undoubtedly have Paillou at his right hand." The quintessential, obnoxious American marine, Gunnery Sergeant Paillou, USMC, was the American version of Sergeant Major Menzies. They looked remarkably similar in a general way – close-cropped hair, skin bronzed by years under the oriental sun. All muscle and no bullshit.

Officers quickly realized that with both men, do not ask their opinion unless you want it unfiltered, rapid-fire and dead on target. The weak and political officers avoided them; the warriors sought their counsel, no matter how bluntly it was delivered.

The gunny had been raised in the tough streets of South St. Louis. He was a China marine; except for a fun-filled year of stomping around Nicaragua during the banana republic wars, he had spent his entire seventeen years of service in the Orient.

The Sergeant Major, being British, was infinitely more polished than his colonial brother. Gunny Paillou could often be heard barking one of his curse-laden soliloquies to anyone in earshot, regardless of rank. While being twin brothers of different mothers in constitution, they were the yin and yang of delivery.

Within a few hours, this diverse band of a hundred warriors, knit together by a mutual sense of duty, slipped into the night. The social climbers and politicos of the British Army were left behind to reap what years of their ilk had sown. The Tigers began their journey with a sense of purpose and vengeance. Japan had to pay for its transgressions on humanity – they were intent on collecting that debt.

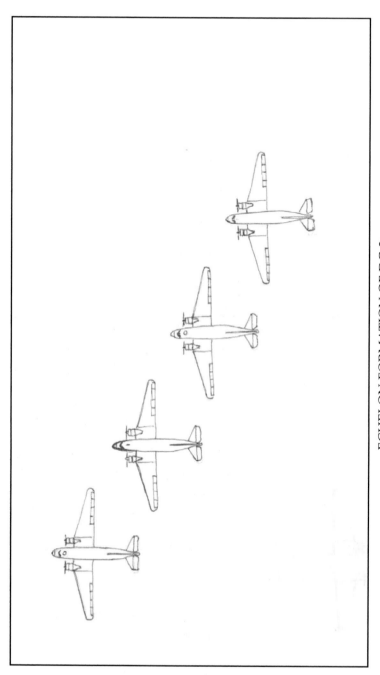

ECHELON FORMATION OF DC-3s

Chapter 6

Goodbyes
10 December 1941

The mid-morning sun warmed the unseasonably pleasant December day. Charles Henry and Trey were loading bags into the trunk of a 1932 Ford coupé. Behind them, David, 17, and William, 12, played catch in the yard.

The eye of Hurricane Laura had passed and now the rest of the storm was blowing in. The boys joined Kaitlyn, 15, on the porch, seeking shelter from the impending storm. Laura Brennan, true leader of the Texas Brennan clan, burst through the screen door and swept across the yard toward the car. She was furious – furious with a tinge of panic. She had lived this before: the separation, the financial hardship, followed by the dreams and the night sweats that she knew would come with her husband's return.

Add to all that, four kids with a father on the other side of the world – enough! She had done enough. Life was supposed to get easier, not harder. Damn pilots. They were always involved in some hair-brained scheme. Always promising life was just about to come up roses.

She glared down at Charles Henry with white-hot intensity.

"You did your part."

Charles Henry wisely did not engage.

"You did your part!"

Laura's voice was rising with a righteousness that would not be ignored. Charles Henry spoke softly.

"I have to go."

"No, you don't," was her rapid-fire response.

"Laura, J.T. is going. I have to."

"J.T. doesn't have kids."

Charles Henry froze. Laura immediately regretted saying it. J.T. and Kate were their lifelong friends. Her own Kaitlyn had been named after her. Laura had often felt a sad guilt that she and Charles Henry had four beautiful children while J.T. and Kate had not been blessed with any.

She looked at her oldest son, his blonde hair shining in the sun.

"Trey, talk some sense into your father."

Trey shifted uneasily on his feet.

"I can't. I'm going."

Laura spun on her heel, facing Charles Henry. She was looking straight through him.

"Bullshit!" she raged.

The entire family froze in place. They wanted to run but didn't dare move. They sensed a showdown of epic proportions. Trey stepped toward his mother; the crunch of the gravel under his feet broke the silence.

"I volunteered first, Mom."

Laura was still staring at Charles Henry, her eyes filled with accusation. He shrugged his shoulders.

"I couldn't let him go alone," he said.

She surrendered, bowed her head slightly and willed herself not to cry. David walked over to his mother and stood awkwardly, not knowing what to do or say. She softly brushed his hair back, then walked to Trey and gave him a long hug; a shorter one was received by Charles Henry. Laura stepped back into the house without saying another word.

David turned to his brother but again fell silent. He had always been the quiet one. Laura always said still waters run deep when asked about David. She was right, of course. A thousand thoughts ran simultaneously through his mind, so many he couldn't choose one to verbalize.

Trey spoke. Like his father, he was never at a loss for words.

"David," he said, "you are going to have to step up to the plate while Dad and I are gone."

"I know. I will."

They hugged a half-hug that was more of a pat on the back. Trey went to the car. Charles Henry put his arm around David.

"Dad, what do I do?"

"Do the right thing, Davy," he said. "Always do the right thing. You will know what that is. You are a good young man, I believe in you." Charles Henry tousled his son's brown hair. "We've got to go. How about some hugs from the rest of you little knuckleheads!"

The three kids hugged Charles Henry as he rubbed their heads with his knuckles. Trey leaned out of the coupé's window.

"Hey David, have Mom drop you off at the airport after the smoke clears. You can use my car until we get back."

"Thanks, Trey." David glanced over his shoulder at the house. "I'd better wait a couple of days."

"Roger that," added his big brother, "and don't wreck it."

Charles Henry jumped in the passenger seat.

"Let's go," he said. "Hey, what are you doing behind the wheel?"

Trey winked at David.

"This is my rig, Pop. You ride now."

He eased out the clutch and they accelerated down the gravel road, disappearing into the dust.

C.R. Smith stood in the corner of the American Airlines operations office at the Dallas city airport. He was wearing the uniform of a full colonel in the United States Army Air Corps. Cardboard boxes filled a good third of the hot, humid room. Sixteen volunteer pilots were crammed into the remaining space. J.T. stood in front of them. C.R. moved to the center of the boxes.

"Okay, gents," he said, "I have a new outfit for everyone."

He began handing out A-1 leather flight jackets first. He knew pilots – he was one. He knew they'd love the leather jackets and thus, whine less about the uniforms that came with them. Next came khaki shirts and trousers. Last came the hats, assorted identification pins, and rank.

Jon Gaus, one of the sixteen pilots, looked at his uniform.

"Does this mean we are in the Air Corps, Mr Smith?"

J.T. looked back at Jon, impatient.

"That's Colonel, numb nuts."

C.R. spoke up.

"Boys, I'll be honest. We don't really know right now. We are simply known as Project Seven Alpha. It is a highly classified program. The United States military is in a huge ramp-up, but we need pilots now. So for this project, you will be reserve officers in case you are shot down. J.T. and Charles Henry have been activated; they are now Lieutenant Colonel Dobbs and Major Brennan.

The young first officers looked at each other with nervous smirks at the mention of possibly being shot at. In a community dominated by machismo, none of them wanted to betray the tightening in their stomachs.

J.T. followed C.R. to the door as the flight crews finished changing into their uniforms. C.R. stopped.

"Sorry about jamming this down your throat with 24 hours notice, J.T. Do you think these kids can hack it?"

J.T. turned and looked at the young first officers, who were laughing and chattering nervously. They looked even younger than they were .

"They'll have to, Colonel. This is gonna be their war."

C.R. looked at the young men, and then the old war dogs mixed in with them. He recognized the look on their faces, the blank stare. In the Great War, they called it the trench stare. It was the look of a warrior at idle. But C.R. knew it was more a form of protection, a withdrawal within himself – not just to recharge depleted batteries, but also to focus on the inner strength that allowed him to do unpleasant or heroic deeds. It also insulated him from those memories. He knew the look all too well.

"Well, J.T.," he said, "I think the greybeards are going to get a second dose as well. Hardly seems fair."

C.R. turned and walked out the door. He stopped at the bottom of the short steps and looked over his shoulder.

"Try and bring them all back, J.T."

J.T. nodded. "Yes, sir."

Lieutenant Colonel Dobbs walked to the chalk board at the front of the small room.

"Attention to brief!"

The noise and the chatter diminished but back round shuffling and whispers continued.

"ATTENTION TO BRIEF!" boomed Major Charles Henry Brennan, Jr., United States Army Air Corps. The sound resonated through the room.

Instantly the group fell silent. J.T. let it hang over them for a few seconds. He neither responded to nor acknowledged Charles Henry. The backup was expected, a given. To acknowledge it would have been an insult to his second in command.

"Gentleman, we have a long way to go."

J.T.'s easygoing manner was gone. Now he was curt, authoritative and to the point.

"We've been configured with long-range tanks. Our legs will be: Los Angeles, Pearl, Wake Island, Legazpi, Philippines, Calcutta, then our new home, Dhemaji, India in the Assam Valley."

"India?" Jon popped off without thinking. "Shit, J.T., I thought we were getting into the war. What the hell will we do in India?"

Lieutenant Colonel Dobbs shot an icy glare at Jon, one he had never seen. It was distant, cold, menacing, and it startled Jon into silence. J.T. resumed his brief.

"We will be supplying the last remnants of the British, Chinese, and soon, American troops in the China-Burma theater," he told them. "Malaya has been invaded by the Japs; they are driving south to Singapore. Washington doesn't expect the Brits to last long. Once Singapore falls, they expect the Japanese Army to turn north and invade Burma. They will drive north to Rangoon, then Lashio to cut off the Burma Road at both ends. If – more like when – Burma falls, we will be the last source of supply to Allied forces in China."

"Not the Hump!" murmured Irish, a short, wild-eyed Dubliner, just a hint of accent betraying his origins.

J.T. paused, rubbed his chin, then responded.

"Yeah, the Hump."

The grizzled Captains all groaned and grimaced as if they were headed to a flight physical. The youngsters just looked around confused. Finally, Trey couldn't stand it anymore.

"What's the Hump?"

"What the Hump is, young Lieutenant, is the nastiest piece of real estate in the world. It's the highest, most rugged, desolate terrain on the planet, with mountains that reach heights of up to 20, 000 feet. As a bonus, it also has the worst and quickest-changing weather – thunderstorms, winds hundreds of knots strong, and ice that will glaze you like a donut. We will be crossing the Himalayas twice a day. Every day."

Charles Henry piped in from the front row. "As an added double bonus, we will be getting shot at."

The first officers stared straight ahead in stunned silence, not daring to look around, wondering what they had got into. The greybeards stared at the floor, knowing.

J.T. straightened and looked at the sixteen pilots, each individually.

"Good. I have your attention. You just learned the most important lesson in the military."

Again, it was Trey who spoke up.

"What's that, Lieutenant Colonel?"

All the greybeards in unison chanted:

"Never volunteer for anything!"

Trey looked down to the floor, embarrassed. Charles Henry slapped him on the back, gave him a wink and whispered into his ear.

"I wouldn't have missed it."

J.T. bowed deeply and formally, in appreciation of the collective chant.

"Thank you, gentlemen, thank you. As the good Major said, we will be getting shot at. You won't just be flying the Hump – you will be doing it in battle-damaged aircraft. You young guys are lucky. All eight of these aircraft commanders – military-speak for Captain – have been there. We won't have to struggle through the standard rooky learning curve, lessons always written in the blood of inexperience." He continued, "Combat flying is different, very different. You young guys, shut up, listen up and suck it up. I have no intention of nursemaiding anyone. If you can't hack it, you will go home. Greybeards, I wish we had time to train. We don't. We will have to knock the rust off en route. You will also have to train your copilots in formation flying. I want these pups proficient in formation flying by the time we reach the Assam valley. Any questions so far?"

Irish raised a hand. "Skipper, I noticed you said legs."

J.T. nodded with a big smile.

"That's correct. We will stop for fuel only. We've got racks in each aircraft for sleeping and fine airline cuisine for your dining pleasure."

Irish looked pained again. "Yeah, if it doesn't kill us first."

His comment received knowing laughs from the entire group.

"Okay, listen up!" said J.T. "Division leads will be me and Major Brennan. In my division, Two Dogs is dash two, Thumper will be my section lead as dash three, and Ski will be dash four. Major Brennan's division is Roper dash two, Irish will be section lead and dash three, with Bluto being tail-end Charlie at dash last. We will go in one big gaggle, all eight ships in a single flight, two divisions in finger four. Major Brennan, you are free to maneuver your division as you see fit. The rest of you, keep it tight. We don't need to trade any paint out there."

He went on. "If the weather doesn't hold, we will break up into four sections to penetrate it. That means two at a time for you new guys. From now on, we do everything in flights of two or more. Starting with section takeoffs today. You boys listen to your flight leads – they are all aces from World War I."

Danny leaned over to Irish and whispered. "I've never heard the Great War referred to as 'One'."

"That's because this is shaping up to be number two, numb nuts." Irish whispered back.

J.T. continued. "Irish was with the RAF. Charles Henry, Thumper and I were with the Hat in the Ring with Rickenbacker."

Trey leaned over to his father.

"You were an ace?"

Charles Henry was looking at his sectional chart and responded without looking up.

"It was a long time ago."

J.T. continued from the front of the room. "In fact, Major Brennan was a triple ace."

Trey stopped listening and stared at his father in disbelief. No wonder he never let Trey read books about the fighter pilots of the Great War – he was in them.

Man-child raised his hand. He had been given his nickname the day he walked into American Airlines operations eight months earlier. It was Irish who hung it on him. He took one look and asked loudly, "Who's this Man-child?" The name stuck. Man-child looked fifteen; nobody could ever remember his real name.

"Question?" J.T. snapped.

Man-child stood; he had perfect manners.

"Sir, why are we leaving so late?"

"Because I don't want to be looking for islands at night," said J.T. "The route has been planned so that all the island arrivals will be in daylight. Are there any other questions?"

All the crews were silent.

"All right, guys. From here on out, we are at war. I've been told enough by Colonel Smith to know that if we get delayed, our route will be in jeopardy. Make no mistake: the Allies are reeling. We are losing this war. Our job is to help the current forces hold on until the cavalry arrives. That will take time. We have to give them enough time to get our military up to speed."

J.T. let the message sink in for a moment.

"All right, let's man up."

The pilots stood, somber, and quietly moved toward the door, each lost in his own thoughts.

"Gentlemen!"

They turned to see J.T. holding a parachute.

"Don't forget these. We are in a new world now."

The crews swiftly made their way to their assigned aircraft.

The eight DC-3 aircraft were lined up at a 45-degree angle in front of the operations shack. They were still in the American Airlines colors of brushed aluminum with blue and orange stripes. Each sat majestically, tail down, nose high in the air. The single, low wing was attached at the bottom of the fuselage with an engine mounted on each side. It was the quintessential airliner of the thirties and forties; design specifications had been set down by C.R. Smith himself.

The airlines liked the economics and reliability of the DC-3. With only two engines and twenty-six seats, it was a profitable machine. And if the airlines liked them, the pilots loved them. They were reliable, well balanced, predictable and comfortable-truly a pilot's airplane. They had proved over the years to be very durable, and would soon prove to be survivable in a hostile environment.

The crews had performed their preflight checks prior to the brief, so they went straight to the cockpits. Within seconds, half the engines were coughing to life. The Pratt and Whitney R-1830 Twin Wasp engines had nine cylinders, big as coffee cans, that produced 1,200 supercharged horsepower.

The radial engine had a quality unlike any other engine. A simple arrangement, much like a daisy, the pedals were cylinders and the center the block, holding the crankshaft and all the other parts together. Radials have a romanticism, an instant nostalgia about them. Perhaps this was due to the symmetry of design, or the smell of AVGAS and oil, maybe the baritone rumble. It was probably the sum of all of these. For the pilots, it was the power – the instant power at your fingertips. Couple that with great reliability, and the DC-3 becomes an aviator's dream. Eighty percent of U.S. airliners in service in 1941 were Pratt and Whitney-powered DC-3s.

Irish moseyed into the cockpit, late. As he slid into the captain's seat, Dan looked over from the copilot seat.

"You know, you don't sound Irish, but I guess you are."

"Really," responded Irish, sarcasm dripping from his voice. "You don't sound like an asshole but…" He shrugged his shoulders.

Dan retreated to the checklist.

Irish smiled and barked out, "How 'bout a prestart checklist, Junior," in a thick New York accent. He just loved screwing with the kids, as he called them.

Dan called off the checklist items as Irish answered.

"Engine start checklist, cold."

"Clear prop," Irish yelled out his open window. "Clear number one."

"Starter select."   "Number one."
"Boost pump."   "Number one."
"Magnetos."   "Off."

Irish palmed the gangbar to engine number one and pressed the starter switch with his middle finger.

"Okay, Danny boy, we're cranking number one."

He counted as six prop blades rotated through the twelve o'clock position, switched both magnetos on, then hit the ignition boost with his ring finger. At the same time, he pressed the primer switch with his index finger at one-second intervals. As the engine popped to life, Irish released the starter and ignition booster buttons and dropped his hand to the throttle quadrant.

Three pairs of levers, with round knobs on top, were on the quadrant, a raised console between the pilot seats. The two tallest levers were bent toward the captain. They controlled the pitch and rpm to the variable pitch propellers. Next in height, and located in the middle, were the throttles. They controlled the power output of the engine by metering fuel through the carburetor. The power was measured as manifold air pressure, MAP. The shortest levers on the right, and painted red, were the fuel mixture controls. They controlled fuel to the carburetor. Their range was from *idle cut off, no fuel,* to *auto rich.*

Irish moved the left knob to auto rich, the forward position. He tweaked the throttle and steadied the engine at 800 revolutions per minute. He repeated the entire process for engine number two, then called for the before-taxi checklist. Dan read aloud over the engine noise as Irish responded:

"Radio master."   "On"
"Boost pumps."   "Off"
"Hydraulic pressure."   "Checked"
"Temperatures and pressures." "Checked"
"Controls."   "Free"
"Navigation lights."   "Off"
"Altimeter."   "3007 set"
"Directional Gyro."   "Set"

J.T.'s voice came over the radio:

"American flight, let's do our run-ups here."

Irish didn't wait for the checklist. In one continuous motion, he locked the tail wheel, reset the parking brakes, checked that both mixtures were in *auto rich*, slid his hand down the console, set the carburetor heat to cold, opened the cowl flaps and set the engine rpm to 1,700. He checked the amps and electrical loads, then set thirty inches of manifold pressure and cycled the prop levers to ensure that they changed pitch on the blades. Next, he positioned the magneto switch from *both* to *one*, then *two*. He checked for a maximum drop of 100 rpm while operating on a single mag, then returned the switch to *both*. Checks complete, Irish pulled the throttles back to *idle*, closed the cowls and unlocked the tail wheel. Dan sat quietly, awed by how smoothly his captain had accomplished the run-up checks.

Run-ups complete, Irish looked to his left and visually inspected the aircraft on his left, then waited for a thumbs-up to be passed to him. His wingman was Bluto, number eight out of eight in the line. Bluto looked over Irish's left side, and then passed a thumbs-up. Irish looked over the aircraft to his right and passed a thumbs-up to that pilot. The process repeated up the line until it reached J.T. on the far right.

Once J.T. had received a thumbs-up from Two Dogs, he knew the entire formation was ready for taxi.

"Okay, Jon," he said. "Call for taxi."

"What do I say?"

"Friggin' new guys", J.T. thought as he shook his head and grabbed his mike.

"Dallas Ground Control, American Zero One, taxi flight of eight."

The ground controller in the tower responded immediately.

"American flight, you are clear to taxi runway three six, altimeter setting 3007."

J.T. clipped off a response: "Clear three six, three zero zero seven. Jon, let's run the before-takeoff checklist."

J.T. gave a hand signal to the ground crew to pull the wheel chocks: two fists touching at their base, thumbs extended laterally, away from each other. The ground crew reacted immediately, as always. The only difference from the norm was that after saluting the captain, they got on board the aircraft. Each captain, seeing the aircraft in front of his pull chocks, gave the signal to his plane captain.

Plane captains were mechanics who were assigned as the coordinator to an aircraft. In the air, the captain owned it, but on the ground it belonged to the plane captain, or PC. Air crew and their PCs had a special bond. The PC got the bird ready for flight; he fueled it, checked fluid levels and coordinated maintenance, if needed. He was the last person to certify the aircraft safe for flight. The pilots trusted PCs literally with their lives on a daily basis, and the plane captains took their responsibilities very seriously.

The lead DC-3 started to pull forward, then deflected the rudder right and tapped the right main brake, swinging the tail and taxiing south to the threshold of runway three six. One at a time, they slid out of their tie-down spots to follow J.T. in order.

Charles Henry watched J.T.'s flight of four slip out, one by one. When his turn came, he ran his engines up to 1,000 rpm. As they caught, he goosed them to 1,500 rpm to get his heavy aircraft rolling, then pulled the throttles back to idle so he wouldn't blast the aircraft on his left with his prop wash. He looked up and saw his wife and three younger kids standing on the edge of the tarmac with J.T.'s wife, Kate. Laura gave a slight wave. Simultaneously, Charles Henry tapped Trey with his right hand, pulled open his side window with his left hand, and kicked hard right rudder. He tapped the right brake slightly and swung the big tail to line up with the taxiing aircraft. As he did this, he poked his head and left arm out of the open window, blowing a big, exaggerated kiss to Laura. She tried to suppress a smile, then mouthed, "I love you," to them both. Trey waved from behind his father. David smiled back mischievously, dangling the keys of his brother's coupé. Kaitlyn and William raised their arms in big waves.

All too quickly, they were out of view. Charles Henry sighed to himself and called for the before-takeoff checklist.

The eight DC-3s slowly S-turned as they taxied toward the runway, turning in large, S shapes because of the visibility problem associated with the high nose attitude. Tightly spaced at 25 feet, the line of eight aircraft looked like a long, silver snake slithering along the taxiway

J.T.'s voice crackled across the radio receiver.

"Flight, switch tower."

Jon looked at J.T., obviously irritated.

"I can handle the radios, Captain-I mean Colonel."

"All right, Jon," said J.T., "you got the radios. Call tower for takeoff, a flight of eight. Tell the section leads to set METO power."

METO power was a reduced power setting for takeoff that would allow the wingman on the section goes, or takeoffs, to have a power advantage. The wingman might need a power advantage to match the acceleration rate of the lead. Aircraft were like people – no two truly were alike; each had its own peculiarities. Even of the same model, no two were ever matched perfectly. So, the wingman had to have a power advantage to maintain position. METO power was a reduced power setting of forty-three inches of manifold air pressure (MAP), which the airlines used if weight and runway length permitted, to save engine life. It would also allow the wingman a five-inch advantage in MAP if they needed it to maintain position on takeoff.

Jon's voice came over tower frequency.

"Tower, American Zero One take off, flight of eight. Section leads set METO power."

J.T. nodded his approval.

"American Zero One, cleared for takeoff," replied the tower. "God speed."

There were no secrets in aviation. Weather briefs, flight plans, fuel loads – an uninformed observer didn't need rumors to figure out a destination; he only needed to do the math.

J.T. rounded the corner and took the upwind side of the runway. The wind was from the northwest, so he positioned his aircraft on the left half of the runway. His section wingman, Two Dogs, took the right side. This would add a safety factor for the takeoff. In a section go, the wingman had to divide his attention between maintaining position on the lead and staying in the center of his half of the runway. The effect of the wind would be to blow the wingman away from the lead if he lost concentration, or as pilots referred to it, situational awareness.

Leaving the runway was preferable to running into the section lead, especially from lead's point of view. The concept allows a glimpse at the inside world of aviation. It was a team-based environment, where each team member was responsible for his actions, or lack of correct action. The penalties for not meeting required responsibility were severe. For a check ride, it meant a bust, or being grounded; flying the line, it could mean a smoking hole; in war, multiple smoking holes.

Pilots hung together tighter than a pack of wolves, but if an individual wolf could not keep up, he would be cut from the pack. The inexperienced or weak would be trained and taken under wing. The inadequate would be cut, either by their airline, squadron – or the ultimate cut: Fate.

These sixteen had met their tests, and they not only excelled in the effort, they reveled in the challenge. These sixteen were good sticks – the highest compliment one pilot would ever give another. Not only were they good sticks, they were good shits. This meant much more than merely being a good pilot. It meant they could be trusted in the air and on the ground. It meant that any one of them would be good company in the cramped cockpit, on a wing or in a hotel room, tent, or the shared stateroom of an aircraft carrier.

A good shit was someone who would cover his wingman's six* in a dogfight or a barroom brawl, even if the wingman started it; someone a wingman would lend a $10 bill to and not expect to get it back, and not care. The bond of aviators was too intense, too forged in consequence to worry about such trivialities.

This was the type of man who sat in the eight DC-3 airliners, waiting for takeoff – a takeoff that would transform these luxury liners into warbirds, and the airline pilots in them to Army Air Corps pilots, the instant they broke ground. There was no turning back now – not that any of them would. Adventure and camaraderie had a value that could not be matched with riches.

J.T. looked over at his wingman, waiting for a thumbs-up.

Jon also watched, calling out: "Good thumbs-up," after Two Dogs flashed the hand signal.

*Pilot slang for his six o'clock position: his butt.

"Okay, Jon," said J.T., "run him up."

Jon extended two fingers so the wingman could see them, and made a circular motion. Both aircraft set thirty inches of manifold pressure.

J.T. directed Jon to hold his arm vertically by the side window.

"Okay, Jon, slowly drop your arm forward."

When Jon's arm disappeared below the window rail, J.T. advanced the throttles to set METO power. The prop lever had been set during the before-takeoff checks to takeoff range. The rpm indicator showed 2,600 as J.T. took a quick scan of the engine instruments. He eased off the brakes as the engines started toward a METO power of forty-three inches manifold air pressure.

"Power set," Jon called out.

Two Dogs ran his power up at a faster rate than J.T. in the lead aircraft. He tapped his brakes to keep from getting forward of wing position and left the power up, waiting for J.T.'s power to kick in. The key to a successful section takeoff was in not getting behind. As the lead aircraft's power stabilized, Two Dogs matched it, now maintaining his position with throttle movement only. His scan jumped from the lead to the runway, continually correcting for drifts.

At 60 knots, Jon called out, "60."

J.T. eased forward on the control yoke to raise the tail. Two Dogs matched his tail to the leads.

At 84 knots, Jon called out, "V-1."

V-1 was a decision speed, if you were under it you could successfully abort a takeoff and stop on the remaining runway; if you where above it, you could not. It varied by runway length, weight of the aircraft, elevation and temperature. It was figured for each takeoff, using charts along with VR, rotation speed and V-2 single engine climb speed.

Jon quickly called out, "Rotate!"

J.T. slowly rotated the control yoke aft, imperceptibly separating the DC-3 from the runway surface.

Jon called out, "V-2."

They were already at their single-engine safe climb-out speed, in case one engine failed in this critical phase of flight.

J.T. called out, "Gear."

Jon dutifully raised the landing gear handle, waited for the indicators to show up, and called, "Up and locked."

J.T. continued to climb at V-2 airspeed. He knew that Two Dogs would be rusty and flailing a bit; he wanted to get him away from the ground. Two Dogs was rough with the pitch control as they rotated, he was over controlling the nose, causing a slight pilot-induced oscillation, or PIO. It had been a while. Even so, the old instincts kicked in and he dampened out the oscillations until he was smoothly matching J.T.'s attitude and power settings. He tucked in close, in parade formation.

At 100 feet, J.T. eased the nose down a few degrees in pitch. As his airspeed passed 90 knots, he pulled the throttles smoothly back to forty inches of MAP, set 2,550 rpm with the prop levers, and left the mixtures in *auto rich*. At 500 feet above the ground, the DC-3 was indicating 110 knots of airspeed. J.T. reset the power to thirty-six inches of MAP and 2,350 rpm on the props for the remainder of the climb to altitude. He began a slow, smooth 15-degree angle of bank turn to the west.

Thumper and his wingman, Ski, had lined up on the runway behind J.T. and Two Dogs. As the lead section's power came up, Thumper started his clock's second hand. He idled into the lead's position as it was vacated, making room for Charles Henry and Roper on the runway. When the second hand hit ten seconds, Thumper's power came up and Charles Henry idled forward, making room for Irish and Bluto in the last section.

Each section launched with a ten-second interval. All eight aircraft were airborne in thirty seconds. As J.T., in the overall flight lead, started his turn west, each section turned inside his turn. They accelerated to 125 knots and began to rendezvous, using the excess 15 knots of closure and radius of turn.

J.T. glanced down the bearing line and saw a lot of movement of the six sections. The rendezvous bearing line was an imaginary line, 45 degrees aft of the lead's wing line. All the wingmen were expected to fly up that bearing line, in order. This procedure would ensure a safe and expeditious join-up.

"Sloppy", J.T. thought, as he watched sections fly acute

(ahead) and sucked (behind) the bearing line. Some were high, some low. They would get better, J.T. knew. He returned his attention to flying a smooth and precise lead.

They were on their way, and nobody would ever be the same.

Chapter 7

C.-in-C. Pac. Fleet HQ
10 December 1941

The commander in chief of the Pacific Fleet (C.-IN-C. PAC) stood at a window overlooking Pearl Harbor. Admiral Kimmel, however, was not contemplating the destruction of the Japanese attack and subsequent flurry of activity it had caused. The outpost on Wake Island was now his primary concern. Thousands of miles away from Pearl and the protection of the fleet, it would be next on the Japanese order of battle; of this, he was certain. After his stunning defeat at Pearl, he had no intention of sitting back for more of the same on Wake Island.

Kimmel had two choices, two courses of acceptable action. First, he could reinforce and defend the island. It was his preferred choice, and yet he knew it to be a difficult task. Before him, nearly his entire battleship fleet was in ruins. His three carriers were all that stood between Hawaii and the Japanese fleet. Fortunately, they had been at sea during the raids three days earlier, and still were. The other option was to evacuate the garrison and destroy what they could. There was a third option that Kimmel refused to even consider: abandon Wake.

Captain Charles McMorris, his staff war planner, knocked twice and entered the room.

"Admiral, I have a contingency plan for the evacuation of Wake Island garrison."

Admiral Kimmel winced at the sound of the words.

"Okay, Soc, what do you have?"

Soc McMorris cleared his throat. He felt uncomfortable even discussing it as an option.

"Sir, first I want you to know I recommend against it."

"I understand, Soc." Admiral Kimmel nodded. "Proceed."

"I estimate the *Tangiers* could hold all 1,500 personnel," McMorris continued, "if we downloaded all stores on board. After assigning her to the *Lexington*'s Task Force, we could steam at best speed to Wake. *Lexington*'s air group could cover the surface evacuation from the air. Weather permitting, we could be in and out in a day – if we left everything behind."

Admiral Kimmel stood motionless for a full five minutes while his subordinate stood at attention. Soc knew the Admiral was reaching a decision on the spot. Finally, Kimmel spoke.

"No, Soc. I'm done running from the Japanese. We will reinforce the island and evacuate the civilians. Have the *Tangiers* loaded with replenishment supplies for the Marines. We will send reinforcements and engage the Imperial fleet at sea. Recall the carriers at once, and work up a contingency for the defense of Wake."

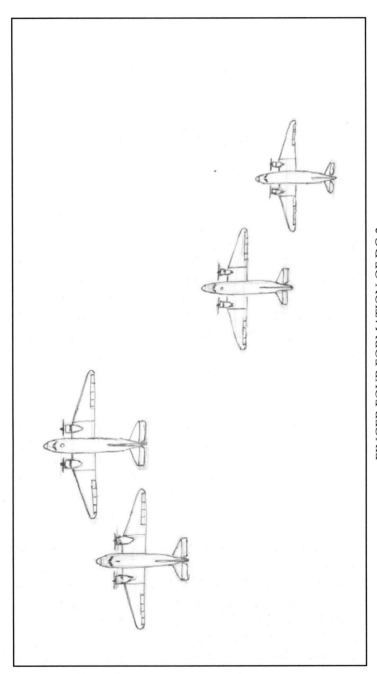

FINGER FOUR FORMATION OF DC-3s

Chapter 8

The Journey Begins
10 December 1941

Upon reaching a cruising altitude of 12,000 feet, J.T. slowly walked the throttles back to thirty-two inches of MAP, pulled the props aft to set 2,100 rpm and closed the engine cowls. It was a faster cruise than normal, initially stabilizing at 165 knots indicated airspeed. He checked the outside temperature: 10 degrees Celsius. He figured their true airspeed was about 205 knots. He would get out his MB4A computer and get a good read once he had time.

Normally, J.T. would plan to reduce power as fuel burned off. The reduction in weight caused by fuel burn would mean increasing speed if he left his power set static. That was fine with him; he was not concerned with fuel economy. The DC-3s all had extra fuel tanks in the cargo bays for long-range legs. This leg, Dallas to Los Angeles, would be relatively short.

J.T.'s concern was time. C.R. had warned him that the window was closing for his fuel stops at Wake Island and in the Philippines. He had to get his squadron west as fast as he possibly could.

"Squadron", he thought to himself, "It's been a long time since I led a squadron."

In fact, he hadn't flown formation at all since he and Charles Henry left the active Air Corps Reserve five years earlier. The peacetime bullshit had finally driven them out. He'd missed it; he was sure Charles Henry did too.

Time had dulled his memories of multi-plane flight. He had always marveled at the sight of an aircraft a few feet from his own in flight. Formation flying was like no other type of flying. The exhilaration was simply unmatched by anything in the air, except air combat. Flying in formation generated a special trust between pilots because the flight lead and his wingman flew as one. The wingman depended completely on the lead for navigation, fuel management and, in bad weather, even basic airmanship. The lead could fly off his instruments, but the wingman always had to reference the lead. The wingman could be flown into a mountain, or stalled off the lead's wing if the lead got too slow. He could be run out of gas or into the ocean. In the event of a disaster, the last thing a wingman would see would be his lead.

A division was two sections, each consisting of two aircraft. The next most experienced pilot would lead the second section, but also maintain position on the lead. He was also the backup division leader. If the division lead had a problem or was shot down, the section lead would take over, so he had to maintain situational awareness for the division as well as his own section.

The preferred formation was the "finger four", which looked like a hand held straight out with fingers spread. The middle finger was the lead position, the index finger was number two, or "dash two", the ring finger was number three as well as section lead, and the pinky was number four. An extra gap was left between the lead and dash three. It allowed dash two to move from one side to the other freely. If the lead crossed him to fill the gap, then pumped his nose, the flight would tighten up with all three wingmen on the same side. This was called an echelon formation.

Echelon was the formation seen most by non-pilots because it was the formation normally used to break up a flight for landing. The lead flew over the runway at 1,000 to 1,500 feet, depending on the set pattern altitude for the field. He separated from the flight after giving the wingman a kiss-off signal, then peeled off and made a 180-degree turn to the downwind leg. While the flight continued straight ahead, dash two followed five seconds later, then dash three and four in sequence. They maintained their spacing, but flew their own landing pattern.

The normal landing pattern was in an oval shape. An aggressive lead would break away as soon as he crossed over the approach end of the runway. Flying a tight pattern, the pilots would go in a descending circle while configuring the gear, flaps, prop, and cowls for landing. Fighters did fan breaks and pitch-up breaks, but J.T. would do nothing fancy with these lumbering DC-3s and their rusty crews. His job was to get everyone to India in one piece, mission-ready. To do that, he had to be on top of his game – he was flying eight airplanes, not just one. Being smooth was the key to a good lead. J.T.'s goal was to make corrections transparent for his seven wingmen. For now, he would enjoy the beauty and art of this technological dance.

Flying was a dichotomy to J.T., a blend of absolute discipline and total freedom. It was a science in which pilots sought the maximum result from the minimum input, even if the minimum input is a high g pull. Being smooth, even if a max performance maneuver is required, can mean the difference between winning or losing a dogfight – or hitting the ground. The dichotomy: long hours of sitting fat, dumb and happy at altitude, then short, adrenaline-filled battles of survival, every nerve ending tingling, every brain cell alive with synapses. They were headed to war but here, now, was the unfettered joy of flight.

As the flight of eight was passing by Guadalupe Peak near El Paso, the chattering on the radios broke J.T.'s spell.

"Trey," Man-child broadcast, "did you get a time hack abeam Guadalupe?"

"Yes," Trey responded. "Stand by."

Danny boy jumped in.

"How about a ground speed?"

Irritated, J.T. picked up his microphone.

"I briefed you knuckleheads to join up and shut up," he said. "All I want to hear from you new guys, besides your check-in sequence, is 'Lead's on fire' or 'I've got the fat chick.' "

The greybeards smiled. They knew that the radio transmitter sucked a lot of joy out of flying. Hand signals, nods, a smile had been all they needed in the Great War. A radio was definitely cheating.

Their route had taken them over Abilene and Midland; the flat Texas plain seemed to run forever in all directions. Now, as they approached El Paso from the east, the western United States unfurled like a master tapestry. The rich color and texture of every ridge, wash, and mountain drew the eye.

J.T. loved the West. The sky was so wide open that just standing on the ground gave the impression of flight. From the air, the feeling was incredible. He never tired of the West, no matter how many times he crossed it.

Unfortunately, western states were famous not only for their beauty but also the severity of their afternoon thunderstorms. J.T. had got a brief from the weather guessers back in Dallas; as usual, they had guessed wrong. In the distance, towering cumulonimbus clouds menaced – boiling and churning, blossoming up to 30,000 or even 40,000 feet. Their enormity and power humbled J.T. – and they too, were a dichotomy: the white purity of the clouds, bathed in sunlight as the aircraft skirted around them, starkly contrasted the dark, lightning-laced fury that crouched inside.

To try and fly over the clouds as they grew was folly; they could out-climb any modern aircraft. An inadvertent or intentional penetration could be catastrophic. The unbridled power of a thunderstorm's updrafts and downdrafts could tear a DC-3 apart. Hail could beat flat every leading edge surface of an aircraft – the wing, tail and cowlings, even the windscreen could be shattered. A lightning strike could short out all power and leave the cockpit without lights or instruments. It could blow holes in the aircraft or even strike the crew. J.T. didn't need to contemplate the strength of the boomers he could see along his intended path of flight. Their severity was a given.

What he was contemplating was avoiding them. In a single ship, he might be able to weave his way through them, but to drag a flight of eight through the tight gaps would be bad head work. He had not survived this long in aviation by exercising bad judgment. No, not today. No jousting with boomers while he was the flight lead.

As they drew abeam the familiar Guadalupe Peak, J.T. turned northwest toward Alamogordo. Fuel was still not a concern, thanks to their long-range tanks, so he bumped up the power to thirty-four inches of MAP and 2,200 rpm. The weather reroute would put them behind. He turned to Jon.

"See if you can tune in Alamogordo," he said. "We are going around this mess."

"Damn", J.T. thought, "we're only in the first leg of this goat-rope to the other side of the planet, and we are already behind."

His concern was not merely with the schedule. He had seen some intelligence reports on how quickly the Japanese had spread through China. The last thing he wanted was to land his squadron at a Japanese-occupied fuel stop.

J.T. picked out a pass in the Sacramento Mountains and headed for White Sands. Jon looked at his sectional chart and double-checked the compass heading. He frowned.

"Hey, skipper," he said, "we're gonna miss Alamogordo on this heading."

"Yeah, I know, Jon," said J.T. "We're heading off the radio airways, and the further west we get, the smaller the towns. We can't afford to wander off course; as of now, we are late. So I'm going to fly a route over major geological points, starting with White Sands. We'll get a time hack over top White Sands, so we will have an updated navigational picture before we cross the San Andres Mountains."

Jon looked at his chart again.

"Why don't we just go over Alamogordo?"

"I want to keep moving us west as much as possible. Besides, even I can't miss White Sands," J.T. replied with a wink and a smile of self deprecation.

As they slid through a pass in the Sacramento Mountain Range, then over the Tularosa Basin, the afternoon sun lit up White Sands like a white neon sign at dusk. J.T. flew to the middle of the Sands, started his clock and called time-hack over the radio, simultaneously initiating a turn. Charles Henry eased his division 15 degrees farther north to match J.T.'s course correction. Then he updated his clock and chart, as did the two section leads. This insured that four separate navigation plots were maintained.

The flight was headed toward Gallup, crossing the unspoiled beauty of the San Andres Range, headed for the Rio Grande. J.T. was too busy with his duties as flight lead to enjoy the rugged scenery. He used the Rio Grande as an intermediate checkpoint, marking the time and using it to figure his speed across the ground.

There are three speeds with which a pilot is concerned in flight. First, and most important, is indicated airspeed. As the name implies, it is the number on the cockpit airspeed indicator, the speed the airplane is moving, aerodynamically, through a mass of air. It is a measure of air molecules through the pitot tube system, a tapered cylinder, approximately an inch in diameter, that sticks out into the air stream. It also represents how many molecules are going over and under the wing to produce lift. If enough molecules don't go over the wing fast enough, the flow of air breaks up, the wing stalls, and the airplane stops flying. As an aircraft climbs, the atmosphere thins. Thus, the indicated airspeed through a mass of air is lower than its true airspeed.

True airspeed is the least important speed, because it is almost always affected by the mass of air that surrounds the aircraft. It is only a measurement used in an equation to figure out ground speed. It is the actual speed the aircraft is moving through a mass of air. When an aircraft climbs at a constant indicated airspeed, the true airspeed increases as the molecules in the atmosphere thin. To the wing, the increase in true airspeed is inconsequential; the indicated airspeed is what is critical for lift.

Ground speed is the speed the aircraft is moving across the earth. At 10,000 feet, 10 degrees Celsius, and an indicated airspeed of 135 knots, the true airspeed of the aircraft would be 162 knots. The ground speed is dictated by the movement of the air mass – simply put, the wind. With zero wind, true air speed and ground speed are the same. A 10-knot tailwind would be added to true airspeed, resulting in an increase for the ground speed. So, from the example above, the indicated air speed of 135 would represent a true airspeed of 162, while the ground speed would be 172.

All these numbers were running through J.T.'s head as he figured them on his MB4A computer. He had been a pilot for so long that he could fly with one hand and work the "whiz wheel," as aviators referred to it, with the other.

Jon watched in amusement.

"How are we doing, skipper?"

J.T. tucked the whiz wheel back into his kitbag.

"We're starting to get some wind off that front," he said. "About 10 or 11 knots on this heading."

Jon reached down and pulled out his own computer. "I may not be the pilot J.T. is," he thought, but "I'm a whiz on the whiz wheel." He smiled in self-amusement as he worked on the wheel the time and the distance covered. It read 10.4 knots.

"Son of a – " he murmured.

"What's that, Jon?"

"Oh, nothing, skipper," Jon said, shoving the MB4A computer back into his kit bag.

The flight of eight DC-3s continued northwest up Mulligan Gulch, crossing the Gallinas Mountains just west of the Alamo Navajo Indian Reservation. J.T. was able to relax and enjoy the flight again as they crossed the lava flow southeast of Gallup. He could see the edge of the storm front now. He figured he could ease a couple more degrees to the west and head for Monument Valley.

"That", he mused, "even Jon couldn't miss."

As the front dissipated, it blew a wispy anvil of cloud over Monument Valley. J.T. examined it for signs of the tight knots of turbulence. He knew that the worst turbulence of a western line of thunderstorms, moving northeast, would be on the trailing southwest corner. Knowing this, he eased the flight out of 12,000 feet to cut under the weather.

Certainly, some of the air crew would think it was a risk. J.T. knew it was not; he had the experience and knowledge that they didn't. Instead of reducing power for a normal descent, J.T. left the power set at the cruise setting. The flight accelerated as they descended into Monument Valley.

At 200 knots indicated, J.T. decided to maintain that airspeed by varying his rate of descent. For now, 600 feet per minute was working nicely. He had to inch the throttles back occasionally; as the air grew in density with descent, the manifold air pressure would rise. If it were to rise too high with the rpm at a cruise setting, it could over boost the cylinders, causing one – or more – to blow.

J.T. was under the overcast with 2,000 feet to spare. He could have leveled off, but with no passengers to spook and plenty of gas, he continued down into the valley. He turned the flight to the southwest, following Highway 163. As they dropped below the top of the buttes, they became enveloped in the valley itself. He leveled off at a mere 500 feet above the valley floor.

Altitude, like airspeed, has more than one type. AGL is above ground level, MSL is above mean sea level. Over the ocean, they are the same; once you cross the beach, they change. In Florida, that means only 10 or 20 feet, but in Colorado, you could fly into a wheat field with 5,000 reading on the altimeter. For the altimeter to indicate properly, the current local barometric pressure setting must be entered into a small window in the altimeter by using a knob. Keeping the setting updated at night, or in instrument conditions, is critical – but not now, not among the red giants of Monument Valley.

J.T. knew his altitude was 500 feet AGL; the buttes were 1,000 feet above the valley floor and he was leveling at half their height. Even without this reference, years of experience told him he was correct.

He glanced back at the flight. The others had transitioned to a stepped-up formation instinctively. This would give a bigger cushion for safety, and allow J.T. to maneuver without worrying about dragging off a straggler on the rocks. The flight's speed slowly decayed, from 200 knots indicated down to 185. J.T. continuously trimmed the aircraft as it slowed.

Trimming is accomplished by moving small control surfaces, called trim tabs, to position the main flight control surfaces. Trim tabs are actually smaller ailerons, rudder or elevator. They move in the opposite direction that a pilot wants the main control surface to move. Using aerodynamic force, they reposition the main control surface. For example, if a pilot is holding back pressure on the yoke to keep the nose level, he could rotate the trim wheel for more nose-up trim. The tab would actually move down, causing the elevator to lift up, thus causing the back pressure to be relieved on the yoke. Trim on an aircraft is equivalent to being able to realign the front wheels of an automobile – as it is being driven. By tweaking the trim wheels, a good pilot can trim a DC-3, hands off. Every change in condition, speed, power setting or weight necessitates a trim change. Even a 100-pound stewardess moving in the cabin will cause a change. Good pilots are constantly trimming the aircraft.

Now, with his pilot in command and flight lead responsibilities caught up, J.T. could enjoy the valley. What a sight he beheld: the buttes rose from the desert floor like the great pyramids of Giza, but instead of coming to a point, giant columns of rock erupted out of the tops of the pyramids straight toward the heavens. At first glance, the color seemed constant and drab, but as the flight emerged from under the overcast, the late afternoon sun began to dance across the western faces of the towers. The edifices came alive with the reds, browns, and oranges of the strata.

The cockpits fell silent. The radio hummed, but emitted no captured voice to disturb the serenity. As shadows grew on the eastern faces, J.T. felt a shiver down his spine. They seemed to morph into gravestones, casting long shadows in the late afternoon sun. It was an observation that he kept to himself.

J.T. followed Highway 163 toward Kayenta, Arizona, slipping the flight into a big wash at the western end of Monument Valley. Gradually the wash narrowed, forcing the flight to tighten up its formation. The terrain subtly elevated, and as it rose so did the flight of eight DC-3s, eventually emerging onto the wide open Kaibito Plateau.

Ridgelines rose from the plateau floor like the spines of great serpents. J.T. slipped the flight through a break in one of the ridges, then turned southwest. He was almost on a direct course for Los Angeles now. He should have climbed as they continued over the Kaibito Plateau and expedited to L.A., but he didn't. He had one more staggering sight for his boys. Many of these guys had not seen it; most of American Airlines' routes were in the east. He would show them in a way that only a pilot could experience – he knew that for some, their first sight could very well be their last.

Before them, on a direct course, lay one of the natural wonders in the world.

J.T. dropped to 100 feet above the flat plateau. The stubby desert trees flashed by at an incredible rate. The young copilots had never flown like this. Speed was relative: at 15,000 feet, 220 knots was like standing still, numbers on a dial; at 100 feet or less, it was eye watering – they were flat-out moving. At this elevation, 220 knots indicated was 265 statute miles per hour. The youngsters squirmed in their seats.

They continued to hug the nape of the earth. At this altitude, J.T. knew they would never see what was in store for their delight. He checked his clock; it was getting close. He continued to scan the horizon in the setting sun. They didn't have much sunlight left, but it should be enough.

Then he caught sight of it, the north rim first, and the eight DC-3s screamed toward the eastern precipice. Sixteen Pratt Whitney R-1830 "Twin Wasp" engines howled at near takeoff power. Just prior to the razor sharp edge, J.T. pushed over the nose of his DC-3. Those who knew what was coming smiled. Those who didn't, the youngsters, recoiled in horror. A couple of them started to grab for the controls in an effort to save themselves from this apparent mass suicide as the flight flashed over the edge – and the Grand Canyon ripped open beneath them.

Sheer terror transformed into stunned awe before the second hand on their clocks ticked. So incredible was the sight, especially for the first-timers, that they forgot the cruel trick played on them. Strangely, it seemed to punctuate the experience.

J.T. continued to push forward on the yoke, plunging the flight of eight into the canyon's purple shadows. In the cabin, the ground crews stirred and glued themselves to the windows. They could not experience it like the pilots; they would have to settle for their sideways peek. All except for one.

J.T. sensed a presence in the cockpit and glanced over his shoulder. There stood his maintenance chief, wearing a smug grin.

"I figured you were up to something when the power came up," he said.

J.T. laughed, descending deeper into the glorious canyon.

Charles Henry had taken a trail position, with his division stepped up 25 feet in altitude and 100 feet aft of J.T.'s lead division. His son, Trey, marveled at the juxtaposition of the lead flight of four, below the desert sands, yet 1,000 feet above the canyon floor. It was as if they were forging into the earth itself. He would remember this sight for the rest of his life.

The purple hue of the late afternoon sky intermingled with the reds, browns, and whites of strata revealed by millions of years of labor from the force of the Colorado River. It was too much for his conscious mind to process, so Trey let his senses soak it in: a natural masterpiece of God, and in the middle of it, the shiny, silver, ultimate achievement of man. It was a fitting homage to the most incredible sight he would ever see.

They followed the canyon, weaving around the internal fingers, taking the same course that the river below took. Finally, the setting sun drove them from the canyon and they climbed out, crossing the rim onto the Sanup Plateau. All that was left of the afternoon sun was an intense iridescent edge, highlighting an orange layer of cloud that was capped by the soft pastels of blue and pink. Climbing through 10,000 feet, they saw the last of the sun slip away.

Now, the desert and mountain ranges disappeared under a blanket of black. The sky above was still lit with the lively color of the last remnants of the day, but the earth melted away below them.

Before them, down in the darkness, lay the mountain area known as the Devil's Playground. J.T. felt a foreboding as he read it on his chart. However, he could not dwell on it. His plan, with its perfectly laid-out timing, had come apart. The full moon would rise in an hour and a half, but now it was dark, and he had to get eight DC-3s on the ground – on deck, as pilots called it – without going bump in the night.

Jon took over flying so J.T. could devote his full attention to the current complication. The original plan had been to be on deck at sunset as a group. Once on deck, the ground crews would have serviced the aircraft without having to wait for stragglers, then launched with the rising of the moon. The plan would have given them an hour-and-a-half to two hours on deck, to ready the aircraft for the Hawaii leg. Now, he would have to string them out into four, two-plane sections. They'd have to service the airplanes in less than an hour, not impossible but significantly harder than planned.

The lead DC-3 was level at 14,000 feet, indicating 165 knots of airspeed. J.T. picked up the microphone.

"Boys, we are going to bust this party up," he said. "Charles Henry, detach your division and slow to 155, descend to 13,000, leave Irish's section at 14,000, and slow him to 150. I'm descending to 11,000. I'll drop Thumper's section at 12,000 and 160 knots. Everyone hold their speed for ten minutes, then resume 165. Stand by for a time hack. Ready...hack."

The wingman of each section turned their external lights on steady and bright. Their flashing anti-collision lights would bathe the lead aircraft in red light. The flashing was fast enough to allow the wingmen to keep the lead aircraft in sight. The leads turned off all their lights except the tail and wing lights, which they kept on dim so they wouldn't blind the wingmen.

The flight broke up, and within ten minutes they were separated into four sections spaced by 1,000 feet in altitude and approximately a mile laterally. On the horizon glowed Los Angeles. All other reference to the ground was indistinguishable; where sky met land was impossible to discern. Each section leader was now on instruments. The visual reference to the earth had evaporated into the night sky. With it went the wingmen's peripheral reference to the horizon; now, their only visual reference was the flickering lead aircraft. The danger of vertigo would now lurk into the flight.

With the anti-collision light intermittently lighting the lead, and reference to the earth in the background gone, the wingmen's inner gyro could tumble. A pilot could get the sensation that the lead was doing rolls or continuous steep turns. He would desperately cling to the lead's wing; his rough inputs to the flight controls would give a hint to his condition and exacerbate it. A pilot with vertigo would become rough and uncoordinated. The only fix was an occasional peek at his own aircraft's instruments. A quick peek would re-gauge his internal gyro, and the entire process would then repeat. It was an exhausting experience, expanding time and turning an hour into an eternity.

As they closed on L.A., all contour on the ground below remained lost, with the exception of the ridgeline that encircled the Los Angeles basin. The four separate flights continued to churn towards the glow. The black mountains encircling Los Angeles began to surrender bits of the city through their passes. The undefined glow gave way to the bright, well-defined, man-made grid of light that was Los Angeles at night. J.T. descended through a pass and into the L.A. basin. Clear of the mountains, he dropped to 2,500 feet.

The night was crystal clear. The bright lights of streets, homes and businesses filled the cockpit. The intensity was surprising and caused the crews to squint. It was as if they were flying over an immense pinball machine. Most streets ran east – west or north – south. Major thoroughfares and highways, with origins set on top of ancient foot trails, wound through the grid like white snakes, alive with the headlights of cars and trucks.

The edges of the grid were uneven on three sides as they ran up to the bases of foothills and mountains. The fourth side, on the western border, was a gentle curve of invisible coastline. The eight aircraft appeared as black forms racing across the effervescing landscape, their lights lost in the clutter of iridescence. Only the blue flame of exhaust remained as a reference for the wingmen.

J.T. reached for the microphone.

"Los Angeles, approach control American Zero One, flight of eight at 2,500."

"Roger, American," came the radio. "You are cleared direct LAX, altimeter 2-9-9-2, switch LAX tower at five miles."

"Wilco," was J.T.'s only response.

Jon looked over at his captain, who was peering excitedly out the window like a little boy. He hated to disturb J.T., but it was against his nature to keep his mouth shut if he had a question.

"Skipper, why didn't we tell them we were broken up?"

J.T. sat back, scanned the instruments in a snapshot glance, then responded.

"Because they would have tried to help, and we don't have time for normal arrival procedures. We'll maintain our own separation and go right into the overhead pattern."

He leaned forward in his seat.

"Okay Jon," he said. "I've got the airplane."

"You got it, boss," said Jon, relinquishing the controls.

J.T. turned toward the coast, looking for the airfield. He got sight of it at ten miles and turned his section to intercept the extended center line that was drawn in his head. There was no wind, so they ran straight in with no crab correction, descending to 1,000 feet. At five miles, they tuned the tower frequency into the radio and transmitted that they were five miles out for the overhead pattern, with three sections in trail at one-minute intervals. The tower cleared the entire flight to land, in order.

As the lead DC-3 crossed the threshold of the runway, J.T. flipped on his anti-collision light, signaling break up, then rolled into a left 45-degree angle of bank turn. Two Dogs continued straight ahead on runway heading for a count of five, then rolled into a mirror image of the lead's break turn. J.T. slowly pulled the power in the turn. As he passed through 180 degrees of turn, he had it all the way back to idle. Now abeam the landing area of the runway, he glanced out the side window to check his lateral distance from the runway. He scanned the airspeed: it was below 140 knots, so he called gear down and half flaps, as he eased his turn to 25 degrees angle of bank and simultaneously initiated a 1,000 feet-per-minute rate of descent.

Coming through the last 90 degrees of his circular turn, J.T. checked his position in relation to the runway. His altitude was good, showing 500 feet AGL. Speed was coming down to 120 knots. He detected a slight overshoot of runway center line, so he tightened his approach turn to 30 degrees angle of bank. As he entered the last 45 degrees of his turn, J.T.'s scan shifted from mostly inside, on the instruments, to mostly outside. His priority was glide slope, runway center line, then airspeed. The DC-3 continued to decelerate as he rolled, wings level, on center line. J.T. called for full flaps and set approach power as the DC-3 slowed through 100 knots indicated airspeed. The power caught and stabilized the airspeed at 85 knots. He continued to trim throughout the entire approach turn. Once on centerline, J.T.'s scan focused on landing area and airspeed.

Once he was sure his DC-3 would reach the runway, he

relaxed pressure on the yoke and let the nose fall through slightly, aiming for a touchdown point at the threshold of the runway. He scanned airspeed one last time on short final. At 20 feet, he began to slowly pull the power toward idle, simultaneously easing the yoke back in a flare. The DC-3 rolled smoothly onto the runway as the throttles touched the idle stops.

J.T. began slight but increasing pressure on the foot brakes, located on the top half of the rudder pedals. He continued to fly the tail until it touched the runway. While the braking pressure dramatically increased, the DC-3 slowed rapidly. It was a tricky dance; most did not attempt it. Instead, they would put the tail firmly on the ground before applying the brakes.

Jon had called out the landing checklist and moved the landing gear and flap handles on command. Then he sat back and watched the show – and it was a good show. As they rolled out on the runway, Jon watched the second section in the overhead. Each section followed in order; within seven minutes, the last DC-3 in the flight had touched down.

J.T. was out of the cockpit already and watching as the tail-end Charlie touched down. The chief had the ground crew hoppin' and poppin': fueling, checking oil levels, and doing turnaround inspections.

A young Army Air Corps Captain marched across the tarmac, headed directly toward J.T. Even in the dim light, his green uniform was obviously starched and pressed – perfect, in fact. He moved with purpose toward J.T. at a surprisingly brisk pace, giving the impression that he was crossing a parade field. He snapped to attention 4 feet from J.T. and rendered a crisp salute.

"Lieutenant Colonel Dobbs?"

J.T. was standing, arms folded, with most of his weight on his left leg. He was the antithesis of the young Captain. His khaki shirt and pants were rumpled and soiled from the long flight. Hatless, he made a half-hearted return of the salute.

"Yeah, I'm Dobbs."

The young Captain was unimpressed. He was the type of officer who was more concerned with the cut of a man's uniform than the cut of his character, more concerned with career than cause.

"Sir, I have charts and a flight plan for your navigator, as well as codes and frequencies for your radio operator."

J.T. looked at him with disgust. He knew the type: self-serving and ruthless, with loyalty to no one but himself. Men like him had driven J.T. to leave the peacetime Air Corps Reserve. They strutted around, all dressed up like pilots, but they were more like seagulls; you had to throw rocks at them to get them to fly. Then, when the shooting started they scurried off like cockroaches caught in the light, to some safe staff job. J.T looked at the braided cord around the arm of the young Captain. Attached at the shoulder, it signified that he was on a general's staff. It was brand new.

"Man", J.T. thought, "this weasel didn't waste much time finding a hiding spot."

"Sir, your navigator?" asked the young captain.

J.T. finally made eye contact.

"We ain't got one, Captain. I'll take it."

"No navigator for an ocean crossing? Most irregular, Colonel!"

"Yes, most – CAPTAIN." J.T. accentuated his rank, a not-so-subtle gesture of putting the twerp in his place. "We have neither time nor the space to deal with regularities."

The Captain stiffened.

"I assume no radio operator as well, then?"

J.T. shifted his weight and glared at the staff puke.

"That, I should think, is obvious even to you, Captain," he replied.

They stood locked in silent, motionless combat – the only combat this young staff officer would ever see. Even though they had just met, they both knew they were mortal enemies. To the Captain, J.T. was a simpleton who just didn't get it. For now their paths would diverge, the warrior to the charge of cannon fire, the bureaucrat to the promise of promotion.

J.T. took the leather attaché case from the Captain and moved toward his aircraft.

"Sir," protested the Captain, "that is my personal attaché case."

J.T. didn't bother to turn.

"I'm sure you can requisition another, here in the back echelon."

He continued to walk toward his aircraft and noticed Jon standing close by. The young first officer had been watching the exchange.

"Wow, he's kind of locked up!" said Jon.

J.T. smiled.

"Dope on a rope, Jonny boy," he said. "There will be more. Let's get out of here."

Chapter 9

The Conquest of the Malayan Peninsula
10 December 1941

The pre-dawn hours found Colonel Jessip in his makeshift headquarters. Spread before him was a large topographical map with the tactical picture detailed on it. Various colors and shapes represented the units available to him, free-fire zones for artillery and their preset coordinates. His pickets, or listening posts, were also charted. Already, four of his listening posts were offline, all of them on the western flank. He had equipped them with field telephones connected by landlines, the most reliable communication one could get in the bush. The likelihood that four would fail almost simultaneously was zero; he had to assume that the main Jap force was attacking from the west.

Assume, assume. All that kept running through his mind was the old military axiom he first heard at Sandhurst as a young cadet: "ASSUME makes an ASS out of U and ME." He had sent a patrol with one of the two remaining radios, but there had been no contact thus far.

Sporadic small arms fire from the area had been reported throughout the night, at times intense. Was it a probe, or was it the lead element of the main force? The sun would be up soon; he had to act. With nothing else to go on, Jessip ordered what little artillery he had, as well as his heavy automatic weapons, oriented to the western flanks.

Singapore was a large, fortified city at the southern tip of the

Malayan peninsula. It represented the choke point at the entrance to the Straits of Malacca. The straits separated the Indian Ocean from the South China Sea; their strategic value could not be understated. If they fell into Japanese hands British India would be cut off from Australia and the United States. The Royal Navy would secure the southern flank – the northern land approach had fallen to Colonel Jessip to defend.

General Percival had expected the main thrust at Singapore itself via an amphibious assault. Jessip had argued that the Japanese would come from the north after landing unopposed. It was no comfort to know he had been correct. The invasion force had landed as he expected.

Reinforcements were on their way. He did not expect them to reach his position in time. He would have to defend along a wide approach from the north. Rather then spread his forces thin, along a line east to west, Jessip had brought them in tight, around a section of hills northeast of Kuala Lumpur. There, he had dug in and fortified his position. His hope was that the Japs would pass him by and attack Singapore, allowing him to maneuver from the rear and engage the Japanese. This, he knew, was not likely. The Japanese were an army of maneuver; they knew its advantages. They would not leave a unit intact to maneuver on them. No, they would attack and destroy his unit first.

The logical route of the Japanese was down the flatter, western side of the Malayan Peninsula. That was the nucleus of his doubt. It was too obvious an approach. Doubt continued to nag at Jessip's subconscious until his apprehension suddenly morphed to comprehension. He snapped a quick order to his communication officer.

"Contact all eastern and central pickets. Order them to imme-diately check for signs of movement between each post, quickly!"

The Com O replied with a nervous "Yes, Sir!"

The doubt that had nagged at Jessip's subconscious was now surfacing as action. The Colonel was intensely worried. He could not wait for confirmation of what he knew to be true. He whirled around to face his staff and exploded into a staccato of rapid-fire orders.

"Arty!"

"Sir?"

"Re-orient all artillery to the eastern flank."

The artillery Captain protested.

"But sir, the western pickets are not reporting."

The Colonel raged. "Do it NOW!"

"All automatic weapons to the eastern flank; stand by for action from the east. I say again the east!"

"COM O!"

"Sir I have no word…"

The Colonel cut him off.

"I need no verification, Lieutenant; the attack is coming from the east. Get the Royal Navy on the net."

The Colonel stood motionless in deep thought. The COM O abruptly stood; his chair tipped behind him to the floor. The racket of the chair striking the wooden planks caught Jessip's attention. He looked up to see the COM O standing with an absolute look of shock on his face.

"What is it, man?" demanded the Colonel.

"Colonel, the Royal Navy reports the *Repulse* and *Prince of Wales* have been engaged by Japanese dive bombers and torpedo aircraft. All communication was lost – a destroyer in the area reports both sunk!"

Silence fell across the room.

"Sir, our flank is exposed!"

The Colonel held up his hand. "Worse than that I fear, it means we will face the entire landing force."

Jessip scrambled out of the makeshift headquarters. When he reached the edge of the slit trench encircling the HQ, he rested his binoculars on the sand bags scanning the valley below. In the background the COM O, now near panic, rattled off.

"Sir, pickets Tiger and Wildcat report evidence of large troop movements between posts."

The Colonel didn't bother to look up from his binoculars.

"Yes I know son, sound the alarm."

He continued to scan the valley below. In the predawn light, he could see the mist pouring down the hill sides like a stream. He demanded, willed the sun to rise faster. He began to detect movement just below the surface of the ground fog. It moved like salmon in a shallow stream. The sun relented to his order and emitted just enough light that he saw what he expected.

The Imperial Japanese Army was moving with a speed and stealth he had never seen. They seemed to be not individual soldiers but a single mass. Splitting, rejoining, and then splitting again with the quality of quicksilver running down a rough surface.

"Magnificent," he muttered.

Already, at least two battalions had passed inside minimum range for the artillery. He slowly turned to his staff and, in a quiet and matter-of-fact tone, gave his orders.

"All artillery minimum range, fire zone alpha and bravo, fire for effect, fire for effect."

In the end, his men fought bravely. Colonel Jessip accomplished his limited goal by bloodying the Japs' nose. But ultimately, that was all he had to offer to British Command in Singapore when he advised, "overrun imminent" in his final communiqué. His command post was overrun as that last message was sent. Two of his staff officers pulled their side arms and killed the first three Japanese troops to enter the HQ. They were quickly riddled by the swarming Japanese.

Colonel Jessip stood and faced the Japanese major in charge of the assault force. He straightened his tunic, then gazed at the dirty, blood-splattered officer and came to attention.

"Well, that is that," he said, "eh, chaps?"

The words had barely left his lips when the Major's samurai sword flashed in the dim light of the command post, and the Colonel's head was severed, swiftly and cleanly.

P-40 WARHAWK

Chapter 10

Feet Wet
10 December 1941

The full moon was rising over the Pacific as Seven Alpha launched. It seemed as big as the sun. The illumination was so bright the crews could read their checklists without the help of manmade light. As the flight climbed into the moonlit sky, J.T. thought: *"Good. We are back on schedule, back on plan."*

Not that the huge full moon was planned; it wasn't. That was luck. All good planners took advantage of luck. They never relied on it, but always capitalized on it. *"Better to be lucky than good"*, J.T. assured himself with a smile.

Seven Alpha was back on schedule, J.T. knew, because the ground crews had hustled and made it happen. *"They never get the credit they deserve for keeping these techno-marvels aloft."* J.T. vowed to himself that as always, he would take care of his boys. It really didn't take much, no more than genuine concern. They were smart and perceptive, with the ability to smell bullshit from 10,000 feet. A pat on the back, a night on the town, could motivate like no order or threat. J.T. knew this as a given, a truth the young staff officer back in L.A. would never get, ever!

"Enough philosophy", the term that over-educated men gave to common sense. All J.T. wanted now was to enjoy the moment, the moon, and the Pacific. Seven Alpha became a part of the night as they moved west. Each element, man, machine, star was now an integral piece of the equation, the sum of which was unknown.

J.T. reached for the microphone of his R/T.

"American, ah, belay that, Army seven eleven expedite the

rendezvous. We are tight on fuel and need to stay on our plan, lead is 110 knots."

Jon looked over at J.T. and asked, "Why 711, boss?"

"Because this whole operation is one big crapshoot, Junior."

The eight DC-3s continued their majestic climb-out. With the moon so full it seemed like day, even the ocean glistened below as the two came together. With their interior lights turned down low, the darkest places in the December night were the eight silent cockpits. As the aircraft moved out over the Pacific and away from the artificial light of L.A., the ocean light intensified when the stars joined in. Trey glanced back, straining to see the lit coast slip away, wondering how long it would be before he saw it again.

The incredible night seemed without boundary: the moon, the depth of stars. All external lights on the DC-3s were off; there was no need for them. The Seven Alpha crews maintained their position in formation by using moonlight and the blue flame of the exhaust gas escaping from within the R-1830, the DC-3 engine. It spilled through the exhaust pipes and over the engine nacelles, creating a beacon of soft blue. The night held an aura that seemed so omnipotent that it would never surrender the sky.

The forces of nature would not be denied, no more than the force of fate that pulled these men toward the white hot fire of war. After ten hours the night sky succumbed to the dawn. The first officers, Air Corps copilots now, had cycled back to the passenger compartments for rest. Upon their return the captains, now transport aircraft commanders, caught some sleep. To a man, they did so in the cockpit, awakening at the slightest miscue of power or over control of the yoke. The neophyte, formation-flying copilots were doing a great job, but they were still green.

Trey stole a few moments for himself on his way to the cockpit. He stood on a small platform and put his head all the way into the celestial bubble, a rounded window shaped like a large punch bowl. Navigators used the bubble to take bearings from the stars with a sextant. Trey was using it as a window to heaven itself.

The solar symphony of sunrise had started; the color spectrum began to come to life in the east. The primary elements of the color wheel Trey had learned in high school art class illuminated the night sky. Deep red at the base, along the eastern horizon, faded to red, then to orange and yellow softening into the cool colors of green, light blue, blue, and deep blue to purple. Venus and Jupiter still shone brightly in the early morning sky, witnesses to the glory of a new day. The moon's light was no longer the primary force of the sky as it retreated to the horizon. The piercing stars began to fade in the east as the coming sun slowly smothered their light, while the stars in the western hemisphere fought for dominance on the limitless stage.

Trey stood reverently in the window, in awe of God's creation. A product of St Gertrude's Catholic School, he had learned his religious lessons well, but it was here that he felt the presence of God. Separated from heaven itself by a mere quarter-inch of Plexiglas, he found God in the stars, not in the books of catechism.

Looking back to the east, the red began to burn hot with the coming sun. The scattered orange clouds grew white-hot edges, further lighting the morning sky. They were pathfinders to the dawn, chasing the stars from the sky before the sun broke the horizon. The planets and a few stars clung stubbornly to the sky, resisting the dawn; they burned brighter than the rest.

"Like men", he thought. *"Some had an intensity that refused to be cowed"*. They would not relinquish the sky until the sun itself pushed them from it, surrendering only to proximity, not intensity. His father was like the last of the morning stars: he stood out among many. Trey only recently had realized how bright. As the new day dawned, he reflected on yesterday and what he had learned about his father. He moved forward into the cockpit, strapped in, and looked over at his father. Trey could not understand why he had kept his glorious past a secret.

The red fireball broke the horizon, consuming the light of even the brightest. The ocean began to swim out of the darkness. Even from altitude, its movement and currents began to reveal themselves. Out of the dawn's mist rose the emerald jewels of the Pacific: the Hawaiian Isles. With the sun beginning to rise behind the eight DC-3s, the indirect lighting colored the ocean a soft purple, broken only by the jagged outlines of the blue-green islands, barely discernible on the horizon. As the orange dawn sun broke free of the hazy horizon, its refracted light became direct. The colors of the ocean and islands transformed in front of the air crews' very eyes. The Pacific changed from purple to turquoise and the islands' blue tint faded. Seemingly lost in the morning splendor, Trey turned toward his father.

"Why didn't you tell us?" he asked.

"Tell you what?"

"That you were a hero."

Charles Henry looked uncomfortable as he tried to formulate a proper response.

"I didn't feel much like a hero."

Trey looked perplexed. To a young pilot, a fighter pilot – especially an ace – was the top of the heap.

"I don't understand, Pop."

Charles Henry looked past Trey, out the side windscreen, and nodded.

"You will, son. Very soon."

Trey looked out his window to see a menacing shark-toothed grin, painted on the nose of a P-40 War Hawk.

It had rendezvoused silently, guns armed and charged. The P-40 pilot had been briefed on the scheduled arrival of Army 711, but nothing was left to chance now – not after the attack on Pearl Harbor.

The P-40's pilot had slipped his agile fighter through the widely spaced DC-3s. Now he was tight on the right wing of Charles Henry's aircraft, peering into the cockpit at Trey. Suddenly, he jammed on the power to his Allison V-1710-81: all the horses came alive instantly. Smoothly, the pilot pulled straight up. As the nose reached 30 degrees in pitch, he initiated a slow roll to the left. Trey pressed his face to the windscreen to watch the slow, graceful roll from their right wing to the left wing of Roper in dash two. At the apex of the roll, the P-40 was inverted right over the top of the DC-3s. Throughout the maneuver, he never took his eyes off the DC-3s.

"What the hell is he doing?"

Charles Henry glanced left to see the completion of the exacting maneuver.

"It's called a canopy roll."

"I know that, but why is he doing it?"

Charles Henry looked at his son and winked.

"I'm guessing he wasn't too thrilled with your Mama's blonde hair and my blue eyes, *Liebchen*. He's mutt-checking Roper over there. I figure Roper is flipping him off about now, and that ought to certify our bona fides."

Trey looked out his side windscreen, and for the first time noticed the fighter's wingman in a high perch, watching. Trey didn't need to ask what he was there for. He knew that if anyone twitched, the wingman would come off his perch, guns blazing.

Trey was learning quickly.

Chapter 11

Pearl Harbor
11 December 1941

The Seven Alpha Squadron was still under escort as they approached the Hawaiian Islands. Abeam the garden island of Molokai, the fighter escort detached. J.T. watched the little fighters pour on the power and pull up into a tight chandelle turn. A chandelle is a climbing turn that changes an aircraft's heading 180 degrees, thus reversing his direction. A tactic developed in WWI, it was used by fighters to meet an enemy aircraft head-on after the enemy appeared behind and above. By reversing direction, a fighter was able to meet his adversary neutrally (head-on) instead of having the disadvantage of a tail-on attack. The critical component of the tactical turn was to maintain maneuvering speed, enabling the fighter to fight aggressively at the merge.

The lightweight P-40s, with their big Allison V-1710-81 engines, performed the chandelle effortlessly. They quickly disappeared behind the flight, returning to their combat air patrol station. J.T.'s glance fell from the molted green fighters to the vibrant colors of Molokai. The blended, flowing richness of the jungle was punctuated by the grey pinnacles of Kamakou jutting from the interior. The white sand border separating the greens of the jungle from the blues of the ocean was just the right accent.

"Perfect", thought J.T. Jon was flying. so he could afford an extended, longing look at the white sand beaches as they slipped by. He glanced at his watch. *"Time to get my head back in the game."* J.T. pulled out his flight log and checked his ETA

(estimated time of arrival) against his ATA (actual time of arrival) to arrive abeam the Kalauppa Peninsula on Molokai: he was within seven minutes.

"Excellent," he murmured to no one in particular. "We are still on schedule."

Jon knew J.T. well enough to know when and when not to respond. He had learned through experience that if he responded wrongly, it always elicited the same response from J.T. "What?" he would say, and Jon would reply with his own, "What," resulting in both staring at the other like he was a confused idiot. When J.T. was focusing on something, it was best not to derail the train of thought.

J.T. stole one more glance out the side windscreen.

"Okay Jon, I've got the aircraft."

Jon raised his hands to verify that he was off the controls.

"You got it, boss."

J.T. settled in. The controls felt light; the DC-3 neither rolled off nor changed in pitch when he relaxed his grip momentarily. *"Good"*, he thought. *"Jon is learning to trim this thing hands-off."*

Satisfied with the condition of his DC-3, J.T. scanned forward on the horizon. He noticed for the first time the funeral pyres, caused by the Jap sneak attack, rising over Pearl Harbor, Hickam, Wheeler, and Kaneohe Bay Airfields. The dark, dirty smoke fouled the dawn sky. He shook his head, thinking of this trip's continuing dichotomy.

The Air Corps had directed Army 711 to fly "feet wet" until reaching Pearl. "Feet wet" meant over the water, allowing the Army's first-generation radar to pick them up and track them continuously. The Imperial Japanese Navy had cut across the Island of Oahu to get to Pearl undetected. Now, the Air Corps wanted friendlies to stick to their assigned routes, to minimize friendly fire casualties. Any aircraft not on an assigned route would be attacked.

Seven Alpha's route had brought them to a predetermined entry point north of Molokai. Throughout the night, they had flown a southwesterly base course of 243 degrees. They had adjusted a couple of degrees either side of base to correct for the winds, plotting their position and drift using the stars. The lead

DC-3 had a celestial observation window on top of the fuselage just aft of the cockpit. Like ancient mariners, they had used sextants and the stars to figure their progress. Now with the arrival of the dawn and the islands in view, they could navigate visually.

Hickam and Wheeler Army airfields were still a mess, with the runways under repair, so J.T. opted for Ford Island Naval Air Station in the middle of Pearl Harbor. The Navy, being ship-oriented, always wanted to land into the wind. At Naval aviation's inception, aircraft required little room to take off and land, so they had developed circular airfields. Air crew would fly over, look at the windsock, and orient the pattern to land into the wind. "No cross-wind" landings were a big advantage in the early days of aviation. An advantage only recently realized was that because of the big area, circular airfields were hard to put out of service by bombing. A runway, on the other hand, could be cut by a few well-placed bombs.

J.T. put the biggest column of smoke on the nose; he knew it would be Pearl. He checked his fuel: they were fat on gas, so he bumped up the power and started a slow descent as they accelerated toward Pearl, Ford Island – and the aftermath of war.

Passing through 3,000 feet, he saw Diamond Head come into view. The distinctive peak stood out from the rest of Oahu, overlooking Waikiki beach and Pearl Harbor. As they rounded Diamond Head, leveling at 1,000 feet, J.T. glanced at the coastal defenses on top of the peak. He could see their anti-aircraft gun barrels tracking Seven Alpha as the flight cruised by. The beach was running parallel to their course. J.T. took a cut away from Waikiki to go farther off the coast. He eased the flight westward to make the turn into Ford Island easier for his wingman. He porpoised his tail, signaling his flight to close up the spacing and take parade formation.

The smoke rose straight into the air, signifying calm wind. J.T. decided to land parallel to Battleship Row, which would keep the flight clear of the smoke in their break turn. He was indicating 200 knots, with the flight in finger four, as he turned in for Ford Island. Rolling wings level, J.T. raised his left hand with a clenched fist to his side windscreen. Two Dogs smoothly crossed under, coming from J.T.'s left wing, filling the open gap for him between J.T.'s right wing and Thumper in dash 3. Now, lined up in echelon right, they closed on Ford Island at 220 knots.

The devastation on Battleship Row was now fully revealed to the Seven Alpha aviators, though only the copilots could catch a glance. The aircraft commanders were intently focused on maintaining a perfect parade position. They knew all eyes on the ground would be on them, their professional reputations at stake. Even in the face of this complete destruction, a tight, well-disciplined flight was demanded – now more than ever, because it was a payment of respect, an airborne salute to fallen comrades.

J.T. scanned the landing pattern for traffic as Jon witnessed the carnage. This adventure was quickly losing its charm. The pattern was empty, so after looking to the tower and receiving the clear to land signal, he had Jon flash five fingers to his wingmen, setting an interval of five seconds between aircraft. Seven Alpha had been in radio silence since leaving L.A. – there was no telling who was listening.

With a green light from the tower giving permission to land, and the interval set at five seconds, J.T. had Jon wave off the flight as he rolled into his break turn. He pulled a hard left, three "G" turn, and his flight followed in perfect intervals. Charles Henry had extended his flight farther to the west before his turn-in for Ford, to gain extra separation for his four aircraft. He had calculated perfectly, arriving over the field as Ski, the last of J.T.'s flight, was at the abeam position of the landing area. This allowed Charles Henry to break immediately and fall right into line as the fifth DC-3 to land. Their interval was tight, and within a very short time, all eight aircraft were on deck.

The DC-3s had shut down next to an open hanger on the southeast side of the field. The hanger, between the landing field and Battleship Row, was being used as a temporary morgue. What had once been white sheets covered the stretchered bodies. Trey walked closer, drawn by a morbid sense of curiosity. He looked across the hundreds of shrouded bodies, uniformly lined up in rows. As he stood in stunned silence, a

light breeze lifted a sheet, revealing the charred arm of a fallen
sailor at his feet.

Trey recoiled. "My God!"

He turned quickly, feeling like an intruder on hallowed
ground, and bumped immediately into his father, who had
walked up behind him.

"It's worse when you know them," said Charles Henry.

Trey looked into his father's eyes and saw a pain and apprehension he had never seen in this stoic man.

"I had hoped – prayed – that you and your brothers would be
spared this."

Trey now understood what his father had meant this morning,
when he had asked him about the Great War.

J.T. walked by, breaking the silence.

"Come on let's get moving, it's getting ugly out there." He
nodded to the west. "We've got to be in the air in an hour."

In his hand was a message from C.R.

* * *

Cantrell had kept his men moving almost without rest. He knew
the Japanese would be moving fast, heading south. Because of
this, he was sure they would stay out of the mountains. He had
kept his company to a mountain trail going up the spine of
Malaya. His intent was to follow it to Burma, then hook up with
the Allied forces there.

But Sergeant Major Menzies had tossed the proverbial wrench
into his plan. He had put out a scout patrol as well as the normal
point man. The conundrum presented to Cantrell was a fat,
undefended target. The overachieving Gunny Paillou had been
the patrol leader. He had found a Japanese supply depot that
was virtually defenseless. His orders were to egress undetected.
Now the two senior enlisted men stood in front of him, waiting
for an answer to a question that had not been asked.

Major Cantrell turned to Captain Russell.

"Let's set up a classic pincer attack – hit and run."

Russell nodded. The sergeants smiled.

Then he added, "We need to be in and out. This will upset the
apple cart; they will come after us."

The company of raiders split into two groups and stalked down the ridgeline to the flat land between beach and hills. The Japanese supply depot was moving supplies from landing craft, then loading them onto trucks to move south. They were mostly stevedores; the few armed troops were not in a tactical position and definitely were not ready for action.

Major Cantrell attacked from the south, Captain Russell from the north – they caught the Japanese completely by surprise. The raiders swept through the shocked troops like a scythe, cutting them down in a single pass. The victory was devastating and complete. The raiders set fire to everything and melted into the jungle. The entire operation took less then half an hour.

After the raid, they moved for twelve hours without stop. When they finally stopped, there was an after-action debrief. The common thread was how crushing and one-sided the raid had been; they hadn't taken a single casualty. They were shocked at how effective it had been. And they were convinced they had a very effective tactic with which to fight the Japanese.

Date time group: 00422Z, 11 DEC 1941
From: COMMANDER AIR TRANSPORT COMMAND
To: COMMANDER SEVEN ALPHA
Subject: WESTPAC INTEL UPDATE
Classification: TOP SECRET SCI/EYES ONLY COM7ALPHA
Text: HONG KONG, NORTH EAST MALAYA, KRA ISTHMUS THAILAND
INVADED BY IMPERIAL JAPANESE FORCES. INVASION FORCE SIGHTED
NORTH EAST PHILIPPINE ISLANDS. EXPEDITE BY ALL WAYS/MEANS. WATCH YOUR ASS.
C.R. SENDS

Chapter 12

Wake
11/12 December 1941

Seven Alpha was now literally on the other side of the world, having crossed the International Date Line. The eight DC-3s were picking their way through a massive line of thunderstorms. The boomers seemed endless, rolling at the aviators one after another. The constant weaving had caused two problems on this, the longest leg of their journey. First their DR, or dead reckoning, plot had become a mess of course and altitude changes. Unable to shoot stars in daylight, they weren't really sure of their exact position. Even more critical, they were low on fuel, thanks to all the course and altitude changes.

J.T. knew things were going south fast when Charles Henry broke radio silence.

"Lead, division two fuel critical."

J.T. responded with one word: "Copy."

Nothing else need be said. He already knew; he was watching his own fuel inch toward *Empty*. He also knew that fuel burn was inverse to flight order. The wingmen burned at a higher rate because they had to maintain position by adding and pulling off power. The pumping effect wasted fuel. The net effect was like cracking a whip; the tail end would have the greatest movement. Bluto was at the back. Even if he was as smooth as possible with the power, he had to be in trouble – the same trouble in which J.T. found himself.

Every aircraft is different; some are easier on gas than others. J.T. knew these eight machines. He knew that their fuel burn varied surprisingly, when in theory they should be the same.

That is why he picked the airplane that he did. It was bent, either in manufacture or from a hard landing. Why didn't matter, what did matter was that it burned fuel at a higher rate than the others. One-and-a-half gallons an hour per engine added up, over a thirteen-hour trip, to thirty-nine gallons. J.T. figured he had the lowest fuel state even though he was the lead.

He also knew they were close – they had to be, or they were all going for a swim.

"Jon, see if you can get Wake on the radio and we will DF* off his signal. Go ahead and tune the ADF* to this frequency."

"Roger that, skipper. What is their call sign?"

"Outpost."

"That's appropriate," said Jon. "Outpost, Outpost, American Seven Eleven."

J.T. tapped Jon on his forearm.

"Oh, yeah," said Jon. "Outpost, *Army* Seven Eleven."

Jon tried for twenty minutes with no result. The tension was building exponentially as the fuel dwindled. Every man knew that if they ditched here in the most desolate spot on the planet, they were done.

"Now what?" asked Jon, looking at J.T., who was rubbing his chin.

"Call out a Mayday."

Jon realized they were now deep in it. To an aviator, calling Mayday was tantamount to saying the f-word in front of your mother: once out, you couldn't take it back. It was a call for help that no pilot ever wanted to admit he might need; an admission that he may not be able to handle the situation.

"MAYDAY, MAYDAY, MAYDAY. Outpost, this is Army Seven Eleven. MAYDAY, MAYDAY, MAYDAY."

An answer came immediately. The ADF needle swung on the compass card and steadied up, 30 degrees to the right of their present course. J.T. turned the flight, putting the needle on the nose.

*Direction find.
*Automatic Direction Finder.

The radio crackled.

"Army Seven Eleven, Outpost, weather below minimums. Stand by for holding instructions."

J.T. picked up his microphone.

"NEGATIVE, NEGATIVE, Outpost. We are in a bit of a jam; we don't have a choice. We've got eight birds running out of fuel up here."

"Sorry, Seven Eleven. We don't have an instrument approach and even if we did, the weather is zero-zero* down here. You will have to hold."

"Not today, Outpost," said J.T. "Here is what we are going to do: I need you to give me a constant carrier on this frequency."

"Say again, Seven Eleven?"

"Just hold the mike button until you have eight silver birds on your tarmac."

"Roger that, Seven Eleven."

"Flight," said J.T., "switch backup frequency."

Each of the aircraft responded in sequence, saying only their number.

Jon dialed in the pre-set secondary frequency. J.T. checked in the flight on the new frequency and set out the plan.

"Okay, gents," said J.T., "our heading is north and aligned with the runway heading. We are at 150 knots, 3,000 feet. When the needle swings, we will be overhead Outpost. Detach in inverse order, take a 30-degree cut to the east, descend for one minute, then make a standard rate turn west all the way back to the field, and land south. Slow to 100 knots on final, and descend until the field is in sight. We will only have a twenty-second interval, so fly the numbers; that island is flat. Good luck, and call on deck."

J.T. snuggled the flight up, as closely as he dared, to a large thunderstorm that he assumed was overhead Wake. The needle swung, and the Seven Alpha flight initiated its homemade instrument approach.

Bluto detached and transmitted, "Eight descending."

At twenty-second intervals, each aircraft detached and

*Ceiling and visibility.

descended into the weather below. At two minutes of elapsed time, Two Dogs detached.

J.T. continued for his twenty-second interval. Jon looked down at the fuel gauge.

"Skipper, we're banging on empty."

J.T. nodded and began a turn west, not east.

"Hey, skipper – we are turning the wrong way!"

Again, J.T. nodded. Jon began to squirm in his seat.

"We didn't take a cutaway – we won't be lined up with the runway!"

"It'll all work out, Jon," said J.T. "Just hang on."

He rolled out pointed at Outpost, but offset 30 degrees to the west from the runway and the rest of the flight. Jon continued to squirm.

"Are we going to descend?"

"Not yet."

"Eight's on deck," came over the radio receiver.

J.T. continued inbound at 150 knots and 3,000 feet, pointed directly at the thunderstorm.

"Skipper, are we going to slow and descend?"

"Seven's on deck," came the radio.

"Not yet," said J.T.

"We are going to run down our interval!"

"That's why we are offset west."

"Six on deck."

J.T. eased the nose down. Without pulling the power back, their speed began to build.

"Skipper, we are 160 knots indicated!"

Jon's voice was rising in octave and volume.

"Five on deck."

The DC-3 began to buffet as they flew under the thunderstorm.

"190!"

The buffeting began to increase; within seconds, there was severe turbulence.

"Four on deck."

Their DC-3 was slammed with a wall of water that seemed more like a waterfall than rain.

"195 knots, we are going to run down three!"

Number two engine coughed, then died.

"Skipper, the rain is snuffing the engines."

Jon was wrong. Number two was out of gas. The buffeting was making it almost impossible for them to read the instruments.

"Call my altitude, Jon."

"We are 500 feet, 195 knots."

"All I need is altitude," replied J.T., far too calmly to suit Jon.

"Three on deck."

"We are still haulin' the mail here, skipper," said Jon. "180 knots, 400 feet!"

They burst through the other side of the wall of water into a foggy mist, just as number one engine quit. J.T. reached up and feathered both props to reduce drag.

"We are dead stick, boss."

Jon's voice was now calm and matter of fact. He had come to terms with the situation. His anxiety was caused by not knowing the plan. Since J.T. didn't have time to explain – in addition to the fact that he was making a lot of it up on the run – Jon was out of the loop.

As dramatically as they had emerged from the wall of water, they flew out of the mist into smooth, crystal clear air.

"300 feet, shit!" said Jon. "Traffic left, nine o-clock. It's number two."

J.T. looked over and picked up his microphone.

"Two Dogs, I'm your right three o-clock. Let me cut in front of ya here."

Two Dogs, startled by the transmission, looked right and saw the unmistakable sight of feathered props not turning. His response was in action only: he jammed right rudder and aileron and came on with the power in one motion, pulling hard behind J.T.'s gliding DC-3. Seeing his move, J.T. eased toward the runway centerline.

"200 feet, 140 on the speed."

J.T. had the nose pointed at the runway, there would be no straightaway on this landing.

"We are tight! 150 feet, speed 120."

J.T. nodded. "Gear now."

Jon threw down the gear handle.

"Full flaps."

Jon slapped the flap handle down. "100 feet, 100 knots."

The silent DC-3 crossed the beach at 50 feet, in a 30-degree angle of bank right hand turn, to line up with the runway centerline. J.T. eased the turn out as they rolled out on centerline, then touched the main mounts down, smooth as silk at 80 knots.

"Shit hot!" Jon exclaimed, shaking his head.

"Not yet, Jonny boy. We got to clear this runway for Two Dogs."

J.T. eased the tail down but did not touch the brakes, letting the aircraft roll out as fast as possible toward the taxiway turnoff. Holding the brakes until the last second, he hit them hard, then eased up on the left brake, using differential pressure to steer them clear of the runway. Two Dogs was already rolling out behind them as they cleared.

"After-landing checklist, please," J.T. calmly requested.

Jon was all smiles as he pulled out the checklist.

Wake was strangely quiet. Every man on the island knew they would be locked in a life-and-death struggle very soon. The sailors and marines knew the odds on their side: zilch, zed and zero. Even so, they went about the preparation for war quietly and methodically, having made peace with their private destinies.

The pace of the former American Airlines ground crews was much more frantic. The flight was behind schedule. Again, it would be up to them to make up the time. The chief was everywhere at once. He settled in for a moment next to a Marine major who was watching the fueling. Wake had big, high-speed pumps built by Pan American Airlines for their flying boats. The pumps were fitted with long hose and nozzle assemblies, so they could reach the top of the seaplanes' wings. Chief had towed the DC-3s down to the pumps and arranged them in a semicircle so that he could fuel three aircraft at a time. Back on the transient flight line, he had his guys going on a fourth with hand pumps borrowed from the Marine squadron.

The first seven were just topping off when J.T. walked up to the chief and major as they observed his DC-3 being fueled.

"We will only take what we need, Major."

"Shit, Colonel, after that approach I'd think you'd want all you can hold."

"Well, we don't want to run you low."

"We will be out of those antique Wildcats before we run out of gas. Less for the Japs to burn."

J.T. looked across the airfield to the parked F-4F Wildcats. *"Pretty little fighters"*, he thought: dark blue on top, light sky blue on the bottom, almost all engine. He mused at the major's antique comment, thinking back to his own trusty Spad. However, there was no denying that the Wildcat did not measure up to the Mitsubishi A6M2 Model 21 Zero. J.T. turned back to the Major.

"Well, at least that front blew through. You'll have good hunting weather."

The Major smiled and started to respond, then looked past J.T. to a young lance corporal running toward them.

"Major, combat air patrol at Point Tiger is engaging a Jap strike force!"

He handed J.T. a folded message. "Colonel, this came for you from the States."

J.T. stuffed the message into his pocket. The Major reached inside his flight jacket's internal pocket, pulling out a package.

"Colonel, could you mail these for us?" he asked.

J.T. took the package. "Sure, Major."

The Major shook J.T.'s hand. "Well, that's my cue. Point Tiger is only fifty miles out – you'd better beat feet."

J.T. watched for a second as the Major ran to his fighter. *"I never got his name"*, he thought. *"God speed, young major."* Then he pivoted and ran for his DC-3. The Marine F-4Fs were already scrambling, taking off in sections.

J.T. came upon his pilots standing in a group, watching.

"Man up, man up," he told them. "The Japs are only fifty miles out. We have got to be airborne in five minutes. Stay low and maintain total radio silence."

As Charles Henry and Trey ran for their DC-3, Trey yelled over the last two F-4Fs taking off. "Don't worry, Dad. They'll get them for us."

"I'm afraid not, son," Charles Henry shouted. "Even if they had enough Wildcats, which they don't, they are no match for the Zeros. We have got to go, and now!"

J.T. reached his aircraft as it was still being fueled. The fueling had been delayed while they performed maintenance to reset the props after J.T. had feathered them on his approach. The chief was extolling his boys to hurry.

"We got enough, chief?" J.T. asked.

"No!"

"How short?"

"At least fifty gallons, maybe a hundred."

"It will have to do."

Chief shook his head. "Well, it won't."

J.T. winked at the chief and tossed him the package that he had received from the Major.

"We'll make it work," he said.

"Yeah, right. What's this?" asked the chief as he caught the package.

"Wills and last letters home."

Jon was just cranking number one as J.T. clambered into the cockpit.

"Taxi now!" As J.T. got into the captain's seat, number one engine barked to life.

Jon yelled, "Hang on," then released the brakes while the engine ran up to idle. .

J.T. started number two as Jon taxied the DC-3 to the runway. He pushed the throttles up to thirty inches of manifold pressure. Number two balked with a cough, then caught.

"Go!" yelled J.T., and strapped himself into his seat.

"They are still cold," protested Jon.

"Ease them up; they'll work. Now roll this crate!"

The engines strained and rumbled as Jon slowly ran them up to takeoff power. He didn't need to look at the temperature of the oil and cylinders on the gauges to know that they were not in the green band for takeoff. The heavy DC-3 lumbered off the short, coral airstrip.

"Get the gear and flaps," J.T. yelled, still strapping in. "Stay low – 100 feet max – and leave them fire walled."

Jon was all motion, reaching for the gear handle, yanking it up, putting the flap handle in retract, and trimming like a madman as the aircraft accelerated and tried to climb. The aerodynamic forces fought him, and he forced the DC-3 to stay at 100 feet.

"Anything else?" he asked the boss.

"Yeah, go straight south and don't hit the damn water!"

Jon couldn't suppress his laugh; it snuck out even over the roar of the Pratt and Whitney R-1830s.

"Roger that, skipper."

The eight aircraft accelerated one by one, each crewman crossing his fingers that the cold engines wouldn't falter. The aircraft all successfully struggled airborne, holding their noses down as they blasted across the Pacific at wave-top height.

Charles Henry squinted into the evening sun, Trey at the controls.

"Don't lose sight of him."

"I've got him," said Trey. "My eyes are just fine, old man."

"Yeah, yeah. Just keep him in sight, sonny boy."

Trey smiled to himself in self-congratulation. One up on the old man was a rare event, one he relished.

The eight DC-3s continued to scorch south at redline speed into the gathering twilight. J.T. had been figuring on his MB-4A computer. He put it away at last, satisfied with the final numbers.

"How long have we been airborne?" he asked.

"Thirty-two minutes," Jon responded without hesitation.

"Okay Jon, set minimum climb power, start us up, and come right to a heading of 250 degrees. Let's get this gaggle rejoined."

The speeding DC-3s came off the ocean in sequence. The lead aircraft decelerated quickly, simultaneously raising its nose in a climb, and reduced power. The trailing DC-3s kept their power fire walled, also using radius of turn to head the lead off. By doubling the lead's angle of bank and getting inside his radius of turn, they closed quickly on the 45-degree rendezvous bearing line. After aligning fuselages with rudder, they slid up the bearing line, using the excess power to maintain a speed advantage over the lead for closure. They closed on the lead, coming up the bearing line like they were on a rail, much more precisely than yesterday.

"Or was it the day before"? thought Jon as he looked over his shoulder.

Once they were all together and headed 250 degrees, J.T. craned his neck to count his flight. Charles Henry had positioned his division to the left aft, and stepped up on the lead division. It allowed J.T. an easy glance at all four aircraft; a courtesy he appreciated. Satisfied that all chicks were aboard, he looked toward the setting sun and pulled out the message from Washington.

"There it goes again," muttered Jon.

J.T. looked up. "Yep, there it goes."

Even with Jon next to him, he felt an eerie melancholy and strange isolation. J.T. watched as the color spectrum lit up the western sky. It looked like a rainbow that had been stretched out straight and laid on its side. Purple fading to blue, then green, yellow, orange and red. Wisps of cloud, now backlit black-highlighted and interrupted the otherwise perfect color spectrum.

Some scientist was always trying to explain the wonders J.T. saw; he didn't want to know. He just wanted to watch the stars fight to retake the sky.

TOP SECRET

Date time group: O355 ZULU 11 DEC 1941
From: COMMANDER AIR TRANSPORT COMMAND
To: COMMANDER SEVEN ALPHA
Subject: WESTPAC INTEL UPDATE
Classification: TOP SECRET SCI/EYES ONLY COM7ALPHA
Text: BRITISH FORCES REELING MALAYAN PENINSULA.
HMS PRINCE OF WALES HMS REPULSE SUNK. JAPANESE
FORCES INVADING PHILIPPINES. LUZON IN NORTH AND
SOUTH. LINGAYEN GULF IN WEST. LEGAZPI MAY BE IN
DOUBT. WYA.
C.R. SENDS

TOP SECRET

Chapter 13

Philippine Islands
12 December 1941

The sun had been up for an hour when the Philippine Islands came in sight. *"Breathtaking"*, thought J.T. Again, the dichotomy: the Philippines were embroiled in a desperate war, yet from where he sat right now, it was the picture of tranquility and beauty.

An island nation, it was much different from the Hawaiian chain. It was more a gathering of archipelagos, islands of various sizes and shapes, densely gathered in a turquoise ocean. Unfortunately, there could be no sightseeing today.

Seven Alpha was now in the hot war. They had missed it by hours in Pearl, and minutes at Wake, but now they would be smack dab in the middle of a shooting war. J.T. dropped the flight to sea level again and headed straight for Legazpi in the southern Luzon Province.

He hoped it hadn't fallen yet. The Japs had moved faster than anyone thought possible; they seemed to be everywhere at once. If the field was overrun they would turn north for Clark Army Airfield. He knew he didn't have enough gas to make it, but he'd go as far as possible, then pass the lead to Charles Henry. With luck he could drop into a field, abandon the aircraft and jump in with another crew. If no opportunity to land presented itself, then he and his crew would be on their own. He would worry about it if and when it happened. For now, he was intent on getting into and out of Legazpi as soon as possible.

J.T. felt the chief's presence over his right shoulder.

"Skipper, how come we are still flying?"

J.T. smiled and responded, "Because I plan for success, not failure, Chief."

"Yeah, sure. What the hell is that supposed to mean?" The chief sounded annoyed.

"It means I figured all our fuel estimates for max cruise speed, and when we got shorted on Wake, I slowed us to max range speed. We used a lot less gas. That's the good news; the bad news is we are late again."

The chief nodded his approval and pointed ahead with his chin.

"They gonna be open for business down there?"

"I hope so." said J.T., still holding his smile. "We will know when I pop up. If there is an X of white sheets on the runway, then yes."

"If not?" asked the chief.

"Then we turn north for Clark."

The chief looked down at the fuel gauges. "We got enough to make it?"

"Nope."

The chief shrugged his shoulders. "Roger that," he said, and moved back into the cabin.

The city of Legazpi was closing rapidly; at three miles, J.T. popped the flight up to 1,000 feet. He took a quick comprehensive scan of the air and ground. He was looking for Zero's, tracers, smoke – and the X on the runway.

J.T. porpoised the tail of his DC-3 gently, and his division tightened up into parade formation. He crossed Two Dogs to the right side, and the formation tightened further into a perfect right echelon. Charles Henry configured his division in the same formation and dropped into a quarter-mile trail.

The field was located on the western edge of Legazpi. J.T. saw the runway and the X. An X normally means the runway is closed, but in this case it meant the opposite, and that the U.S. Army, not the Japanese, was awaiting Seven Alpha's arrival.

The two flights of four were lined up perfectly as they flew into the overhead pattern; each division moved as one unit. Jon looked over his right shoulder.

"They look a lot better today, skipper."

They broke up in sequence with fighter-like precision; the troopers on deck all stopped to watch the aerial precision. After their circular approach pattern, the eight DC-3s landed and taxied in intervals directly to the fuel pits, and shut down.

A young Army captain, whose name tag read Butler, met J.T. and Jon at the door of their aircraft.

"It's a good thing you guys aren't any later. We pull out in an hour."

J.T. looked surprised "Where to, Captain?"

"Batan. We are going to make a last stand there. Hopefully, we can hold on until reinforcements arrive."

"Jesus! It's that bad already?" asked J.T.

"Yes sir. Damn Japs are all over the Islands. They caught the Air Corps on deck at Clark. We don't have any air cover or bombers to stop the invasion. Haven't seen the Navy at all; they must be licking their wounds in Pearl."

J.T. shook his head in disbelief. C.R. had warned him; he just couldn't believe it. The front lines had been so static in the Great War, they never changed. They would fight and scratch for months for a few hundred yards. Now there didn't seem to be any lines at all, the Japs were nowhere and everywhere all at once. He turned his attention back to the present.

"We'll get out of your hair ASAP, Captain."

"Outstanding, Colonel. It may take some time though; we can only pump a couple simultaneously. Why don't you rest in the shade over there? We'll give you a shout when we are close."

J.T. looked over at the inviting patch of shady, thick grass. "That sounds like a good idea, Captain."

The Captain started to walk away, then turned back to J.T.

"Oh – I almost forgot: here is an "eye's only" for you from D.C. I'd have you sign for it, but not much point in keeping records just to burn."

J.T. nodded in agreement. "Roger that, Captain."

"One more thing, Colonel. Do you know a Joe Butler?"

J.T. looked at his name tag, "Yeah we got a plane captain with us named Butler. You know him?"

"Yes Sir, he's my brother."

J.T. sighed and turned to Jon. "Take the captain to see his

brother He's with Irish." He turned back to the Captain. "Thanks for your help. What's your name, young captain?"

"Dave. You're welcome. I wish you could stay longer, but that's not an option. Take care of my brother, wherever you are going."

"We will. You watch your ass out here – it is getting ugly fast."

They exchanged salutes, and J.T. sought the shelter of shade. Sitting down in the luxurious grass, he read his message.

Date time group: 0300 ZULU 12 DEC 1941
From: COMMANDER AIR TRANSPORT COMMAND
To: COMMANDER SEVEN ALPHA
Subject: WESTPAC INTEL UPDATE
Classification: TOP SECRET SCI/EYES ONLY COM7ALPHA
Text: CLOSE CALL ON WAKE. JAPS MASSING NEAR
SOUTHERN TIP BURMA. CROSS FROM ISTHMUS OF KRA
THAILAND TO BURMA IMMINENT. WYA.
C.R. SENDS

The odyssey was beginning to take its toll. The air crews really hadn't slept for a couple of days; not real sleep. An aviator can nod off into what seems like a deep sleep, but a change in power, aircraft attitude or a radio call will instantly bring him back to exactly where he is. No fog, no "where am I" – instant awareness. It is not a fitful sleep. As each man lay in the shade, he immediately fell into a dreamless slumber.

J.T. jerked awake to the prodding of the chief. "Skipper, skipper."

Instantly he was alarmed: the Army was gone and it was way too quiet.

"I'd love to let you sleep, but we better hi-yacca the hell outta here!"

J.T. wiped the sleep out of his eyes.

"How long has the Army been gone?"

"An hour. I cut them loose."

"Let's do hi-yacca, Chief!"

He jumped to his feet and started kicking boots.

"Come on knuckleheads, let's roll. I got a bad feeling about this place. Move! Now!"

As the groggy crews were rousted, they all awoke with the same sense of imminent danger and started scrambling for their aircraft. The ground crews had already pulled chocks and loaded on board. The engines began to cough to life as the plane captains fired them up in advance of the crews boarding.

The chief grabbed J.T. as he headed for his DC-3.

"Hey skipper, Butler's brother wanted me to light this when we left." He held a long fuse leading to the fuel and ammo dump.

"How much fuse?" asked J.T.

"They told me eleven minutes."

J.T. looked at the eight DC-3s; all sixteen of their engines were turning. "Well light it, Chief!"

"Aye aye, skipper."

The Chief lit the fuse with his well-chewed half cigar and flashed a devilish grin at J.T.

"Now, we most definitely must hi-yacca!"

J.T. returned his grin. "Most definitely!"

With that, they sprinted for their DC-3. Jumping into the captain's seat J.T. made one transmission on the R/T. "This place goes up in ten minutes. Do not dawdle, out."

The aircraft came out of the fuel pits two abreast starting their section takeoffs prior to reaching the runway. Each section was separated by less then five seconds as they rolled. The fuel pit was on the west end of the field, so they took off to the east to save the time they would have wasted taxiing the length of the field.

J.T. extended straight ahead for ten seconds after retracting the gear and flaps, using the time to accelerate to minimum maneuver speed. Then he started a climbing left turn at full power to get back on their westerly course. He was pulling hard, 45 degrees angle of bank, so each section followed his path of flight. They were unable to get inside his radius of turn and wouldn't be able to do a normal rendezvous. Instead, they would execute a running rendezvous, which meant simply running down the lead from a trail position once he eased back his power. Each pair performed their airborne U-turn with perfection, arriving in a straight line of four sections, passing just north of the field at 1,000 feet AGL.

Irish was rolling out in the trail position after his turn west when sporadic tracer fire suddenly streaked across the nose of the aircraft.

"What the heck is that?" screamed Danny as he pointed to the glowing bullets.

"Small arms fire – look." Irish rolled the DC-3 up on its left wing, letting Danny see the Japanese troops swarm over the field, shooting on the run.

"Holy cow, Irish – they almost got us!" As the words left his mouth, a small caliber bullet cracked through Irish's side windscreen ricocheted off the overhead panel and landed harmlessly in Danny's lap.

"A miss is as good as a mile! Here ya go, killer – a souvenir." Irish picked up the hot bullet and dropped it in Danny's breast pocket.

"Gee, thanks," Danny screeched as he flung the bullet out of his pocket.

Irish paid no attention. He pulled a flask out of his flight jacket's pocket, eased the cork out with his teeth, and plugged the circular hole in his window with it. Next, he took a long pull, turned and offered both the flask and a sarcastic remark.

"Don't mention it, New Guy, and don't worry. There will be plenty more."

Danny eyed the flask but resisted. Irish made two subtle jerking motions with the flask toward him.

"Liquid courage. Takes the edge off, Danny boy."

Dan took a reluctant swig.

"You'll be okay," Irish said, giving him a wink and a smile. "You get used to it." He took one more swallow, and stowed the little bottle back in his jacket.

Charles Henry was abeam the dump when he motioned Trey to look out the side windscreen. Trey leaned way over his father to get a look at the dreaded Japs. At that moment, the fuel and ammo dump blew with a force that rocked all eight aircraft. The explosion threw shrapnel and debris 1,000 feet higher than the DC-3s, and it began to rain down on them, banging on the fuselage like hail. Trey jerked back.

"Jesus!"

"Mary and Joseph too!" laughed his father.

Chapter 14

The Road to Calcutta
12 December 1941

The eight DC-3s were at treetop altitude with a redline airspeed of 221 knots indicated. J.T. tried to hold the base course, plus or minus 5 degrees, to the tip of French Indochina. His priority, however, was hiding. By using the terrain, he hoped to mask an entire squadron's crossing of the Philippine Islands. He weaved, climbed and descended, always keeping the flight on the jungle canopy or ocean wave tops, or splitting karsts and plunging into valleys.

After turning west from Legazpi, J.T. had navigated the flight across southern Luzon. They crossed the Burias passage and then flashed over the beach of Masbate Island. Feet wet again, they crossed the 60 nautical miles of the Sibuyan Sea, skirting just north of Tablas Island, then across the Tablas Strait toward the southern tip of Mindoro.

Hiding eight DC-3s seemed laughable, but he was going to do his best. Unfortunately, they had drawn a crystal clear day, not a single cloud to hide in. Had the weather produced a marine layer, they could have "scud run" underneath it, maintaining a visual reference to the earth while staying under the low ceiling. It was unforgiving flying: a momentary loss of situational awareness or navigational error, and the flight would end abruptly, usually in the side of a hill. With a large front, they could climb to altitude, tuck the flight in tight to maintain sight of each other, and plow through the weather. Either condition would have allowed them to become invisible to Japanese fighters.

On an incredible day like today, however, there were only two things to do: run low and fast, and sit back to enjoy the ride. Low-level flying was high-risk; it also required an increased level of attention and skill. But most of all, it was fun. The pilots called it high-speed "raging", and the only way to make it more fun was to add more airplanes to the equation. As long as no tracer fire appeared from the ground or enemy fighters, it would continue to be fun.

Even though the eight transport-class aircraft moved aggressively, it was done smoothly and in balance, with a precision the young copilots had not thought possible for planes that size. The ailerons of the DC-3 were not very effective, so each turn was led with rudder to start the lumbering aircraft in its roll. The technique was quite effective when coupled with a smooth application of the aileron.

Trey watched his father with the deep respect of a pilot watching a master instructor. Charles Henry's maneuvering seemed effortless, automatic. Trey wondered if he would ever get that good.

They popped the ridgeline splitting Mindoro and, pushing over, they descended down the back side of a ridge toward the water again. They thundered across Ilin Island just off Mindoro, then crossed a narrow channel headed to Ambulong Island.

Charles Henry nodded ahead.

"Trey, look at that."

Trey glanced up to see a sight out of one of his childhood adventure novels: an island ringed by a perfect beach of electric tan sand. Inland of the beach was a thin line of vibrant green jungle that separated it from a ring of jagged grey karsts that jutted abruptly out of the heart of the island, almost purely vertical from the lush belt of jungle.

The flight began a rapid climb to clear the circle of conjoined pinnacles. This geological phenomenon was like none he had ever seen before. Tightly grouped and peaked sharply, they looked like the teeth of a crocodile. As the flight crested the granite ring, Trey couldn't believe what he saw. The back of the pinnacles fell steeply into an internal lake. The entire center of the island was a deep blue lake with a fortress-like outcropping in the middle.

As they streaked over the center of the island, Trey saw a mirror image on the other side. "Incredible", he thought, half expecting to see dinosaurs wading in the water. He never knew visual wonders existed like the ones he had seen in the past two days. Not only did they exist, they seemed to roll at him one after another, at a disorienting pace. The flight dropped over the rear of the island heading out to sea again. Another sight to remember forever was logged into Trey's memory.

J.T. returned to base course after traversing the Linapacan Strait. He updated his navigation plot and pushed out to the open South China Sea, feet wet, back to the endless sea. Fifty miles out, they began a climb to altitude. The fighter threat was now behind them; being spotted by a Japanese ship was now the primary concern.

Trey had learned in grade school that three-quarters of the planet was water. Cognitive knowledge was quite different from actually seeing it. The scale of it was mind-numbing. His eyes were starved for relief, but none would come for hours. His intellect told him they were moving over the water at over 200 nautical miles an hour, 230 in statute miles. Yet his eyes told him that he hung motionless, trapped in this noise-generating machine. Resigned that his sentence would stretch for more hours than he cared to count, he settled in, as did the rest of the crews, and the eight DC-3s continued their chase of the sun.

Chapter 15

Calcutta
12 December 1941

The flight of eight glistened in the midday sun as they rounded the tip of Indochina and changed course to the northwest, up the Gulf of Siam. They had made up most of their lost time on the Wake – Legazpi leg of their journey. The Legazpi – Calcutta leg was 300 nautical miles shorter, which translated to one and a half hours, and that further translated to 145 – 150 gallons of extra fuel. J.T. decided to burn the fuel, trading it for time by flying faster.

He had been able to relax the past few hours. Out in the middle of the South China Sea there were no Zeros to fear. Now there would be. The Jap navy and its aircraft carriers would undoubtedly be supporting the invasions in Malaya off his left wing. He knew they would also support the planned invasions of Singapore on his tail, and Burma on his nose. Indochina, on his right wing, was already firmly in the hands of the Japanese. They were virtually surrounded by the Japanese threat as they flew northwest up the narrow gulf.

The Imperial Japanese Navy was definitely in the area. Worse yet, J.T.'s flight would cut across the narrow, and now occupied, Isthmus of Kra and the southern sliver of Burma on its course for Calcutta. Kra held the highest threat for them. A single Jap Zero on patrol could shoot down half his squadron in seconds. The only thing that would save the other half would be the Zero running out of ammunition. Two Zeros? Well, it would not be pretty, and no one would ever know what happened to the eight American Airlines DC-3s of Project Seven Alpha. It would be a total mission failure.

J.T.'s emergency dispersal plan called for everyone to scatter. They were all unarmed, so maintaining a defensive formation like a bomber group would only allow the Zeros to shoot them all; it was a non-starter. Instead, they would scatter in eight different directions. The fighter or fighters would be forced to pick a target and run it down. With any luck, the untargeted DC-3s would escape.

It went against his nature to initiate an every-man-for-himself plan but without guns, there was no option. The Japanese navy, he knew, was only half the problem and certainly not the easiest half. Once they were feet dry over the Isthmus, every land-based fighter in the theater would become a threat. To say, at this point, that they were now committed was an understatement of Biblical proportion.

"So there's no point in sweating it", thought J.T. He'd cross that bridge if, or when, the Japs built it.

Luck had held crossing the Isthmus of Kra and Southern Burma – luck, common sense and the experience of wars past. J.T. had taken them off course whenever a smoke plume appeared on the horizon. Where there's smoke there is fire, and where there's fire there is a cause. In modern warfare, more often than not, the cause was warplanes. Seven Alpha dodged the hotspots and remained unscathed.

The Isthmus of Kra and the tip of Southern Burma were barely 75 miles across, from the Gulf of Siam to the Andaman Sea. The flight returned to course over the Andaman Sea, passing the many mouths of the Irrawaddy River, 120 miles west of Rangoon. They stayed over the water on a direct course for Calcutta. The last body of water to cross was the Bay of Bengal, which was still firmly in British hands.

Now they were finally in sight of Calcutta. A section of RAF Hawker Hurricane fighters had already given them the once-over as they flew up the Hugli River toward their destination at RAF Dum Dum, Calcutta. As Seven Alpha descended, the planes became enveloped in a thick brown haze that hung over Calcutta. It wasn't caused by war or weather. The haze emanated from a dense population of humanity in a booming, industrialized city that sprawled in every direction. The change was a stark contrast from the desolation, the utter emptiness over which they had spent the past three days.

Sixty-five hours spent flying in formation had knocked all the rust off the old dogs and taught the new dogs a few tricks. Their formation was mirror image as they entered the pattern at RAF Dum Dum.

The challenge, after a long crossing like they had just made, was getting back on step for the most critical phase of flight, the landing. This was where the thousands of hours of experience and endless training paid off. The muscle memory, the effortless scan, and the familiarity of task came together to bridge the fatigue. But it was not without risk; a moment's distraction or lapse of attention could end in disaster.

As always, it was ultimately the state of mind that was paramount. The experienced aviators knew this, and had survived because they knew. They began the process of mental sharpening, prior to descent, by physically moving in the cockpits to wake tired muscles. Then the aviators snapped off checklists with an exacting precision, to awake groggy brains. To the uninitiated, it might seem trivial but it was an important part of the process of rousing body and mind. It was time to perform. There would be no second chance for a bad perform- ance, which meant, at best, having to endure the humiliation of not hacking it in front your fellow pilots – at worst, a crash.

The old dogs were on their game. They had no intention of coming this far and stalling on final approach just because they hadn't really slept for three days. It was time to get up to speed and water these Brits' eyes.

They descended further into the thick, Calcutta haze. Combined with the afternoon sun angle, visibility to the field was severely limited. Regardless, J.T. pushed the throttles up on the Pratt and Whitney R-1830 Wasp engines. He pushed them close to max power, but left a couple of inches of manifold air pressure to give his wingmen a little power advantage to maintain position. Inching on a little throttle friction, he held the throttles in place and continued to let the nose descend to pattern altitude.

Finally, the runway revealed itself through the haze. J.T. imperceptibly eased the flight 20 degrees to the left, to line up with the runway. He glanced over his shoulder to the right; Charles Henry had put his division on line. Eight shiny, silver DC-3s in tight, right echelon parade formation, accelerated toward redline speed and the duty runway at RAF Dum Dum.

J.T. turned to Jon.

"Call the tower," he said, "and tell them we have eight pieces of screamin' American steel for the overhead pattern. Also, flash a three-second interval to our wingmen. With eight in a line, we will have to tighten up the interval."

Jon made the radio call to the tower, then flashed a three to the echelon. The actual pace would be set by dash two; if he was late and followed at four seconds, the rest of the flight would match his interval. This would keep their spacing uniform for safety reasons, but more importantly it would look shit-hot.

Two Dogs went at two seconds.

Eight DC-3s charging over the field at full power were hard to ignore. By snapping onto their left wings in two-second intervals, each aircraft peeling from the pack precisely and aggressively, they sent a message: American Airlines was here to save the day. It was a message J.T. wanted sent loud and clear.

The message had been received. The career British officer stood outside base operations, glaring at the impertinent colonials. J.T. and Jon walked up to the Major, after checking with weather and filing a flight plan for the final leg of their journey.

"Must they sleep there?" he asked.

J.T. followed the starched major's glare. There, on his finely manicured lawn, lay a litter of mutts. They were unshaven, dirty, wrinkled and not without a distinctive scent.

J.T. smiled and winked at Jon.

"Yes, they must."

"Yes, quite." The Major cleared his throat. "Well, Lieutenant Colonel, this is Flight Lieutenant Quigley. He will navigate to the Assam Valley for the flight. He's a little scruffy; I should think he will fit right in."

J.T. smiled a Cheshire Cat grin and responded, "Yes, quite, Major."

At that, the Major snapped off a perfect salute, complete with heal-click, did an about-face, and marched back to the operations building.

"Wow," said Jon with a smirk. "Same idiot, different suit."

J.T. let out a laugh.

"Yes Jonny boy, you are learning quickly."

"What's that?" asked Quigs. "Oh, the Major. He is a bit stiff. Easy enough back here, we don't sit on tradition in the Assam. It's a bit basic, I'm afraid."

J.T. was still amused.

"We expected that, Quigs. You from down under?"

"Yes, actually. Say, usually you Yanks can't tell the difference. Do you have any of those marvelous Yank steaks in there?" Quigs looked at the lowering sun. "Well, we should go, Colonel. We don't want to try the Assam and the hole in the dark, eh?"

J.T. nodded.

"You get us up there all in one piece, and I'll personally barbeque you a big, fat New York strip. Fair dinkum, Quigs?"

"Fair dinkum! Cheers, mate – let's go."

Chapter 16

Shangri-La
12 December 1941

The eight DC-3s glided smoothly up the majestic Assam Valley. Each flight of four moved as one on their way north into the recesses of the valley. A cold front had swept through eastern India, cleansing the sky of any impurity, whether it was haze, smoke, or clouds. All that was left was the imperial blue of a perfect sky; only the looming Himalayas interfered.

J.T. had leveled the squadron at 10,000 feet MSL. The valley floor had remained nearly at sea level while great mountains rose on both sides and at the northeast end. The Assam Valley was a geological marvel. Its dominant feature was the Brahmaputra River, snaking down the center. The great Himalayas were off J.T.'s left wing; the Patkai range, off his right. As the flight moved northeast towards the heart of the Assam, the valley funneled down to an average 50-mile width. A giant granite outcropping on the Himalayan side marked the halfway point. Rice paddies and fields began to give way to dense, triple-canopy jungle.

Quigs stood in the cockpit between J.T. and Jon, pointing out the features of the valley.

"Say, when we get another 10 or so miles we need to drop down to the valley floor," he told them. "Keep heading for Dhemaji in the northwest corner of the Assam. As we close on Dhemaji, we will be looking for an ancient Indian fortress. There is a hidden valley to the south of it. Don't get fast in the descent – we want to maintain our best maneuvering speed. We shall need it, mates. It is a bit snug at the entrance, so no more than two at a time."

J.T. nodded and had Jon give the hand signal to Thumper's section to take trail. Thumper slid his section 500 feet directly aft of J.T., and slightly stepped-up. Charles Henry matched the lead division's formation. Within two minutes, the flight had shifted from two flights of four aircraft in finger-four formation, to four flights of two aircraft, spaced in a row behind the lead.

The squadron had dropped to within 100 feet of the valley floor and slowed to 140 knots indicated airspeed, the minimum maneuver speed for the DC-3s at their present weight.

J.T. got sight of the ancient fortress.

"There it is, Quigs."

"Excellent, Colonel," responded Quigs. "We have just enough light to shoot the hole."

J.T. shot a sideways glance at Quigs.

"Shoot the hole? It's been a long day, mate!"

"Yes, sir.," said Quigs. "As I said, it is quite tight at the entrance. By all appearances, it looks as if the ravine will close off completely. We'll start by offsetting east into the Assam, so that we can reverse our turn to the west and come directly at the entrance and valley wall on a perpendicular heading."

Quigs continued:

"The fortress guards the entrance to the hidden valley, which is at the base of the pinnacle that the fortress is situated upon − south side, by the by. Upon entering the ravine, we'll start a left turn, no more than 15 degrees angle of bank. It will appear as if we are surely going to hit the wall. Instead, we'll rapidly reverse our turn to approximately 45 degrees angle of bank to the right − a judicious use of the rudder is required − and swoosh, we'll have shot the hole!"

"Sounds exciting, Quigs," replied J.T. with more than a hint of sarcasm. "Jon, put Two Dogs in cruise."

Jon held his arm up vertically, his hand in a fist with thumb extended, and made a fore/aft motion, much like a hitchhiker. Two Dogs slid aft in a looser formation. The hand signal, he knew, meant they were going to maneuver aggressively. By dropping aft, Two Dogs could maneuver either side of J.T. at will, to maintain position and avoid smacking the ground. The other sections repositioned to match the lead's formation.

J.T. was running in, heading due west. He pointed the DC-3's nose just south of the fortress. He would have loved to study its intricacies and beautiful architecture, but he was preoccupied with surviving by desperately trying to see the entrance.

At a half-mile he began to squirm. Jon noticed J.T.'s discomfort and, having never witnessed it before in spite of all they had already been through, he was about half a beat shy of a heart attack himself. Inside a quarter-mile, and still no ravine, no entrance, nothing. They continued to churn toward the valley wall at 140 knots. The paddies had long ago given way to the triple-canopy jungle clinging to the steep hills that suddenly leaped from the valley floor. The lushness of the jungle gave the preface of the Himalayas a soft, velveteen quality; a quality J.T. knew was in appearance only. Under that velvet façade were tree trunks, dirt, rock, and somewhere – allegedly – a gap.

Jon was hyperventilating.

"You got it yet, skipper?"

J.T. shook his head.

"Nope."

Jon turned to Quigs.

"How about a little help?" He was nearly apoplectic now.

Quigs just smiled.

"We are pointed directly at it," he said. "Patience, and it will come into view."

J.T. squirmed and scanned; Jon just squirmed. Then, almost imperceptibly, the hole revealed itself.

"I got it!" snapped J.T. "Is it always this hard to see?"

"No," Quigs laughed. "It gets worse when the visibility is down."

Jon rolled his eyes.

"Great, I can't wait."

J.T. started the slight left turn. First, his DC-3 disappeared into jungle, then Two-Dog's.

Sitting next to Charles Henry, Trey sat bolt upright.

"They crashed!" he yelled.

"Nope," responded his father in a matter-of-fact voice. "No fireball."

As soon as J.T. had begun his left turn, he reversed hard to the right with lots of rudder. The DC-3 protested; it was stout and maneuverable for its size, but it was still a transport aircraft. Two Dogs, in trail, tried to match the reversal but couldn't. He slid outside the radius of J.T.'s turn slightly, to hack it. Very slightly. It was tight, damn tight!

They shot the hole.

It gave entrance to a vibrant and lush valley. The sides were steep and close, separated at points by no more than half a mile. The valley walls rose rapidly, nearly straight up, quickly reaching thousands of feet above the valley floor. The floor itself was surprisingly flat, with a frothing stream rushing in a mean-dering course down the middle. It reminded J.T. of the Yosemite Valley in California, only quite a bit narrower. Then he realized there was not enough room to turn around.

"The field is two miles up on the right side of the river," Quigs piped up from the back. "Not enough room for the overhead pattern. One way in, one way out."

J.T. nodded.

"Jon, drag Two Dogs."

Jon responded by immediately making a cranking motion with his hand, then waving Two Dogs off. Two-Dog's aircraft dropped the gear and flaps and slowed to 120 knots. Thumper, having just shot the hole, saw J.T. drag Two Dogs and did the same with Ski, then timed ten seconds and dropped his own gear, slowing to 120 so he wouldn't run down Two Dogs. The trailing sections separated in identical fashion.

Standardization is critical in a multi-aircraft flight. Every aircraft has to fly pre-briefed speeds and positions to prevent a disaster. One pilot out of sync could cause a fiasco. It is part of the trust of the brotherhood of aviation; the wing trusts the lead not to prang him in and the lead trusts the wingman not to run into him. All members of a flight trust each other to do the right thing. Standardized procedures are the touchstone that allow it all to look easy.

As J.T. was in the flare, he noticed that the runway had a fairly steep incline of 2 to 2½ degrees, at least. He smiled to himself. *"That's how they operate one way in, one way out, regardless of the wind. Land uphill; take off downhill."*

The squadron of DC-3s, now eight in a line, touched down in sequence, slowing rapidly on the incline and clearing the runway as the next aircraft in line rolled out behind. J.T. cleared the runway and was waved into a concealed revetment by ragged, thin RAF ground crews.

"Won't you need these revets for your own aircraft, Quigs?" he asked.

Quigs shook his head, yelling above the engines as J.T. ran them up to clear them prior to shutdown.

"Oh, I should say not, Colonel. We've crashed them all or they have been shot down in China or Burma. We lost the last one yesterday – you are just in time. Cheers."

After shutting down the engines, J.T. couldn't wait to exit the aircraft and smell some fresh air. He glanced around the valley. At the farthest end was a surprisingly intact palace, nestled right up against the rock wall.

Quigs stepped out of the DC-3 and stood next to him.

"Quite tight, eh, Colonel?"

J.T. looked closer around the valley for signs of bomb craters or patches in the runway.

"Quite tight, Quigs. I imagine that is why the Japs haven't found it yet."

Quigs smiled his infectious grin.

"Yes, sir – that, and the decoy field in the Assam. If we get one shot up and can't shoot the hole, we land it there. If it can't be made worthy of flight, we leave it there after cannibalizing the parts. The Japs come by from time to time and shoot up our junk yard. They are happy, we are happy, and no one's the wiser."

J.T. smiled back.

"Whatever it takes, Quigs. One question for you: how do you keep from running into each other in the hole?"

"Oh, not very creative, I'm afraid. First and third quarter of the hour, out; second and fourth, in."

"Ah, the KISS principle." J.T. nodded. "I like it."

"KISS principle, sir?" Quigs looked puzzled.

Jon had joined them after completing his checks.

"Keep It Simple, Stupid," he quipped. Quigs was clearly amused by the Yank witticism.

J.T. continued to survey his new surroundings, his attention quickly focusing on a set of rundown, rotting wooden barracks. They were obviously uninhabited, although he knew that would soon end.

"'Basic' is a bit charitable for a description of this place, don't you think?" he said.

"Perhaps, Colonel," said Quigs, "but had I told you the truth, I was afraid you would refuse to come. At any rate, here it is – home sweet home!"

Charles Henry walked up to J.T. with a wide-eyed Trey close behind. J.T. noticed his operations officer's approach.

"Hey, Charles Henry," he said. "Send a message to Colonel Smith. Tell him Seven Alpha is on line at Shangri-La."

Charles Henry nodded and proceeded to the only hut with antennae. Quigs was again amused by the Yanks; their relaxed manner was more to his Aussie liking than the upright British manner.

"Shangri-La. Oh yes, quite nice. Cheers – eh, Colonel?"

"Cheers it is, Quigs."

Chapter 17

The White House
12 December 1941

C.R. Smith approached the Map Room of the White House quietly. The President sat with the Chief of Staff of the Army and the Chief of Naval Operations. There had been no good news exchanged between them, and the stress registered heavily on FDR's face. He looked up from the dispatches and saw C.R. in the background.

"C.R. please come in," he said. "I need some good news. Even a shred would be a welcome change. Do you have some for me?"

C. R. stiffened.

"Yes, sir, Mr President. I believe I do."

"Well let's have it – come in, come in."

C.R. eased into the room with obvious discomfort. He still had not come to grips with the fact that he was privy to the most tightly-held secrets of the war.

"Sir, I have received a message from Project Seven Alpha."

The Army and Navy Four Star flag officers looked confused. The CNO spoke up.

"Project Seven Alpha, Mr. President?"

FDR waved him off.

"A little project C.R. and I whipped up," he said. "I'll have you back-briefed. What have they for us?"

C.R. Smith handed him the message. The President read through his half-glasses and let out a roar of a laugh.

"Outstanding! Shangri-La! I love it; I must meet this man of yours, C.R."

Colonel C.R. Smith smiled, but his eyes betrayed the worry his heart felt.

"I hope that you will, Mr. President, I truly hope that you will."

FDR slapped the desk. The message had instantly revived him, filling him with a surge of optimism.

"Excellent," he said. "It is small, but a start – a spark in the darkness that will help to lead us to our eventual deliverance from the abyss."

The President turned away from his desk.

"I'm suddenly hungry. C.R., brief the General and Admiral on Seven Alpha; after all, you do technically work for the General."

Without another word, FDR wheeled his chair from the room.

The Four Star officers peered quizzically at the pudgy, older Colonel in the brand-new Brooks Brothers uniform. This time the General spoke.

"Do tell, Colonel."

TOP SECRET

DATE TIME GROUP: 0300 ZULU 13 DEC 1941
FROM: COMMANDER AIR TRANSPORT COMMAND
TO: COMMANDER SEVEN ALPHA
SUBJECT: WESTPAC INTEL UPDATE
CLASSIFICATION: TOP SECRET SCI/EYES ONLY COM7ALPHA
TEXT: JAPANESE FORCES INVADED SOUTHERN TIP OF
BURMA. CROSSING FROM ISTHMUS OF KRA. WYA.
C.R. SENDS

Chapter 18

The Hump
13 December 1941

The dawn found Charles Henry, J.T., Quigs and his commanding officer, Major Norman Holliday, in a makeshift office at the
end of one of the rundown barracks. The Seven Alpha crews
were sitting on cots outside the open-ended office.

J.T. spoke first.

"Gentlemen, the Major and I have conferred, and we agree
that for the first couple of weeks, we will fly with RAF copilots.
They are going to teach us the ropes. After that, we will cycle in
our own copilots and become stand-alone. The flying here is the
most severe imaginable." He turned over the floor to Major
Holliday. "Major."

"Thank you, Lieutenant Colonel. The RAF has learned many
lessons here, unfortunately most have been written in blood. I
see no reason, and Lieutenant Colonel Dobbs agrees, to relearn
them the hard way."

J.T. stepped forward.

"Okay, any questions?"

Jon stood up.

"Sir, what will the Seven Alpha copilots be doing?"

Charles Henry now spoke up.

"I'm glad you asked, Lieutenant. You will be squaring away
these quarters. The troops will be busy with the aircraft."

A collective groan emanated from the group of youngsters.
Jon sat back down.

"Sorry I asked," he said.

J.T. winked at Jon.

"You can start by building me a wall for this office, Jonny boy. Oh – one more thing," he said. "The good major has graciously offered us the services of Flight Lieutenant Quigley as a liaison officer after they rotate out of theater. Sorry about that, Quigs."

Quigs shrugged his shoulders. "What, and leave all this?"

J.T. slapped him on the back.

"Welcome him aboard, boys!"

The Seven Alpha crews all yelled in unison, "Welcome aboard, asshole!"

Charles Henry raised his hand to quell the laughter.

"Okay, that's it. Go get some chow. It's gonna be a long war."

The crews filed out, leaving J.T. and Charles Henry alone in the ramshackle office.

J.T. sat down at the splintered desk.

"Charles Henry, I don't want us to micromanage this project. These guys are big boys and we need to be in the rotation, not chasing our tails over insignificant details. We need a simple daily schedule, once we figure out the operation, plus an initial training plan until we get up to speed."

Charles Henry nodded his agreement.

"Roger that, skipper. Who do you want to start with?"

"You, me, Irish and Thumper will run the Hump initially. Two Dogs, Ski, Roper and Bluto will shuttle down to the supply depot at Dispur. They don't want to cut a road up here; they're afraid the Japs will follow it and find us. Not much air defense around here. The Tigers are busy in Burma, and the Brits everywhere else. They figure the best plan is to hide us and not have to sweat the air defense of the Northern Assam Valley. So for now, we are going to shuttle supplies in and out. Once we get some air cover, the plan is to move to the floor of the Assam, but for now – "

Charles Henry interrupted, "Standard bucket brigade."

"That's a fact, Charles Henry, so we need to get these guys on step. We are going to be shootin' the hole heavy – damn heavy," said J.T. "Make sure we put together a good brief on short field landings and takeoffs at max gross weights. Get Roper to do it, he operated out of Alaska, he's our resident expert. Also, tell them to go easy on the tail wheel landings, we don't want to prang any on, and bend one at, the aft door."

Charles Henry was taking notes.

"Yeah, that is the weak spot on these aircraft. I'll pass the word, skipper."

"Let's go get something to eat, Major Brennan. We're airborne in an hour, day one of the odyssey."

"More like day five, J.T."

J.T. smiled and nodded. "That's a fact."

J.T. walked down the line of revetments just as the sun was reaching the valley of Shangri-La. Word of the message home had spread, and the name stuck immediately. The revets had camouflaged netting stretched across the top of sandbag walls. The netting was peaked at the center, giving each individual revetment the appearance of a tent. As he passed, he could see that his troops had been up all night, prepping the birds. Each of the American Airlines DC-3s had been painted drab olive green. He could tell they were fully loaded by how they squatted on their struts.

J.T. stopped at the mouth of his revet and watched as the chief shouted a few last-minute orders, a cigar clenched tightly in his teeth. J.T. wondered if it was the same stogie he first saw in El Paso a week ago.

"We're ready, skipper," said the chief.

J.T. nodded his acknowledgment.

"What did you do to my beautiful silver birds, Chief?"

"Made them a little more survivable, skipper. These ain't American Airliners anymore. These are Army transports – warbirds."

The heavily laden DC-3 was hard to taxi on the loosely packed gravel runway. J.T. finally got it positioned at the very end of the Shangri-La runway, pointed downhill toward the hole. He ran the mixtures to auto rich, pushed the prop levers full forward to max pitch, then began to open the engine cooling cowls to the full open position.

Quigs stopped him at the halfway point.

"Lieutenant Colonel, we find that half is sufficient. The engines hardly warm up when we level off and accelerate to shoot the hole. We actually found that when we throttled back at maneuver speed, the engines would shock cool as we ran down hill to the Assam. Half cowls also will reduce our drag and is perfect for climbing, once in the Assam.

"Set and forget," J.T. responded as he cycled the flight controls. "Lesson number one, Quigs?"

"Quite so, and many more to come, sir."

J.T. smiled his easy smile.

"Okay, but do me a favor and call me J.T. in the aircraft."

"J.T. it is," said Quigs. "We're off then – it is on the hour!"

J.T. pushed the throttles up to the stops. His manifold pressure gauge showed 52 inches, the Pratt and Whitneys howled. He strained to hold them back with the foot brakes. Quickly, he scanned the engine instruments. Satisfied with their readings, he released the brakes.

The DC-3 shuddered and shook. J.T.'s initial impression was that it would never get airborne but then a marvelous force kicked in, the single most powerful force in the universe: gravity! The incline on landing was now a decline for takeoff. In short, they were running downhill with a lot of weight. The acceleration was surprising. J.T. mused over the fact that for most of his life, he had fought gravity; it was nice to have it working for him for a change.

By midfield, the tail was up and they were approaching rotation speed.

Quigs yelled over the din, "Delay the rotation; let it fly off at Vy."

J.T. didn't ask why. He held the nose down until max rate of climb speed of 105 knots, then let the airplane fly itself off the runway. As the wheels broke ground, Quigs didn't hesitate, immediately raising the gear handle.

"They frequently overload us," he yelled again. "If you were to rotate on schedule with an overload, it could get unpleasant. By the same token, if overloaded and you lose an engine, you will not be able to accelerate to single-engine climb speed. So we rotate at it. If the end of the runway comes up first, we take what we have and hope for the best."

They had just become airborne, and J.T. was already pulling back the power to maintain his best maneuver speed. *"Yes sir"*, he thought, *"these Brits definitely have their shit wired. I'm going to learn a lot today."*

They shot the hole.

J.T. had worried about an accelerated stall due to the weight and high angle of bank to make the turn. But because they were going downhill he could let the nose down, reducing the angle of attack and thus the danger of stall.

Quigs seemed to read his mind.

"Going back up," he said, "the weight of the fuel is gone and you are higher up on the power so even over grossed you can make it."

J.T. nodded. *"Lots to learn."*

Clear of the hole, J.T. turned northeast in the Assam and pushed the throttles up to 40 inches for climb.

Quigs pushed them to 43 inches.

"We only use two power settings once we clear the hole, max climb and max continuous cruise, once clear of the Hump."

J.T. trimmed the aircraft for max climb and headed for the Himalayas, which were already in view. He was climbing at 1,500 feet per minute but knew it wouldn't last. The enormity of the Himalayas made them seem very close.

"Are we gonna do a turn here until we get to altitude, Quigs?"

Quigs smiled. "They are still 45 minutes away, J.T."

"Wow", thought J.T. *"I most definitely have a lot to learn around here."*

Passing 10,000 feet, they put on their oxygen masks. At 14,000 feet, they shifted the superchargers to high gear to maintain manifold pressure. Leveling off at 20,000, J.T. lifted his oxygen mask.

"How fast do you want to cross the Hump?"

Quigs pulled his mask and replied, "As fast as we can. Sometimes the wind is 100 knots up here. You also have to learn the passes. If you lose an engine, you can't stay above the mountains. Always want a way out, eh, J.T.?"

"Most definitely, Quigs," J.T. agreed.

"I wish we could have let you fly your first combat mission empty, sir," said Quigs, "but the lads on the other side are quite desperate."

"No point in wasting a trip," replied J.T. "Besides, it's not my first."

Quigs looked quizzically at J.T., then glanced over his shoulder at the chief.

"Say, mate, have you strapped the cargo as snugly as possible?"

The chief looked annoyed.

"Yeah, mate! It's secure."

"Cheers, it will get quite bouncy very soon."

As the DC-3 approached the Himalayas, their size was overwhelming. J.T. felt as insignificant as a grain of sand in a vast desert. The ruggedness of the mountains limited the spread of humanity to the periphery. As they climbed their way into the heart of the Himalayas, the desolation was on par with the oceans they had just crossed. To go down in them would be to disappear forever, no different from crashing and sinking in the middle of the Pacific. There would be no sign left behind, no hint of a past existence of man or machine – simply gone, swallowed whole.

Quigs kept glancing over his shoulder looking into the cargo bay.

"Everything OK back there Quigs?"

"Quite!" replied the Australian with a smile.

In the back the chief bounced with loose cargo, scrambling to re-secure it.

Chapter 19

China
13 December 1941

The turbulence ended after twenty minutes. J.T. welcomed the chop on the other side and finally, even that gave way to smooth air. They descended down the China side of the Hump, headed for the auxiliary field of Batang. Batang was more of a clearing than an airfield. It had been hastily built, originally intended as an emergency divert. However, with the Burma theater becoming increasingly in doubt, HQ had decided to drop some supplies in the rear until the situation stabilized. For now, Batang would have to do; much in the beginning of this war would simply have to do. They would have backup supplies and a base close to Burma if – or when – the road fell.

The Allies would fight tooth and nail for the Burma Road. However, the reality of their recent track record was glaring. Batang gave the Army a fall-back position if needed. Today, it also had the advantage of being close. Quigs could get two sorties on the first group of Americans, in one day. Also, this far in the rear, they wouldn't get any ground fire – not today, anyway.

J.T. started to ease the power back for a normal descent. Quigs stopped him.

"We leave the power up," he said. "Come in hot. Speed is life."

"More is better!" J.T. added.

"Quite," replied Quigs. "Now, we normally come in low and fast. Buzz the field, then pitch up to the abeam. We will decelerate in the pitch, drop the gear and flaps, then fly a tight, circular approach. The buzz gives us two things: a look at the field, and the Japs just can't resist shooting when we fly by. If they shoot, we just go away."

J.T. dropped toward the field. The combination of gravity and engine power quickly pushed his speed up to the red line. They buzzed the field, which was always exhilarating, checked the wind sock, and looked for ground fire: all clear. The aircraft felt very heavy at top speed. J.T. pitched up left as planned. At 15 degrees nose up, he started to roll into a 45 degree angle of bank turn. He put on 2 to 2½ Gs as he pulled for the abeam position.

When he started to retard the throttles, Quigs overrode him, pushing the throttles back up.

"We are heavy." he told J.T. "Our old friend gravity will slow us quite rapidly in the pitch."

Just as Quigs had promised, the DC-3 decelerated rapidly, surprisingly fast considering that the power was near max. By the time J.T. eased out of the steep pitch upturn, the DC-3 was down to gear speed, abeam the landing zone. Quigs dropped the landing gear handle automatically. They had reached the apex of the pitch maneuver at about 1,000 feet above the ground. As the gear swung down and locked into place, Quigs set half flaps. J.T. had eased the turn to 30 degrees angle of bank and set approach power. He immediately nosed the DC-3 over, setting approximately 1,000-feet-per-minute descent. It was a tight and steep approach, more suited for a fighter, not a heavy transport. J.T. felt as if he was right on the edge of maintaining control.

The tactic was designed to minimize exposure for the aircraft and crew. It did, but it was a handful for the pilots. Passing through the 90-degree position, with just a quarter of the circular pattern left to complete until becoming aligned with the runway, they were still 25 knots fast. After looking out his left window to ensure that he wouldn't overshoot the center line of the runway, J.T. called for full flaps.

Quigs response surprised him again.

"Not yet. We are slow."

"Slow? How can we be slow?" thought J.T.

Quigs hadn't been wrong yet, so he continued to pull the heavy DC-3 to the centerline of the grass strip. Rolling wings level on short final, J.T. scanned his airspeed again and was shocked to see that he was at his approach speed. Once the wings were level, Quigs dropped full flaps, and the aircraft stabilized for just a few moments. Quigs yelled out encouragement.

"We are looking good J.T.! When we cross the tree line, pull the power to idle and push the nose over to maintain approach speed. Go for the end of the runway."

J.T. nodded in acknowledgment. As they crossed the tree line, he started to ease the power back. Quigs overrode him again, grabbing the back of J.T.'s hand and yanking the throttles to idle. J.T. had to aggressively push the nose over to prevent a decay in airspeed.

"Hold this attitude until you can't stand it," said Quigs, "then flare."

J.T. held the nose down until he had to pull back hard into a flare to break the 1,000-feet-per-minute rate of descent. Even with the hard pull, the result was not what he anticipated. The heavy DC-3 squatted but did not flare. The hard pull reduced the rate of descent enough to prevent a bounce, but they stuck it pretty hard.

"Shit!" muttered J.T.

"Perfect!" exclaimed Quigs.

The heavy DC-3 slowed dramatically, having dissipated a lot of energy plunking it on even before J.T. got on the brakes.

"Outstanding, mate!"

"Outstanding? That was a terrible landing, Quigs."

Quigs laughed.

"J.T., you must remember you no longer carry little old ladies. You are now a combat cargo pilot. We fly into short, hostile fields. We need to get it on deck, stopped, unloaded and off, ASAP."

Quigs continued.

"By landing with authority, we start the deceleration instantly and, as you saw, quite effectively. No flare, no bounce, no time wasted. Now, bump up the power – we taxi fast. Look left, ten o-clock, you can see the men who will unload us. Come in fast and swing the tail so as to point the door right at them."

For the first time, Quigs seemed nervous.

"Do not shut down the engines," he said.

"Okay Quigs, you're the boss."

J.T. swung the tail precisely as Quigs directed. Before the aircraft was stopped, Quigs was unstrapped and moving to the cargo bay. He had pre-briefed the chief to start un-securing the cargo, aft to fore on the starboard side, while he went fore to aft on the port side. Quigs was a lot faster. By the time the chief finished, Quigs had already opened the aircraft and begun pushing out crates of ammunition to the waiting Chinese troops, who were acting as loaders.

"Chop, chop," Quigs barked at the Chinese troops as he frantically shoved the cargo aft and out the door. The chief sensed the urgency and figured it was for a good reason, so he matched the pace.

They had just about finished when a tall Marine captain pushed his way to the cockpit and sat sideways in the copilot seat. J.T. looked up from his chart.

"What the hell is a captain of Marines doing out here?" he asked.

"It's a long and sad story, Colonel," said the Captain. "I doubt you have time. I've got some Intel and KIA reports for HQ, and also some mail, if you wouldn't mind."

"No sweat, young Captain. I wish we had some for you."

"That's okay, Colonel. We are moving forward once we are re-supplied. I don't think it would find us anyway."

Quigs scampered into the cockpit.

"We are off-loaded – we must go, chop, chop!"

The Marine captain got up and slid by Quigs as he was headed aft. J.T. stopped him.

"What's your name, Captain?"

"Russell. Jim Russell."

J.T. held out his hand.

"I'm J.T., and this is Quigs. We'll put our return address on your mail if any comes back for your men. We will carry it around until we find you. Keep your head down."

They shook hands.

"Nice to meet you, J.T.," said Russell. "Fly safe and often. I got a feeling you will be our only lifeline soon."

J.T. nodded. "I'm afraid you're right. The Japs invaded Burma this morning."

"Yeah, I know. That's where we are headed."

Quigs was already pushing his way into the seat and strapping in before the marine exited the aircraft. Once set, he leaned over to check that the captain had cleared the door and pushed up the power.

"Let's go!" he ordered. "Take off the opposite direction, wind is light – go, go, go!"

J.T. manhandled the DC-3, kicking the tail around to the direction they had come from, setting takeoff power before they were on the runway. He lifted the tail as they eased onto center-line; the light DC-3 was airborne within a few hundred feet. Quigs snapped up the gear and settled back into his seat, his normal, calm manner returning immediately. J.T. tried to stifle a grin.

"You don't like being on deck much, do you, Quigs?"

Quigs vigorously shook his head.

"I should say not! I've been caught twice on deck by the Japs. Strafed by a Zero once, went down to ground fire the second time. The last time, it took me three weeks to get out. Most unpleasant in the bush – bugs, snakes – no sir, I did not like it at all."

J.T. smiled. "Not to mention the Imperial Japanese Army trying to hunt you down."

"What? Oh, yes, that too. But mostly snakes and bugs. Most unpleasant indeed."

J.T. was completely amused by the young Australian. Here he was flying combat missions over the most dangerous route in the world, and Quigs' only worry seemed to be critters.

They began their long climb toward the Himalayas. Quigs glanced at his watch.

"Excellent," he said. "We should make it back in time for a second run."

Chapter 20

C.-in-C. Pac. Fleet HQ
17 December 1941

Admiral William Pye sat nervously at the desk, which had been Admiral Kimmel's only that morning. Kimmel had been relieved of command of the Pacific Fleet, for cause. The scapegoating had begun. There would be more blood in the water before it was all over. Pye had been given temporary command awaiting the arrival of Admiral Chester Nimitz. What made him nervous was the relief expedition currently underway. If the expedition ended in disaster, they would rig another noose on the gallows from which Kimmel currently swung.

The relief expedition put the last line of defense in the Pacific at risk. Three fast carriers, the *Lexington, Saratoga* and *Enterprise*, were all that lay between the Imperial Japanese fleet and Hawaii – as well as the west coast of the United States itself. Intelligence had been slight at best, and all of it bad news. The Jap force's composition and size were unknown. Aviation assets continued to raid Wake daily; many were carrier-based. Obviously, the Japanese carrier navy was present, at least in part.

Vice Admiral Wilson Brown had sortied the *Lexington* and Task Force 11 on the fifteenth for a diversionary raid on Jaluit in the Marshall Islands. It was intended to cover Vice Admiral Frank Jack Fletcher's Task Force 14, which included the *Saratoga* as his flagship. TF 14 was the Wake relief force and sortied the next day, headed directly for the island.

"Two thousand miles away, two thousand", Pye thought. He kept dwelling on the distance. A ship damaged that far away would be lost to scavenger submarines or long-range bombers. If both

the *Lexington* and *Saratoga* were lost, the war would be lost. He could hear the trap door of the gallows bang open.

Captain McMorris entered the office.

"Sir, shall I brief you on the rest of the Wake Island relief action?"

"The rest? The rest of what?" Pye responded forcefully. "I don't understand. Task Forces 11 and 14 have both sailed."

Soc McMorris could feel his trepidation, and it worried him.

"Yes sir, they have," he replied, "and tomorrow Bull Halsey sails with Task Force 8 in support."

Admiral Pye squeezed a pencil in his right hand until it snapped. He cleared his throat.

"Am I to understand, Captain, that the entire fast carrier force of the Pacific fleet is committed to the defense of Wake Island?"

Captain McMorris stiffened formally, coming to attention.

"Affirmative, Admiral. We have sortied the fleet to engage and destroy the enemy."

Admiral Pye slowly put the two pieces of the pencil in a large glass ashtray. He let out an almost imperceptible sigh, and then spoke.

"Understood Captain. I want a full brief on this in two hours. Every detail."

"Aye-aye, Admiral."

C.-in-C. Pac Fleet HQ
10:32 Hours
22 December 1941

After four days' of agonizing indecision, Admiral Pye had made up his mind. Before he could send the order, Captain Soc McMorris came running into the office.

"Sir, the Japs are landing on Wake – we just got a message from Commander Cunningham!"

Pye waved him off.

"It doesn't matter, Captain. I've reached a decision: recall Task Forces 11 and 14, and have Bull Halsey cover their retirement with Task Force 8."

McMorris flew into a rage.

"There are men dying out there – *your* men! We can't abandon them! We are in a position to take it to the Japanese. We must attack!"

"Captain, I am well aware of the implications of my decision," Admiral Pye quietly replied. "I am the temporary commander of the Pacific fleet; I will not risk its destruction. If Fletcher meets a force that is not smaller than his, it will be a disaster. I want them unequivocally recalled – now. Is that clear, Captain?"

Soc McMorris stood still, his face turning red. Finally, he replied.

"I will comply with your orders under protest, Admiral."

"Duly noted, Captain. Dismissed."

Flag Bridge, USS *Saratoga*
22 December 1941

Vice Admiral Frank Jack Fletcher exploded in fury, throwing his hat to the deck after reading the message handed to him.

"Verify this immediately," he demanded.

The staff officer subconsciously took a step back.

"We have, sir. Twice."

Fletcher was furious. He had positioned his task force and fueled them for battle. His air wing and pilots were ready to avenge Pearl Harbor. Now, at a time when he should be giving an order of attack, he instead had to give an order of withdrawal.

His emotions boiled over.

"This is an outrage. Damn bureaucrats, damn politicians – why aren't all these pathetic cowards in Washington, D.C.? They should be shuffling paper and kissing ass, not commanding men in battle!"

Regaining a modicum of composure, Fletcher left the Flag Bridge, incapable of watching the task force turn away from the men who were dying on Wake.

TOP SECRET

Date time group: 0300 ZULU 24 DEC 1941
From: COMMANDER AIR TRANSPORT COMMAND
To: COMMANDER SEVEN ALPHA
Subject: WESTPAC INTEL UPDATE
Classification: TOP SECRET SCI/EYES ONLY COM7ALPHA
Text: WAKE FELL YESTERDAY. THEY PUT UP A HELL OF A
FIGHT. ANTICIPATE 7ALPHA ROTATE HOME MID-FEB. HO
HO HO. WYA.
C.R. SENDS

TOP SECRET

A6M2-MODEL 21-ZERO SEN.
JAPAN'S FRONT LINE FIGHTER "ZERO"

Chapter 21

Zero
24 December 1941

Within a very short and intense period of time, the American Airlines pilots had been transformed into combat cargo pilots. They learned to go against many of their stateside instincts. They penetrated thunderstorms now to hide from fighters instead of skirting them, having learned that the best place to transit storms was in the upper third of the cloud formation. Besides, the hammering they took was no different from a normal crossing of the Hump; the advantage of invisibility from Zeros made it worth the ride. They learned to plant their landings without bouncing or being embarrassed. Mostly, they learned to push their DC-3s to their performance limits – and beyond.

The veterans quickly reverted to their roots. It had not taken them long to get their edge back, once the daily grind of combat operations began. They fell back on the habits and procedures that had seen them through the last war.

It was Christmas Eve, and the day could not have been clearer – not a cloud in the sky, no place to hide. Thumper nervously scanned the sky behind and above his DC-3. Man-child, in his right seat, seemed oblivious to Thumper's anxiety. Instead, he was enjoying the trip. A beautiful and unusually smooth day, even the Hump had spared them the normal, bone-jarring ride. Now, on their return leg, he hoped the smooth weather would hold.

He didn't even comment on the occasional turns Thumper made to the left, craning around to scan behind the lumbering

DC-3, then returning to course without a word. Something had the hair up on Thumper's neck. Man-child had got used to the twitchiness of the vets. He figured, what the heck – it kept them alive in the last war; who was he to question their nerves? Besides, he had read a report from Intel saying the Zeros wouldn't come up this far north.

Thumper started another turn to the left, leaning way forward over the yoke and scanning the sky aft and above his ship. Suddenly, he saw what he had been looking for: a glint of sunlight off a wing, as the hunter performed a low reversal turn to align fuselages for a high-deflection gunshot.

Even before Thumper's brain could fully process the information, his muscle memory reacted instantaneously, instinctively, in full survival mode. He simultaneously snapped on full left aileron and full left rudder, while pulling the yoke into his lap. As he manipulated the flight controls with his left hand, his right jammed on emergency full power. The empty DC-3 reacted surprisingly, even violently. Man-child banged his head on the right windscreen frame. The chief, who was acting as crewman, went flying across the empty cargo bay, bouncing off the right bulkhead before being pinned to the floor by the high G-force.

Thumper never took his eyes off the glint, watching it transform from a black dot into a Mitsubishi model A6M2 Zero-Sen. Just as Thumper got the full 4 Gs that he wanted on the DC-3, the Zero's wings began to sparkle with gunfire. The 20-millimeter cannons and 7.7-millimeter machine guns were throwing a combined 1,800 rounds per minute – 30 rounds per second – at the maneuvering DC-3. From a past life's experience, an experience he once thought he would never call upon again, Thumper knew the rounds would fall behind him.

The Zero did not have enough lead pursuit. His nose wasn't far enough in front of the DC-3's. Thumper could see the tracers arc away from him because of the G-force. The Zero pilot had not anticipated a fighter-type break turn from a DC-3. Because of the abrupt move from the DC-3, he couldn't get his nose out in front of it in time to score any hits. Under high G, bullets made a curving arc falling away from the direction of the pull, much like water from a hose.

Had his attack been unobserved, the Japanese pilot could have bore-sighted the DC-3 and blown it from the sky. But Thumper had refused to cooperate, keeping the four-G pull on. His nose was now passing through 45 degrees, nose low; he was rolled, almost inverted. His plan was to complete an oblique turn, a modified split S, pulling for a valley below and slightly offset to the south. As he buried the DC-3's nose toward Mother Earth, Thumper pulled the power to idle. He didn't need to look inside at the instruments to know that his DC-3 was at the redline speed. He scanned alternately between the valley and the Zero – and then pulled directly at the fighter. The young Zero pilot matched the DC-3's move, rolled inverted and pulled 6 Gs to regain a firing solution. When he rolled inverted and pulled, his canopy and windscreen filled with the mountains, valley and ground below. Startled, he subconsciously eased his turn, not wanting to bury his nose and hit the ground, and overshot the flight path of Thumper's DC-3.

The fighter pilot rolled back upright, pulling off target to get his situational awareness back. He realized the valley floor was thousands of feet deep. He had been duped by the fleeing DC-3 pilot. Infuriated, he rolled back inverted, went to combat power and executed a six-G split S in pursuit of the DC-3. Had the transport been a fighter, he would have lost it easily in the ground clutter. The large DC-3, however, was easy to spot as it completed its oblique turn, running for the valley floor.

The Zero pilot knew that even with the head start it had, he would quickly run the DC-3 down. He would relish this kill; his honor would be restored. Coming through the bottom of his split S, he pulled until he was pointed directly at the lumbering DC-3. After pulling straight toward the earth at full power, his acceleration was dramatic. Pulling through the bottom of his maneuver, he was now at 30 degrees nose low, chasing the transport down the valley at 300 knots. Now with his nose on the target, he could see it through his gun sight. With his sighting rings, he could measure the distance: it was almost 4,000 feet away.

Easing forward on the stick, the Zero pilot put his fighter in a zero-G dive. With no positive or negative G on the airframe, it produced no lift and thus no induced drag. Gravity, aided by the 925 horsepower of the Nakajima Sakae engine, turned it into a rocket. He intentionally over-sped his aircraft, exceeding his redline by 50 knots – now at 350, he ran Thumper down quickly.

Thumper's plan had been to run down the valley and hope that either a) the Zero wouldn't follow him into the weeds, or b) it would lose sight and thus couldn't follow him. Neither, he knew, was likely to happen.

After getting his head banged on the windscreen frame, then pushed down to his right knee by the G-force, Man-child was regaining his personal bearings. He looked around, trying to figure out how they had wound up in a valley, going the opposite direction.

"What the heck is going on, Thumper?"

Before he could get an answer, the chief burst into the cockpit.

"Where's the Zero?"

"What Zero?" shouted Man-child.

Both the chief and Thumper ignored him.

"Did you lose him, Thumper?" asked the chief.

"I don't know. Get up in the celestial window and check our six, left side high."

"Roger that, Thumper." The chief seemed to levitate into the celestial window just aft of the cockpit. Within four seconds he was back in the cockpit.

"He's coming, seven o' clock high, doing the speed of heat!"

"Shit, hang on!" Thumper pulled the throttles to idle and put the aircraft into a violent slip, by full-deflecting right aileron and full left rudder.

By cross-controlling the aircraft, the attitude remained static, wings level. However, all of the flight controls in the wind stream acted as speed-brakes. Cross-controlled and at idle power, the DC-3 slowed as dramatically as the Zero accelerated.

"Get back up there," Thumper told the chief, "and yell when he shoots."

"Eye, eye, Thumper."

Man-child couldn't take it anymore.

"Why are we slowing? Let's run like hell!"

Thumper leaned far to his left.

"He's 100 knots faster than us; we'd never get away. I'm going to make him come down and fight *my* fight."

Chief had barely got into position when the Zero, now at 1,500 feet, started firing. He ducked and yelled to the cockpit:

"Incoming!"

Thumper held the slip and unloaded the airplane, pushing to negative G.

The Zero pilot had decided to make a long, slashing attack, then come off target by pitching up and left to a high perch, and re-attack if necessary. He had just pulled the trigger on his two 20-millimeter cannon and 7.7-millimeter machine guns, when the DC-3 disappeared below his nose. He pushed to reacquire his target, but had to release the trigger. Negative Gs would jam his guns.

It was then that he noticed the unbalanced flight of the DC-3 – a slip! His closure was not the 100 knots he expected; it was 200. As he blew past the DC-3, he chopped his power to idle. Enraged, he pulled off, pitching to a high perch left of and 1,000 feet higher than the DC-3. Bending his Zero to its perch, the Japanese pilot roughly cross-controlled in an attempt to slow it down. He had lost his composure, driven now by pure blood lust; all he wanted was the kill. He slid slightly forward of the DC-3. Instead of steadying his aircraft and methodically maneuvering into a firing position, he immediately re-attacked.

The Zero was much harder to slow than the DC-3; it was still doing 225 knots on its high perch. Thumper had slowed the DC-3 to 150 knots, close to best maneuver speed. The Zero pilot initiated a barrel-roll attack. He pulled the nose of his fighter 30 degrees straight up. Passing 30 degrees nose up, he started a slow roll to the right while still pulling up. His nose reached an angle of 45 degrees high, as he slowly rolled inverted. At the halfway point, he was perfectly inverted and let his nose fall through the horizon, pointing directly at the DC-3. Their courses were 90 degrees offset so that the DC-3 moved down the valley while the Zero continued the slow right roll in the opposite direction, continuing to descend.

The maneuver gave the fighter pilot the separation he needed. As he completed the roll, he ended up slightly aft and below the

DC-3, in a perfect firing position. The move was quite spectacular. Thumper admired the precision as only a pilot could – and
it was exactly what he expected. In fact, he had counted on it.

Now they were both low and slow: his fight. The wings of the
Zero sparkled. Thumper anticipated the shot, released the slip,
went to emergency power and pulled another four-G break turn
to the left and into the Zero. Again, the tracers missed.

This time, the Zero stayed in the saddle; he pulled his throttle
to idle and wrestled on 5 Gs. The Zero was buffeting wildly, on
the edge of stall. Thumper over-banked, still at 4 Gs, feinting for
the valley floor, which was closer than the Zero pilot realized.
He bit, jerking his control stick left to head off his prey, pulling
harder. He stepped on the bottom rudder to bring the gun sight
piper back on the DC-3.

The high G, coupled with the low airspeed, combined to raise
the angle of attack on the wing to a dangerous level. Angle of
attack is simply the angle between the wing and the relative
direction of the air flow. If the angle gets excessive, caused by
the pilot pulling too hard, airflow over the wing becomes
turbulent, causing buffet. If the pilot continues to pull, the flow
will separate from the wing and it will stall, or stop producing
lift, regardless of the speed of the aircraft. The result is a
departure from controlled flight – most of the time, quite a
violent ride.

Thumper knew the Zero pilot was pushing his aircraft to the
edge of its performance envelope. He answered the Zero's move
by rolling back, wings level, and pulling straight up. The young
fighter pilot, while still in heavy pre-stall buffet, reversed the
controls again aggressively to get the piper back on his target.
The wings sparkled again with deadly fire from his weapons,
but because of the unbalanced condition of his aircraft, the fire
was poorly aimed and not concentrated.

The aircraft began to uncouple: as he started to roll right, the
nose yawed left, causing the airflow to his left wing to be
partially masked by the nose of the aircraft. As the airflow
separated on the left wing, it stopped producing lift while the
right wing was swept into the wind, so was still producing lift.
The left wing had stopped flying while the right wing

continued. The Zero shuddered. Then, even though the Zero Pilot was trying to turn right, the aircraft snap-rolled left and departed controlled flight in a classic, adverse yaw stall.

The Zero pilot panicked and exacerbated the critical situation by jamming on combat power. It was a fatal mistake. The torque caused by the engine power and propeller created more momentum as the aircraft actually rotated around the prop. The sum of these forces rolled the Zero left violently. The nose dropped below the horizon and, after its second snap roll to the left, it hit the valley floor, inverted and 20 degrees nose low. It exploded into a huge orange and black fireball.

Thumper rolled up on his left wing and watched the impact.

"Holy shit!" chirped out Man-child.

The chief poked his head into the cockpit just in time to see the fireball.

"That's a kill," he deadpanned.

Thumper nodded and added, "We got any holes back there, Chief?"

"Yeah, a couple, nothing vital."

"Good," said Thumper. "Let's get the hell out of here. He might have a wingman."

Man-child sat up straight.

"Wingman?" he said, his voice two octaves higher.

Thumper turned the DC-3 to the right and flew out of the valley. He set climb power and began the long climb to a crossing altitude. Man-child spent the rest of the trip looking over his shoulder, intently scanning behind them. There were no wingmen. The rest of the flight was uneventful.

After they landed, Man-child sprinted to the makeshift operations office. By the time Thumper and the chief walked in, Man-child was jabbering like a monkey, dog-fighting with his hands. The youngsters were gathered around, soaking in every word. Thumper sat down next to Charles Henry.

"Rough day, Thumper?"

"I've had better, Charles Henry."

"Rock killed a Zero, eh?"

Thumper nodded slowly. "Damn lucky."

Man-child heard the statement.

"Lucky? That was the best damn flying I've ever seen or heard of! I didn't think a DC-3 could do that. How can you say that was luck?"

The room full of pilots was now looking at Thumper. He stood slowly, wearily, and counted off on his fingers.

"One," he said, "we were lucky that we were empty. Two, we were lucky the valley was below us. Three, we were lucky he jumped us on the left side. Four, we were lucky he followed us down to the deck and fought our fight. Five, we were lucky he wasn't as good as he thought he was, and stalled that airplane. If any one of those things hadn't happened, we'd be the smoking hole, not him."

Thumper started to head for the door but Trey stopped him.

"We are all just trying to learn, Thumper. Help us – tell us how you beat that Zero."

Thumper stood with his arms crossed over his chest.

"Okay, sport." He looked over and winked at Charles Henry. "Listen up, knuckleheads. First, I didn't defeat that Zero. I defeated his weapons, then the pilot."

He got a look back from his young students that could be best described as the trout look: eyes wide open, mouths agape. Thumper couldn't help but laugh.

"Okay, boys, here's the deal: in a high-G turn, to shoot another airplane down, the shooter has to get his nose way out in front of the targets. Then he has to hold steady on the target and walk the bullets onto something critical on the aircraft or into the cockpit. It ain't easy. If the target starts wiggling, it is damn hard; 90 percent of air-to-air kills are unobserved."

"What does that mean?" Trey interrupted.

Charles Henry piped up from across the room.

"It means the target never saw the shooter – his first clue being rounds impacting all over the aircraft. Luck counts, but in combat you gotta make your own luck."

Thumper went on.

"First, defeat the initial shot." He demonstrated with his hands. "Move the airplane, don't be a compliant target. Pull right at him; force him to commit his nose for a shot. Then move again to get out of plain or phase. Get your nose low, to keep or get some energy by using gravity."

Danny raised his hand as if in school.

"How did you keep from pulling the wings off?"

"The DC-3 is a utility class aircraft; that means it's stressed for 3½ positive and 1 negative Gs. I didn't pull more than four. Engineers always build in a little buffer, the fudge factor. The DC-3 is as strong as a horse, it is over-built. Remember: you have to be smooth and coordinated."

"Even when you are being aggressive?" asked Trey.

"Especially when you are being aggressive, you have to be in coordinated flight."

Man-child looked confused.

"What do you mean by coordinated?"

"You have to keep the tail behind the nose. That Jap got sloppy. He was more focused on killing us than flying his aircraft. He killed himself, I just talked him into it."

Trey asked one last question.

"What did you mean when you said he wasn't as good as he thought he was?"

Thumper smiled.

"Trey, no pilot is as good as he thinks he is."

The young copilots all looked to the floor, assuming he was talking about them individually.

"By the same token, no pilot is as bad as his buddies think he is, either."

That brought a relieved laugh from the group.

"Look," he continued, "you have to wander into the valley of the shadow of death thinking that you are the meanest S-O-B in the valley. But, in the back of your mind, know – expect – that you will make at least one mistake every flight. Always be on guard for that mistake. When you recognize it, you can fix it."

Thumper headed for the door again and this time, Charles Henry stopped him.

"Thumper, you are a double-pump today," he said. "You take off in a half hour. Want me to take it?"

Thumper looked over at Man-child.

"No thanks, Charles Henry, the Man-child and I will take it. Come on, Junior. Let's get some chow."

"Ho, Ho, Ho," mumbled Man-child. "Merry Christmas."

DATE TIME GROUP: 0031 ZULU 04 JAN 1942
FROM: COMMANDER AIR TRANSPORT COMMAND
TO: COMMANDER SEVEN ALPHA
SUBJECT: WESTPAC INTEL UPDATE
CLASSIFICATION: TOP SECRET SCI/EYES ONLY COM7ALPHA
TEXT: MANILA HAS FALLEN. US FORCES DIGGING IN ON
BATAAN. JAP FORCES ENCIRCLING KUALA LUMPUR
INVASION FORCE HEADED TO DUTCH EAST INDIES
(BORNEO, CELEBES). WYA.
C.R. SENDS

Chapter 22

Ding Hoa
5 January 1942

Bluto had received his nickname honestly. He looked like Popeye's cartoon nemesis: 6 foot 5; 285 pounds; broad shoulders and a barrel chest; and no matter how much he shaved, he had a perpetual five o'clock shadow. His appearance was menacing – men instinctively backed away when he entered a room. Yet, he seemed oblivious to the effect his presence had on strangers. Those who knew him were amused by the phenomenon; to his friends, Bluto Klaus was a docile sweetheart of a man.

An animal lover, Bluto always had a dog in tow, whether it was in Dallas, St. Louis, Cleveland or New York. Every American Airlines operations office seemed equipped with a stray dog that greeted Bluto before he reached the operations building. The other crews thought it was his size that caused him to stand out, but his observant first officers knew the real reason: he goosed the engines on short final to announce his arrival. To the dogs, it was his gentle manner – that and the treats he carried in his pocket.

Bluto and his normal copilot, Hass-Man, were quite a pair. Hass-Man was a full foot shorter than Bluto, and 150 pounds lighter. The big man was gregarious and loud, the small man reserved and stoic. Hass-Man was second generation Prussian; Bluto was a second generation Pole. Even with all that was now going on in Europe, they were very close friends. They had been flying together longer than any of the Seven Alpha crews.

Bluto and Hass-Man were on the southern route to Chengtu, and they were being hammered by the weather. Ironically, it was the bad weather that allowed them to fly the southern route; it kept the Zeros on the ground. Even with the bad weather their normal cockpit banter went uninterrupted. Bluto was boisterously telling a story, with hands and arms gesturing wildly, Hass-Man nodding and laughing in amusement. Not that Hass-Man sat like a bump on a log, when the conversation turned more esoteric he would jump right in. Quite obviously they both enjoyed the long hours of discourse, because they had been crewed together for so long.

They were headed due east across the Hump. On their route, they would cross some of the biggest rivers in the world – the Irrawaddy, Salween and the Mekong – but they would see none of them today. They would have to fly a DR (dead reckoning) plot for three hours; the DR plot, being little more than an educated guess, depended on accurate wind predictions. They would plot a wind-corrected course, and time their progress, hoping that the forecasted winds would be close. It was all about time, heading, and faith. They took their faith with a healthy dose of covering their bases. They would climb to an altitude that would clear all obstacles, just in case.

Once over the Hump, they had hoped the weather would clear enough that they could navigate via pilotage (visually). But it didn't clear up, so they flew a DR plot toward Kunming. Upon reaching the Kunming area, they were still in the weather; they turned northeast and tuned in the radio navigation aid at Yangkai, 40 miles away. They marked on top at Yangkai: the mark established their position directly over Yangkai, so they reset their clocks and updated the navigational plot. Next, they turned northwest for Chengtu, which was now an hour away.

Bluto started down over the flat plain between Chunking and Chengtu. The barometric pressure was forecast to be stable, so they would descend no lower than 500 feet above the high plateau. If the forecast had been for unstable pressure, they would go no lower than 750 AGL, as an added safety buffer. After descending to their minimum altitude, if they didn't break out of the clouds, it would be back to the Assam. This morning, they broke out at a comfortable 1,500 feet AGL. They picked up their course visually and landed without incident.

Chengtu was in a relatively secure area, allowing for a more relaxed unloading of the aircraft by Chinese workers. It also allowed the crew an hour on deck, which enabled them to enjoy the one delicacy available to them: eggs – real eggs, fresh eggs, eggs from a chicken, not a box. Cooked any way you wanted them.

Everything in India was powdered or canned, and tasted like it. For many of the crewmen, the powdered food had an unpleasant side effect: it acted as a laxative. For those individuals, it was best to skip the powdered eggs for breakfast before a mission; a gastrointestinal incident while crossing the Hump would be unpleasant for the entire crew. Bluto was one of these unfortunate individuals. Now he was hungry and making a beeline for real food.

The airport restaurant was a crashed DC-3 that had lost an engine while attempting to takeoff overweight. Returning to earth, the aircraft had bounced hard and veered off the runway, severing the landing gear and coming to rest off the side of the runway – where it still sat. After stripping it of serviceable parts, crews had converted the wrecked hull to a restaurant.

The Chinese cook who inhabited the unusual diner had somehow picked up the nickname Frenchie; no doubt an aviator with a sarcastic sense of humor was the source. No matter – Frenchie seemed to love his *nom de guerre*. A chef of haute cuisine he was not, but he could make a mean plate of "eggeses", any way you wanted them.

Bluto banged through the swinging doors like a gunslinger in the Old West. He made his way to the counter, where all ten stools were empty. Behind the counter, the old Chinaman was bent over a crackling, gas-fired stove. The smell of fresh eggs cooking in sesame oil filled the air.

"Frenchie, mona' mi'," boomed Bluto, "eggeses for all my men."

Frenchie looked up, his face lit up. "Big Man, how you?"

"Good, my friend – good and hungry!"

"How many eggeses for you?" Bluto held up ten big fingers. Frenchie immediately went to work. "How many for Little Man?" Hass-Man held up four fingers, as did Slim, their air crewman. Frenchie was already in a flurry of activity. "Okay, okay – me make, you sit."

Bluto, Hass-Man, and Slim sat down for their feast of fresh eggs. Frenchie quickly whipped up the delicacy and slapped down three metal GI plates. The crew leaned over the eggs, inhaling the magic aroma. Bluto waved the precious smells of sesame, eggs and "secret spices" into his nose, then quickly devoured the meal.

After finishing, Bluto wiped his big mug with a rough paper napkin. His five o'clock shadow, already present, pulled fibers from the napkin. As he brushed the fibers from his chin, he saw movement under the swinging doors – something small and furry: a head. He put his hand on his shoulder-holstered .38 caliber Smith and Wesson.

"Rat – I hate rats!"

Frenchie looked up. "No, no! Him dog."

Bluto relaxed his grip on the .38, and a tiny ball of black fluff waddled in. The puppy sniffed around, scrounging for any morsel of food it could find.

"Well look at that," Bluto laughed. He got up and walked over to the small dog, sweeping it up in one of his huge hands. It was soft as silk and surprisingly clean. It looked up at Bluto with big, dark eyes.

"This is just what OPs needs at Shangri-La," said Bluto.

Frenchie shook his head, laughing. The giant American always entertained him.

"You like, you take, Big Man."

Bluto slipped the pup into his leather flight jacket.

"Time to go, boys – thanks for the dog, Frenchie." He slapped an extra five-dollar bill on the countertop.

The air crew slogged out to their DC-3 through ankle-deep mud. The aircraft was already fueled and loaded, a process that had gone quickly since the cargo was self-loading: Chinese troops headed to Myitkyina Burma.

The troops sat flat on the cargo bay floor. They were brand new, "green" troops, their fresh denim uniforms stiff and uncomfortable. As the air crew made their way to the cockpit, stepping over the nervous peasant troops, they gave a thumbs-up and let out an enthusiastic, "Ding Hoa!" which translated roughly to, "Everything is okay." It was the inexperienced soldiers' fervent wish. Most of these Chinamen had never been in an automobile, let alone an airplane.

In the cockpit, Bluto sat in the left seat, the puppy's head poking out of his zippered jacket, and looked over at Hass-Man.

"I think," he said, we have a name for this critter: Ding Hoa."

Bluto got Ding settled inside his flight jacket, leaving off his shoulder harness to make the pup as comfortable as possible.

Like the Chinese passengers, the little dog had never flown and didn't appear to be looking forward to the adventure. As the engines ran up for take off, Ding ducked his head inside Bluto's jacket. When they began their climb to altitude, he showed his fear further. Hass-Man started laughing, then pointed to Bluto's leg. His khaki trousers had a small dark stain that was growing from under his jacket.

Bluto looked down. "Shit. Give me something, Hass-Man."

Hass-Man shook his head, still laughing. "Your dog, pal. Not my problem."

Bluto reached over and grabbed Hass-Man's chart.

"Hey, that's mine," he protested.

"Now it's both our problem," responded Bluto as he shaped the chart into a makeshift diaper. It ended up more like an envelope than a diaper but the purpose was the same; he slipped it under his jacket and around Ding's bottom.

Bluto shared his oxygen with the dog, who trembled all the way to Myitkyina and Shangri-La. He couldn't tell if Ding was cold or just didn't enjoy the experience of flight.

Once on the ground again, Ding quickly became a permanent fixture outside the Ops shack. The pilots and crewmen loved him, and he thrived under the attention – and the flow of goodies from the mess hall. His belly was always round and plump, and he began to grow rapidly.

After a few days, Ding was settling in as the happiest dog on earth when a large vulture decided to share in his bliss; the bird of prey just could not resist that plump belly. It had watched from its jungle perch for days, and now it swooped down, sharp talons plunging deeply into the helpless dog's back. Ding struggled as the winged beast beat its way back into the air, but he was too small.

Fortunately, Bluto had put Ding on a leash so he wouldn't get run over by taxiing aircraft. After only a short flight, the leash played out and yanked the puppy back to the earth, leaving the disappointed vulture to look for easier prey. The leash had saved Ding, but for how long was uncertain: the poor dog lay motionless on the ground with deep gashes in his back.

Trey had seen the attack from the barracks and ran over to the pup. He found an ammo crate lid and gently slid it under Ding, using it as a stretcher, then rushed him to the medics. They dressed the wounds but were not optimistic about the puppy's chances; his gashes were deep.

When Bluto returned, he sprang into action, setting up a schedule of volunteers to nurse Ding in his absence. Slowly, in Bluto's care, the dog got stronger but it became obvious that he would never be quite right.

Date time group: 0051 ZULU 20 JAN 1942
From: COMMANDER AIR TRANSPORT COMMAND
To: COMMANDER SEVEN ALPHA
Subject: WESTPAC INTEL UPDATE
Classification: TOP SECRET SCI/EYES ONLY COM7ALPHA
Text: FULL SCALE INVASION OF BURMA UNDERWAY FROM CENTRAL THAILAND. RANGOON PROJECTED TARGET. WYA.
C.R. SENDS

Chapter 23

Invasion of Burma
21 January 1942

The day started with frantic activity, and the schedule was scrapped. An all-out effort was underway to support the Burma front. Every available asset was being put into Burma, which meant that Seven Alpha would be responsible for getting them there. Their aircraft were reassigned to shuttle fresh troops into Burma from Imphal and fly the wounded back. By the panicked nature of the messages from Burma, it was obvious that things were going badly for the Allies.

Bluto ambled in at 04:45 with Ding limping along behind him. It had been almost three weeks since Ding's impromptu flight with Vulture Air, and it was obvious that he would never be normal. That didn't matter to Bluto; in fact, it endeared him to the dog even more.

In OPs, J.T. watched Bluto and Ding's entrance. "How's Ding doing, Bluto?"

"He's hanging in there, but I think he has some permanent spine damage from those talons."

J.T. nodded. "Well, you did good by him, Bluto. I thought he was a goner."

"He's a scrapper, skipper. He'll be fine."

J.T. held out an op request from Burma. "Japs invaded Burma – it's ugly already. We've been reassigned to reinforce the Brits."

Bluto took the sheet. "Roger that, skipper."

He walked out of the OPs shack and got Ding settled in a wooden lean-to he had built, under which the dog could hide from the feathered airborne threat. He tied Ding to the leash, tenderly fluffed his pillow, and disappeared into the darkness as J.T. watched from the doorway, Ding from his shelter.

Bluto taxied his DC-3 to the runway in the dark, and launched in the predawn grey of a new day. They were on their second run of the day, from Imphal, India to Lashio, Burma and back. On the first round-trip, they had brought in 30 fresh troops and returned with 15 wounded. Bluto thought about that ratio, knowing it was unsustainable. On the second run, no wounded were ready for transport but more significantly, the fuel depot was empty. Hass-Man ran the fuel numbers and reported to Bluto.

"Hey, Big Guy – we can make it but it will be tight."

Bluto had just returned from the weather shack. "Well, the weather is supposed to hold in the Assam, but I got the usual disclaimer about the instability and thus unpredictable nature of the area, blah, blah, blah."

Hass-Man laughed. "Well what do you want to do?"

Bluto watched as more DC-3s landed. The field was beginning to get jammed up with all the arriving aircraft.

"We can't stay here and wait for fuel; there isn't room. Plus, I don't want to get caught on deck by the Japs. Do we have enough for a divert?"

Hass-Man responded immediately: "No."

Bluto rubbed his scruffy chin, "Well then, I suppose the question is would you rather run out of gas or get blown up, worst case scenario?"

His trusty copilot thought about it for a ten-count.

"Run out of gas. We can always bail out."

Bluto nodded agreement. "Me too. Besides, all these aircraft can't stay. Some will have to takeoff to get more in. We might as well be the first."

The weather was marginal as they reached the Patkai Range; they were in and out of the clouds. The bad visibility prevented them from seeing the weather building in the Assam Valley. Cool air flowed out of the Himalayas into the Assam thanks to a lower-than-expected drop in the ambient pressure. The cool air mixed with the humid jungle air of the Assam and as a result, the entire valley was soon covered with a thick blanket of fog. Bluto climbed out of the clouds to get a look at the valley before he committed to crossing the Patkai Mountains.

In the clear area between cloud decks, two Mitsubishi model A6M2 Zero-Sen fighters were on patrol, looking for Allied aircraft. The DC-3 popped out of the clouds just below and in front of the fighters, and they immediately rolled in on the fat target. Hass-Man scanned over his shoulder just in time to see the lead Zero open fire.

"Break right, break right!" he yelled.

Bluto responded instantly, and his turn was quick enough to get the DC-3s fuselage out of the Zero's crosshairs. However, the Zero pilot had 60 rounds from a 2-second burst already on the way. They missed the fuselage and cockpit but seven high-explosive, 20-millimeter rounds hit the left wing. The first round smashed into the outboard attaching hinge for the left aileron, and the next six stitched across the wing, exploding on impact.

Under the four "G" load of Bluto's evasive turn, the damaged wingtip separated. The aileron, now only attached by two hinges, began to flutter. The aircraft buffeted heavily, mercifully throwing the fluttering aileron from the DC-3. Bluto quickly stuffed the nose and disappeared back into the clouds.

With the Zero threat neutralized, Bluto was now preoccupied with wrestling the damaged aircraft under control; it took both pilots on the yoke to manage it. Bluto trimmed the aircraft, full right wing down. He used about half the available rudder trim to hold course for Imphal. Even with the assistance from the trim tabs, it took the physical strength of the crew to overpower the imbalance in lift caused by 3 feet of left wing and the aileron being shot off. Somehow, they managed to keep the wounded bird flying toward the assumed safety of the Assam.

Once they had regained control of the aircraft, Hass-Man assessed the damage. Slim had reported no hits in the back; Hass-Man turned to examine his wing. He wasn't pleased with what he saw. A single 7.7 millimeter round had hit the right wing smack dab in the middle of its fuel tank. This model of DC-3 was an airliner, not the military C-47 version of the aircraft; it had no self-sealing tanks. They were losing precious fuel.

They nursed the stricken DC-3 over the Patkais, only to find the valley socked in with fog. Bluto descended into the Assam to shoot the instrument approach at Imphal. As he slowed, the DC-3 became harder to control, so he slowed in 10 knot increments until he dared go no slower. As they struggled down the final approach course, Bluto did an incredible job of wrestling the aircraft right down the chute.

"Call the tower," he said. "Get us clearance to land and the weather again."

"Roger that." replied Hass-Man. "Imphal tower, Army six-oh-six request permission to land and current weather."

The tower responded with bad news: "We are zero, zero down here. Six-oh-six, say intentions."

Hass-Man answered, "We don't have a choice, tower, we are streaming fuel and will only get one, maybe two looks."

"Okay, six-oh-six, you are cleared for the approach and clear to land runway one eight. Good luck."

The tower controller didn't have to ask: he heard the DC-3 go around on a missed approach. He immediately cleared them for another try. Again, the same result. It was now time for Plan B. With the fuel gauges reading empty, Bluto climbed straight ahead to 3,000 feet.

"You and Slim get your chutes on," he said.

Hass-Man started back, then turned. "What about yours?

Bluto struggled with the dying aircraft. "Bring it forward."

Hass-Man came back with Bluto's chute. "Slim jumped," he said. "Come on, Bluto, let's get out of here."

Bluto looked up at his old friend. "I can't, Hass-Man. I can barely hold it. You get out – now."

Hass-Man looked at the controls. They were full-deflected and the aircraft was barely flying. "Speed it up, then we will go!"

Bluto shook his head. "No can do. We'd hit the tail when we jump."

Hass-Man knew this was true, but he frantically looked for an escape plan that would get them both out. He found none.

"You get out," he said. "I'll hold it. I'm smaller – I can get out easier when it rolls off."

Bluto was now sweating profusely with exertion.

"No offense, Hass-Man, but you'd never be able to hold it."

Hass-Man's heart sank. He knew the big man was right – Bluto was barely holding the aircraft's wings level – but he didn't want to accept it. *"There are always options"*, he thought, *"always a way out – we have to find it."* The engines suddenly coughed and then died. Now they were out of time.

"Go, now!" Bluto yelled. "I will be all right. I can make it."

They both knew that was bull. Hass-Man stood frozen with dread.

"Get your Prussian ass out of here – I can't hold it much longer!" Bluto grabbed Hass-Man and threw him down the tunnel into the cargo bay.

Hass reluctantly walked to the open door and plunged into the fog with tear-filled eyes. He pulled his rip cord and floated down silently, blindly, defeated by fate. His agony grew when he heard the unmistakable impact of a metal machine on Mother Earth. There was no explosion, just a gut-wrenching crunch.

When they found Hass-Man, they thought he was in shock. He was still lying on the ground where he had landed. But it was not shock that left him totally debilitated – it was deep grief and an overpowering sense of guilt.

Date time group: 0151 ZULU 24 JAN 1942
From: COMMANDER AIR TRANSPORT COMMAND
To: COMMANDER SEVEN ALPHA
Subject: WESTPAC INTEL UPDATE
Classification: TOP SECRET SCI/EYES ONLY COM7ALPHA
Text: KAVIENG, NEW IRELAND. RABAUL NEW BRITAN INVADED. SITUATION DIRE. PORT MORESBY, NEW GUINEA ALL THAT STANDS BETWEEN JAPS AND AUSTRALIA. ALL AVAILABLE ASSETS SHIFTED TO THAT THEATER ROTATION IN DOUBT. SORRY ABOUT BLUTO. WYA.
C.R. SENDS

Chapter 24

Shangri-La
24 January 1942

J.T. sat on a desk in Operations looking at a map of the Pacific theater. The Japanese Imperial military seemed unstoppable. They were within weeks of consolidating their forces. The last Allied strongholds were barely hanging on: Rangoon, Burma to the northwest was covering India; Port Moresby, New Guinea was covering Australia to the south; Singapore stood at the Straits of Malacca, cutting off the Japanese navy's access to the Indian Ocean; Bataan and Corrigedor in the Philippines were preventing the Japs from moving on Midway and the Hawaiian Islands.

"They have to hold", he thought. If they didn't, then Australia, India and the United States would be next. He also had a more immediate and closer problem. He had to get his boys' heads back in the game. Bluto had been a popular aircraft commander and member of the squadron. His death had rattled the Seven Alpha crews, especially Hass-Man. He had not spoken or eaten in four days.

To add to his leadership challenge, J.T. was sure they were going to be extended. He turned to face his air crews and most of his maintainers, and walked toward the map.

"Gentlemen," he said, "I'm not going to bullshit you. Things are bad."

Irish pushed his way forward. "How bad, skipper?"

J.T. was silent for a long five seconds.

"What I'm about to tell you is classified Top Secret." He pointed to the map and touched Rangoon, Singapore, Bataan and Port Moresby. "These are the last Allied strongholds in the Pacific theater. If they all fall, the war is lost." His fingers touched India, Australia, Hawaii, and Alaska, and slid down to the west coast of the United States.

Silence seemed to fill in for air in the crowded room. No one breathed; they couldn't. J.T. let the silence hang for emphasis.

"I don't have to tell you how things are going in Burma; you can see it for yourself. From the message traffic I've seen, I'd say it is going about the same in Bataan and Singapore. When we got into this war it was about keeping China alive and fighting. It still is, in our day-to-day grind. But the big picture, the world picture, has shifted. We absolutely must stop them here on the Burma-India border, and at Port Moresby on the front step of Australia. The Australian Army is in Africa and on the other side of the world; they are virtually defenseless at home."

Quigs nodded in agreement. "It wouldn't take long."

J.T. paused. "After that," he said at last, "it would be the United States. "

"Gentlemen," he continued, "the Allied command is shifting everything they have to the defense of Port Moresby. I have no doubt that will include our relief. This is bigger than any of us now – you, me, Bluto. We aren't on some grand crusade to save freedom for the world. It's more than that now. It is about saving our homes, our families. I intend to stand and fight here. Anyone who does not, I need to know now."

Nobody moved or said a word; the air was still out of the room. The great adventure had taken on an ominous and deadly change of course. Finally Irish spoke up.

"Well we'd better get busy; it's going to be a long war."

The Seven Alpha personnel started to file out – everyone except the chief and Charles Henry.

J.T. looked up. "What's up, Chief?"

The chief stuck out his chin. "I got five whiners, skipper."

"What do you want to do?" asked J.T.

"Fire the bastards."

J.T. couldn't help but smile. "Won't that leave you short?"

"Yep. Look, skipper, these guys are a cancer already. We will be much better off with them gone."

J.T. knew he was right. "Okay, Chief, it's your call. They will be on the next flight out of here."

The chief was still standing fast.

"Something else on your mind?" queried J.T.

"Yep. Any idea how long I've gotta keep these airplanes flying?"

J.T. shrugged his shoulders. "I wish I knew, Chief. I wish I knew."

The chief strolled out with a little pep in his step, in search of a certain five troublemakers, soon to be unemployed on the other side of the world.

J.T. turned to Charles Henry. "I don't suppose you are waiting to invite me to chow."

"Nope," responded Charles Henry.

"Okay what's up with you?"

"What do we do about Hass-Man? He's beating himself up pretty bad. You want to send him back?"

J.T. appreciated how Charles Henry kept a close eye on the crews.

"No, that's the worst thing we could do. They were close, flew together for years. Hass-Man is senior; let's upgrade him. Give him Bluto's replacement ship; that will keep him busy."

Charles Henry raised an eyebrow. "Good idea," he said. "I'll do the designation letter today."

Date time group: 0231 ZULU 16 FEB 1942
From: COMMANDER AIR TRANSPORT COMMAND
To: COMMANDER SEVEN ALPHA
Subject: WESTPAC INTEL UPDATE
Classification: TOP SECRET SCI/EYES ONLY COM7ALPHA
Text: SINGAPORE HAS FALLEN. SUMATRA, TIMOR INVADED. JAVA NOW IN VICE. ANTICIPATE ALL OUT PUSH ON RANGOON. PORT MORESBY HANGING ON. STILL WORKING YOUR RELIEF. WYA.
C.R. SENDS

Chapter 25

The Grind
16 February 1942

The grind continued, mission after mission. It seemed endless, the only variation being the weather. On average, for the past two months, each crew had flown between eleven and twelve hours a day – a spine-numbing 300 hours a month – per pilot. At least the double pumps had been halved; as the front stabilized in China, they were going deeper on half the flights. Because of the longer flight lengths, only one per day was possible.

The relief was welcomed by the ground crews. They were still pulling 18-hour days, but at least the tempo had dropped. Charles Henry had the operation running smoothly and pretty much on its own, which allowed him to take a normal rotation. When they first got to Shangri-La, one of the mechanics had let slip that he knew how to type. Charles Henry pressed him into service as assistant operations officer and scheduling officer. The man hated his new job and quickly acquired a new nickname: Grumpy.

The boilerplate schedule launched four crews from the supply depot at Dispur. They would be wheels-in-the-well at 0400, allowing them to shoot the hole at sunrise. They would refuel, eat breakfast, and if they weren't given an emergency reassignment, go on the originally scheduled run. Charles Henry had decided to add this flexibility instead of going directly to Burma at first dawn, because they got a lot of emergency reassignments in the Burma Theater, thanks to the fluid battle lines. The Dispur aircraft went exclusively to Burma, double-pumping out of the supply depot, then returning to spend the night.

The other four crews launched from Shangri-La at first light, going directly to China. After off-loading and refueling, they flew to the depot at Dispur. There, they had dinner while being reloaded, and launched in time to shoot the hole at twilight, requiring only fueling for the next day's launch. The China routes were better – less legs and less bullets – so Charles Henry swapped crews every week.

The only variation, besides the weather, was destination; after a couple of weeks, even that became a non-event due to familiarity. Grumpy coordinated the proper loads to their proper drops; he didn't like doing it, but he was good at it.

With Quigs in the rotation, they had an extra Transport Aircraft Commander or TAC, also known as Captain. The chief had pieced together two of the RAF's wrecked DC-3s; one replaced Bluto's aircraft and the other was used to run fuel. It was nicknamed Buff or Buffalo, short for fuel buffalo.

The Buff was used to run fuel from Dispur to Shangri-La, all day, every day. Command still wanted a hidden base in the event things got even worse. They had worked the logistics to keep loading to a minimum at Shangri-La. However, they needed a lot of fuel in order to run the daily schedule. On most days, that meant four trips for the Buff.

Every eighth day, a TAC would be rotated to the Buff. It was a nice break, not having to worry about getting shot at. They trained one of the mechanics to read the checklists and lower the gear and flaps, and he took to it like a duck to water. His name was Ermond Bryant, so naturally they called him Mink. Within three weeks, Mink was shooting the hole and landing at Shangri-La.

On days when any of the China crews had short hops, they'd hang around and have breakfast with the Burma crews. Once in a great while, all of the crews would meet at the breakfast table. Today was one of those rare days. Normally, the squadron breakfast was a rowdy event, complete with backslapping, loud laughs and lots of "hand flying". Today, the mood was different, very subdued.

The crews seemed numb. They were nine weeks into the grind of flying the Hump, running from Zeros, dodging anti-aircraft

artillery. With the exception of the occasional weather day, they
had gone nonstop since leaving Dallas 2½ months ago. It was
beginning to show. At breakfast, Charles Henry had studied
each face intently. The youngsters had visibly aged ten years.
His vets were picking up little twitches that he recognized from
the Great War.

He knew that weak men collapsed mentally under the strain.
Strong men began to manifest physical signs as their brains
looked for release. Tics, skin problems – there had been a lot of
twitching and itching at the breakfast table. The stress of
ceaseless combat operations was taking its toll. These guys
needed a break.

Now, standing in the door of the OPs office looking out over
the tarmac, Charles Henry could see that the ground guys
needed a break as badly as the air crews. There were multiple
arguments going on, including one pushing match that wound
up in a mud wrestling contest.

He turned around and saw J.T. leaning back in a chair, hat
pulled down over his eyes, apparently asleep. Quigs sat in the
corner at an old desk, reading messages.

Charles Henry broke the silence. "Hey, skipper?"

J.T. responded immediately without raising his hat or sitting
up. "Yeah, Charles Henry?"

"We need to get these guys a break, some R&R, anything to
break the monotony."

J.T.'s chair came forward and hit on all four legs. He pushed
his hat back, got up and walked to the door. He knew that if
Charles Henry thought it worth mentioning, something was up.
He followed his second-in-command's glance across the
mayhem on the tarmac.

"Yep," he said. "You are most definitely right, Charles Henry.
Hey Quigs, you got any ideas there, mate?"

Quigs closed his eyes and pinched the skin between his eyes.
"Let me put on my thinking cap." He sat motionless for a full
thirty seconds while J.T. and Charles Henry smiled at each
other.

Suddenly, he bolted for the calendar on the wall.

"Yes, yes, perfect!" Quigs exclaimed excitedly, tapping the

calendar. "Two days after tomorrow: a fortnightly party at the Governor's mansion in Calcutta."

J.T. rubbed his chin. "Governor's mansion...is that a good idea?"

Quigs was very animated now. "Absolutely, I should say so: great food, free booze – and nurses!"

"Okay, Quigs, if you say so. Charles Henry, have Grumpy spread the word. We stand down day after tomorrow for the Governor's Ball."

By the time J.T. had manned up his aircraft twenty minutes later, the entire mood of the small base had changed. There were smiles aplenty.

Chapter 26

Shoot Down
17 February 1942

J.T. and Jon were the last of the Shangri-La crews on deck that evening. J.T. had a habit of counting airplanes, and his made four so all the Shangri-La boys were home. Next, he would check with Grumpy on the Dispur bubbas, or crews. Charles Henry was the detachment officer in charge, so whether he was in Dispur and J.T. in Shangri-La or vice versa, he always radioed J.T. with a head count.

J.T. shut the engines down and looked out of his side windscreen. He saw Grumpy waiting, his normal scowl replaced by a look of worry. J.T. left Jon to finish the checklist and hurried out of the cockpit. Grumpy was standing next to the door as he exited.

"What's up, Grumpy?" J.T. asked before his feet hit the ground.

The mechanic replied in a rapid-fire staccato. "No word came from the depot so I called: two missing."

J.T. grimaced. "Who?" he asked, already knowing, if no word had been passed, what the answer would be.

"Charles Henry and Quigs," responded Grumpy.

J.T. now shared his look of concern. "Any radio transmissions?"

"No."

"Sightings?"

"No."

"Shit!"

J.T. stood in stunned silence for a few seconds, his mind racing with thoughts and options, trying to grasp one and formulate a plan. Suddenly, he snapped to action.

"Where were their drops?"

"Deep, both."

"Hot?"

"Probably."

"Exact location?"

"E-68 and E-67; China, French-Indochina border."

J.T. paused to think. "Okay, let's chart them and organize a search and rescue."

Grumpy snapped off an uncustomary salute.

"Yes, sir!" The two of them started for the operations office.

Not knowing was the worst part; the unknown always invited the imagination to disaster. It was excruciating to the crews. The finality of knowledge, the word, even if it was unpleasant, always seemed a relief.

Today, they didn't have to twist in the breeze long. The distinctive roar of Pratt and Whitney R-1830's stopped them in their tracks. They spun on their heels to see a DC-3 charging up the valley, trailing vapor from both wings.

Jon walked up quickly, joining J.T. and Grumpy.

"Man he's hot! What's he doing, skipper?"

"He's bleeding out fuel, wings are all shot up," replied J.T.

Jon shook his head. "He's too fast – he will never make it!"

J.T. allowed a slight smile. "Yes he will. Watch this."

As if on cue, the DC-3 went into a max deflection slip, and the roar from the PW R-1830s went silent. The aircraft shuddered from its drastic deceleration, and the gear and flaps started their methodical mechanical extension, unhurried by the extremis of the situation. The DC-3 held the slip until 10 feet above the runway, returned to balanced flight, and touched down.

The aircraft fast-taxied clear of the runway, pointed right at J.T., Jon and Grumpy, and rapidly closed on the small group. At close range, it pivoted on the right main mount as the engines shut down and the tail swept toward them, the door ending up within 10 feet of where they stood. Charles Henry was instantly in the door.

"Quigs is with the bugs!" He jumped from the DC-3. "The

Japs were waiting for us! Damn sky filled with hot lead on our fly-by. We took some small caliber hits and bugged-out. We received an HF transmission from Quigs as we crossed the Hump. Apparently, they had the same receiving committee but took a lot more damage. They only made it twenty-five miles, crash landing at Echo 66. Too close to the Japs – they will definitely go after them. We couldn't go back because we were bleeding out our fuel. So we told them to hunker down, that we'd be back at dawn."

J.T. nodded. "Okay, let's get our collective shit together and be ready to pick them up ASAP!" He caught sight of the chief running up to the group. "Chief, I need a plane ready with nothing but gas at 0300. No need to risk a crewman; Charles Henry and I will go alone."

"Aye aye, skipper." responded the chief. "It will be ready at 0200."

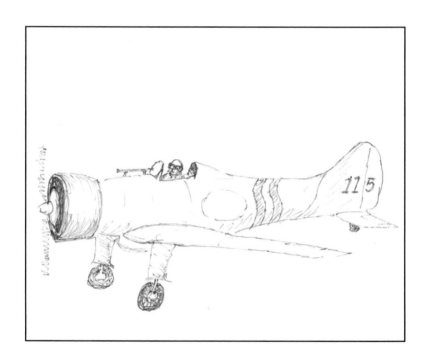

MITSUBISHI A5M4 CLAUDE

Chapter 27

Rescue
18 February 1942

At 0300, J.T. found Charles Henry, the chief, Grumpy and four other mechanics standing at the Buffalo. They were all in field gear and heavily armed, each with a .45 caliber side arm, Thompson sub-machine gun and hand grenades.

"What's going on, Charles Henry?"

Charles Henry looked exasperated.

"They want to go."

The chief stepped forward.

"Correction," he said. "We are going!" His face had a look of determination, discernible even in the moonlight.

J.T. couldn't stifle his smile. "Is that a fact, Chief?"

"That's a fact!"

J.T. looked into his old friend's eyes. They were resolute and unflinching – he was indeed going, or nobody was. J.T. threw up his hands.

"Okay, okay, chief. Any other surprises, this fine morning?"

Now it was the chief's turn to smile.

"Funny you should mention it." He stepped back, making a grand gesture towards the Buff.

J.T. hadn't noticed in the predawn dark when he walked up, but the boys had been busy last night. The most obvious modification to the Buff was a rather large .50 caliber machine gun, or "fifty," mounted on a swivel to the cargo door frame. The door itself was gone, and on closer inspection, J.T. saw that so were some of the windows in the fuselage. He walked up to the door and looked inside, a fifty was rigged opposite the cargo door as well, in the space a window had been.

"Pretty impressive, Chief. Anything else?"

"Yes, sir. The celestial bubble is removed, and an internal fuel tank is installed and fueled in case we take some wing hits. Also we rigged some armor and loaded some spare parts, food and water, just in case."

"Outstanding, Chief. Any weapons for me?"

The chief shook his head.

"Nope. You fly, we shoot."

"Fair enough, let's get some chow and be ready to go. We need to be on the runway, engines turning, when dawn breaks."

"Roger that, skipper. One more thing, though." The chief flicked on his flashlight and pointed it toward the front of the aircraft.

J.T.'s eyes followed the beam of light. It came to rest on the fuselage nose just forward of the captain's side windscreen, illuminating a painting of a brightly colored, snorting buffalo.

"Nice, Chief – who's the artist?"

The chief's chest swelled with pride. "Me!"

"You never cease to amaze me, Chief."

The two men started toward the chow hall. Charles Henry glanced over at one of the ground crew. It was Grumpy, and he was armed to the teeth.

"Where the hell do you think you are going?"

Grumpy's response, as always, was succinct:

"China. I've pushed enough paper."

Charles Henry started to respond, then stopped. Grumpy didn't stick around to hear it anyway; he was headed for the chow hall. Then Charles Henry noticed his son walking up to the Buff.

"Good morning, sunshine."

Trey looked up. "Mornin', pop."

He stood quietly for a few seconds, shuffling his feet in the mud.

"Maybe I should go with J.T. – I mean Colonel Dobbs."

Charles Henry crossed his arms. "Why's that, sport?"

Trey continued to shuffle.

"Well, if something happened, losing the number one and number two guys wouldn't be a good thing." He looked up, meeting his father's eyes in the bright moonlight. "This didn't turn out like I thought it would," he said. "I shouldn't have got you in it."

Charles Henry put his arm around his son.

"I appreciate it. You got a set, which makes me proud. Look, I did know what was coming. I would have come anyway."

Trey looked at his father with doubt in his eyes.

"Still, you shouldn't both go."

"We will be okay. Besides, all you boys are self-loading. You know what to do, and how to do it." Charles Henry smiled. "Let's go eat, I'm hungry."

The colors of dawn, vibrant and alive, were contrasted against the black of the earth. The jagged outline of the Himalayas seemed torn from a bolt of black fabric. As they approached, the mountains were even more foreboding than normal. Regardless, they were across them quickly, enjoying a 60-knot tailwind. The crossing had been surprisingly smooth. Sunrise was glorious as always, especially from the top of the world. The predawn colors danced above them as they descended into the black-grey of China. By the time the morning sun broke the eastern horizon, they were ripping across China at redline speed.

They had shot the hole in the moonlight of a clear night's sky. Even so, it was more by Braille than sight. No one on board had protested or squirmed when the power came up on the engines well before the sun. They knew the race was on. The rugged bush would slow but not stop the Japanese troops, who would march through the night to get at a crew that supplied their enemies with bullets. Seven Alpha had to win the race

As soon as they cleared the Hump, Grumpy went to work on the HF radio. The HF, or high frequency radio, was actually comparatively low frequency. VHF stood for very high frequency and UHF, ultra high frequency. The lower the frequency, the higher the power and thus, the further the range.

After forty minutes, Grumpy made contact. The hardest and most important step of a combat search and rescue was complete; they had established communications. Unfortunately, the information exchanged was not good news. A Japanese A5M4 Claude fighter was snooping in the area.

Ten minutes later came worse news. The Claude had caught sight of the downed DC-3 in the early morning light. It flew low over the DC-3, then went into a climbing orbit overhead. He was obviously climbing to get better range for his UHF radio, to call in the position to Japanese ground troops.

Grumpy went forward and relayed the ugly news. J.T. mulled it over for a few seconds.

"Charles Henry," he said. "How far out are we?"

Charles Henry checked his plot and watch.

"One hour and thirteen minutes."

J.T. gave Grumpy a wink. "Go get the chief. I've got an idea."

Grumpy rolled his eyes. "Here we go again."

Charles Henry looked quizzically at J.T.

"You want to tell me what you plan to do about that Claude?"

J.T. didn't hesitate: "Kill it!"

"Really?" Charles Henry raised an eyebrow.

The chief reached the cockpit.

"Skipper," he said. "Grumpy filled me in. What's the plan?"

"Chief," said J.T., "I need you to pull that fifty off the starboard side and put it on the same side as the door gun. Also, pull all the windows out of the port side. You and Grumpy man the fifties; get everyone else on a Thompson. I'll send back Charles Henry too."

The chief flashed a devious smile.

"We gonna set a trap, skipper?"

"That's a fact. I'll make us a big, fat target that the Claude driver won't be able to resist. The last thing he will expect is a face full of lead from a cargo plane."

"Roger that, skipper. I'll get us ready."

Charles Henry smiled and shook his head.

"This just might work, J.T. Man, I can't wait to give him a little surprise, up close and personal."

"You gonna get some pay back, Charles Henry?"

"I intend to, with malice."

"Okay, killer," J.T. laughed, "why don't you go back and help them set up. I've got it up here."

"You got it." With that, Charles Henry slipped into the cargo bay.

J.T. had time to think about his decision. To put himself in harm's way was one thing, but to put seven others, men he knew and loved, was quite another. He prayed it wasn't false bravado. He wished he was alone but knew he couldn't do the mission by himself. His choice had been to leave three of his men behind or risk the lives of seven brave men to try and save them.

These seven men had helped to ease his decision merely by being here, by demanding to be here. In fact, had he not relented to them, this mission would already be over – and ultimately unsuccessful.

J.T. leaned down the tunnel between cockpit and cargo bay and yelled to Grumpy.

"Tell Quigs we are an hour out and to hunker down with the bugs, but be ready to move. Tell him not to sweat that Claude."

J.T. would sweat the Claude enough for both of them.

The chief's boys worked rapidly, moving the right fifty-two windows down from the left door gun on the same side of the aircraft. They pulled the Plexiglas out of enough windows so that each Thompson had a clear shot as well. The two fifties and five Thompsons were readied, test-fired and reloaded.

"We all ready, Chief?" asked Charles Henry after the last Thompson had been test-fired.

"That we are, Major."

Charles Henry slapped him on the back and went forward to the cockpit.

"We are all set, J.T. How far out are we?"

"Sixteen mikes," J.T. said, using aviator slang for minutes.

"What's the plan?" asked Charles Henry.

"I'm going to buzz the field just like we always do, then pop up in a left-hand orbit. I'll keep us low so he can't get under us. I'll set and hold a 15-degree angle of bank turn and be smooth like silk. He will come high to low on the inside of the turn. Hold your fire until you can't stand it; have the others cue on you. Remember if he twitches – "

Charles Henry cut him off.

"Yeah, I know: he sees us and the guns, we'll let all hell loose if he does."

Charles Henry returned to the cargo bay. After briefing the shooters on the plan, he added one last order.

"Go for the engine, not the pilot," he said. "His center windscreen is bulletproof. If we get the engine, it doesn't matter if the Claude pilot's dead or alive, because the airplane will no longer be a threat. We'll grab our guys and get the hell out of here in time to make that party tomorrow night, got it?"

The six men nodded in acknowledgment. Charles Henry sat on the floor under his station, looked at his watch and settled in for the longest twelve minutes of his life.

J.T. overbanked the DC-3, descending for Echo-66. Charles Henry, sitting between the fifties, felt the move.

"Hang on – here we go!" he yelled.

The DC-3 roared across the field at 235 knots, exceeding redline by 15 knots. J.T. wanted to make the DC-3 look as fast as possible to the Claude overhead. He had to draw it down and make it commit. He pitched the DC-3 up, going for 500 feet over the field.

As the aircraft pitched, Grumpy let out a loud cowboy yell. The chief, who was hanging on to his fifty, looked over at Grumpy in surprise; it was totally out of character. Grumpy shrugged his shoulders.

"I'm a Texan, Chief," he shouted over the din.

J.T. leveled the aircraft and began his orbit at 15 degrees angle of bank and 150 knots. The trap was set.

Overhead at 10,000 feet, Flight Lieutenant Ichiro Yamaguchi could not believe his good fortune. A big, fat target was orbiting below him. He had been stuck in these ancient Mitsubishi A5M4 fighters for over two years. He had requested transfer to the A6M2 Zero-Sen, the latest and best fighter in the Imperial Japanese inventory. His request had been turned down, and now he was stuck doing menial missions as the air war raged over Burma with the P-40s of the Flying Tigers.

His Claude fighter had been designed in 1935, an awkward transitional time for aviation. The industry had moved from open cockpit, wood-and-fabric biplanes to single-winged, enclosed cockpit aircraft in less than a single decade. The horsepower of the engines seemed to double every other year, going from a norm of 500 horsepower to 3,000 plus. The advances were so rapid that an aircraft design could be obsolete before it went into production. The Claude was a prime example: it was an underpowered, fixed-gear, open-cockpit dinosaur. The huge leaps in aerodynamic design and engine technology that occurred in the late 1930s were represented by the performance of the A6M2 Zero.

The China theater had received the first Zero fighters. Lieutenant Yamaguchi was in the air over Chungking in August of 1940, when the Zeros zipped by them to engage the defending Chinese air force, sweeping the skies clear before his squadron could even get into the fight. After that, Imperial Command relegated his and all other A5M4 squadrons to the backwaters of the war. Today's mission had been the final insult: here he was, a fighter pilot of Imperial Japan, ground spotting for the Army.

He'd had no idea how fortune would smile on him today. An air-to-air kill, sealing the fate of not just the airborne crew but the one on the ground, would force Imperial Command to approve his transfer. *"Yes, fortune is truly on my side today"*, the Japanese pilot thought as he rolled in on the DC-3 from 10,000 feet above. This would be like picking cherries from his mother's tree.

His antique fighter accelerated quickly as the nose fell through the horizon. He was trading altitude for airspeed to close on his quarry. Lieutenant Yamaguchi was positively ecstatic, yet he knew he would have to attack and kill with perfection. He would not get a second chance.

Passing through 5,000 feet, he switched his master armament switch to 'on'. As he slid behind the DC-3, he maneuvered to a firing position and flipped the toggle switch that charged his two 7.7 millimeter guns and scanned the target through his tube gun sight. The old fashioned sight was a two-foot long, one-inch diameter tube. It was crude technology, the biggest drawback being that it greatly restricted the pilot's view.

Yamaguchi continuously trimmed his aircraft to balance it exactly. At 220 knots, he eased back the throttle to maintain that speed. He didn't want to accelerate to redline and have to deal with the high-speed buffet it caused. He scanned the target, then checked the balance ball again to ensure that he was trimmed perfectly.

"I will only get one shot", he told himself again. His Claude fighter was only capable of 236 knots. Its Nakajima Kotobuki 41 engine had a mere 710 horsepower. It was only able to power a pristine aircraft to redline speed. Because his squadron was forced to operate out of rough Army fields, the wheel fairings had been removed to prevent mud and grass from jamming into the wheels, then freezing at altitude and locking the wheels. If he missed, the DC-3 would merely run away.

Back to the sight tube, the fighter pilot sweetened up the gun solution. Closing to 1,500 feet from the DC-3, he scanned again through the gun sight, putting the crosshairs where wing met fuselage. At 1,000 feet, he slipped his index finger onto the trigger; his scan was now through the gun sight only.

Lieutenant Yamaguchi's intention was to close to 500 feet and open fire; this would ensure a devastating concentration of fire. At 700 feet, he noticed the door was gone on the DC-3. Distracted, he didn't shoot at 500 feet. That is when he saw the guns. Concentration lost, his hand involuntarily moved.

The entire left side of the DC-3 exploded in a withering fusillade of automatic weapons fire. The tracer streams melded together into a single impact point, the Claude's engine. Two of its nine cylinder heads were blown off cleanly. Hot oil erupted from the crankcase and flared. A round reached the carburetor, smashing it. High-octane fuel continued to pump out, until it reached the burning oil. When it did, the Nakajima Kotobuki 41 engine exploded. All the tracer fire held on the engine except one; it moved to the open cockpit as the Claude flashed by and below.

The center windscreen was bulletproof; the open side cockpit obviously was not. Lieutenant Yamaguchi died of head wounds two seconds before impacting the ground. Charles Henry had his payback.

He knew his hits were good; his personal reaction was not. Instead of exhilaration or a feeling of revenge, he felt a strange twinge of remorse, even guilt. He replayed the battle over in his mind, visualizing the impact of the .45 caliber rounds on the skull of the Japanese pilot. He could not tell if he was filling in the detail with his imagination.

With only 70 knots of advantage, the pass, by air-to-air standards, was slow, allowing his brain to record it. Whether real or imagined, Charles Henry had an empty, cold feeling in the pit of his stomach that tugged at his soul. He had crossed the line, his line. This day, he knew, would come back to him in the dark of night.

J.T. immediately dropped the gear and flaps; he was in a position to make a play for the runway. He initiated his move when he saw the engine of the Claude explode. Pushing the nose over, he dove for the runway.

Quigs and crew were on their feet and moving as soon as they saw the gear come down. J.T. had the DC-3 on deck within eight seconds. He kept the power up on both engines, looking for Quigs and his men. They broke from the brush just to the left of the nose, 1,000 feet ahead. J.T. goosed the power and closed the distance in a few seconds.

J.T. slowed the DC-3 to the pace of a man's run, and the three adrenaline-filled crewmen easily caught the aircraft and clambered on board. Quigs went through a window. As soon as the last man hit the cargo bay floor, Charles Henry scrambled to the cockpit, yelling:

"Go, Go, Go!"

J.T. cobbed the power. They were starting halfway down the runway; it would be close. Sporadic gunfire popped from the tree line as they cleared it by less than 10 feet.

Quigs scampered up to the cockpit.

"Absolutely in-friggen-credible!"

"How was the night, Quigs?" asked J.T. with a knowing smile.

"Bugs, creepy-crawly bugs; everywhere I looked, damn bugs!" he shrieked.

J.T. and Charles Henry laughed.

"You ready for a party, Quigs?" asked Charles Henry.

"Yes, sir! That's a fact, Charles Henry, that's a damn fact.

Chapter 28

The Governor's Ball
19 February 1942

Thirty-three happy campers crammed into the back of the Buff. An airline-configured DC-3 held twenty-one passengers comfortably; with troop seats, it could hold twice that number, although not comfortably. The troop seats were wood-framed benches with canvas seats, bolted to each bulkhead.

The crew faced each other, competing for legroom. Even in that cramped space, the Seven Alpha boys couldn't stop smiling. Chief had rigged the seats the night before. It was tight, but they fit.

As the plane accelerated down the runway they sang, "99 Bottles of Beer on the Wall" at the top of their lungs, trying unsuccessfully to compete with the Pratt and Whitney engines. The faster the DC-3 went, the faster their tempo became. The group broke out in a riotous roar as they shot the hole and began the three-hour journey to Calcutta.

At the controls of the Buff, J.T. looked over his shoulder down the tunnel to the writhing cargo bay, and turned to Quigs.

"So you're sure your Brit buds won't mind us crashing the Governor's party?"

Quigs smiled his most mischievous smile.

"Of course they will! They will absolutely – ah, how do you Yanks say it – crap a bustle of hostile cats?"

"Shit a litter of angry kittens, actually," J.T. laughed. "But close enough."

The old saying about best-laid plans came to J.T.'s mind as they stood in the hot afternoon sun on the tarmac at Royal Air Force Base, Dum Dum. The Seven Alpha Warriors were stranded. Apparently their good friend, Major Perkins of His Majesty's Air Force, had noticed the flight plan from Shangri-La, with the extensive manifest of passengers attached. He put one-plus-one together and figured out their plan. After a little investigation, he discovered their transportation request and canceled it. And to insure that there would be no rescheduling, he closed the motor pool at noon.

It was now 1600. The Governor's party started at 1700. Even if they had transportation, they would be late. To top it off, Irish and Danny boy had gone missing. So far, this R&R was neither restful nor relaxing.

Charles Henry walked up to J.T. and Quigs.

"The natives are getting restless, skipper. Any ideas?"

"Quigs?" asked J.T.

"Run like the wind before they form a lynch party, is my suggestion."

"Thanks a lot, mate."

Trey sauntered up to the group.

"What in the hell is that?" he asked, pointing down the tarmac.

All heads turned to see an old bus, literally steaming toward them. It was at least fifteen years old with exposed front wheels, a long hood, and a hissing radiator at the front. The passenger compartment was square and constructed of rotted wood.

The bus ground to a screeching halt next to the disgruntled revelers. Irish was behind the wheel.

"Get in!"

The boys let out another hoot. Their enthusiasm for life, which had waned of late, instantly restored.

The chief raised the vehicle's long hood, shook his head and let it fall back into place.

"Couldn't you have stolen something at least from the last decade?"

Irish threw him a cold beer.

"Shut up and get in. I had to run it a little hard to make my escape."

The chief took one last disdainful look as he walked around the front end and climbed on board the bus. Danny boy was handing out bottles of beer. The chief snatched two, grumbling as he moved down the aisle.

"That's the ugliest damn stewardess I've ever seen."

The pump was primed. J.T. and Charles Henry slipped into the last row of the bus with a couple of beers apiece. Charles Henry could sense the groundswell.

"Ugly is right, J.T. This little sworee' is getting ugly early!"

J.T. looked around at his men.

"That's a fact. Oh well, what are they going to do, shave our heads and send us to the front?" He pulled off his hat and rubbed his close-cropped hair. Flashing his smile, J.T. clinked bottles with Charles Henry and sat back to watch the opening act of the show.

The ancient bus survived the traffic of a bustling Calcutta and almost made it to the Governor's mansion, sputtering to a halt within half a mile. The chief pronounced it dead and they set off on foot, each man loaded down with beer and nursely ambition.

They met their first obstacle at the gate of the stately residence. A huge, grey stone edifice, it looked less like a house and more like a library from a major city in the States. It was definitely out of place in Calcutta. A large courtyard with center garden and fountain lay between the Seven Alpha boys and the front door – not to mention the tall, heavy cast iron gate and stone wall.

They should have been impressed by both the security and the architecture, but they were impressed by neither. At the stone sentry booth by the gate, J.T. and Quigs were engaged in discussion with the Sergeant of the Guard, who pointed out in painstaking detail the proper procedures for entry and the fact that their names were absent from the guest list. Meanwhile, Thumper crept into the corner between the gate and the sentry post. J.T. saw him out of the corner of his eye and stepped slightly aside to cover him from the good sergeant's view. Thumper motioned Trey to join him while J.T. distracted the sergeant.

"I am Lieutenant Colonel Dobbs, United States Army Air Corps," he said, "and I can assure you that we are in fact invited. Check your list again."

The sergeant was now getting irritated.

"As you wish, Colonel, but I can assure you that you are not!"

As he glanced down to his list, Trey went silently over the gate, boosted by Thumper, unlatched it and quietly opened it a crack. The Shangri-La Warriors began creeping through the breach. Almost half of them made it into no man's land before the Sergeant of the Guard noticed.

"Hey! You men, stop!" he bellowed. Then he made the mistake of chasing the men already inside, instead of securing the perimeter. The sprint was on.

Quigs and J.T. were still standing at the sentry booth. Quigs shook his head.

"Classic tactical error," he said. "Wouldn't you say, Lieutenant Colonel?"

J.T. nodded in agreement.

"Classic indeed, Mr Quigley. Shall we?" He bowed toward the gate which had been flung open wide.

"Indeed!" answered Quigs. "Major Brennan, care to join us?"

"Why yes, Mr Quigley, I believe I shall."

The three calmly walked through the gate.

"Do secure the gate, eh, Major?" said Quigs. "Most shoddy security here, wouldn't you say?"

"*Most* shoddy, Mr Quigley," Charles Henry agreed. "We shall have to notify the proper authorities, I'm afraid."

Quigs was barely able to suppress his laugh.

"Right you are, Major!"

The Sergeant continued his chase of the first group while being closely followed by the second group of wild sprinters. Both groups, properly lubricated, ran with an awkward, exaggerated gait. Full beer bottles were jostled out of pockets and popped like flash bulbs on the stone driveway. The second group, by a strange twist of fate, was faster than the first. They swept up the Sergeant in their wake and caught the first group just as they hit the door to the grand entrance.

Inside, the Governor's Fortnightly was moving along at its normal snail's pace. It was a stuffed-shirt affair and by all appearances, positively painful to most attendees. The men present were in mess dress uniforms and almost exclusively old and fat. In drastic contrast, the nurses were young, beautiful and shapely. They were also obviously bored and sticking to the opposite side of the room from the paunchy staff officers. All the eligible studs were on the Burma front, and the nurses had no intention of mixing with those left behind. What had once been the highlight of the month had become forced fun.

The doors burst open, swinging until they banged off the walls behind. The Seven Alpha group rushed through en masse, not seeing the single step, 5 feet inside the foyer. Suddenly, beer bottles, Yanks, and one poor Sergeant of the Guard sprawled onto the fine marble floor.

The commotion was so intrusive that the room fell silent. Even the band abruptly stopped. A buxom blonde, a little older than the others and obviously their CO, broke the awkward silence.

"Oh, look," she said. "The Yanks are finally here."

The group's favorite RAF Major stepped up, barring the way.

"What's this?" he said. "I don't believe the Colonists were invited."

Jon pushed himself off the floor and got in Major Perkins' face.

"Thanks for arranging our ride, Major."

The situation had grown instantly tense and appeared to be rapidly sliding toward a physical confrontation, when J.T., Charles Henry, and Quigs came through the door. The Major, retreating from Jon's presence, stepped in front of them.

"You Yanks are most resourceful, aren't you?"

"Most! That's why we keep winning all the wars, Major." J.T. topped off his snide comment with a wink.

Perkins was getting visibly aggravated.

"Still," he bristled, "you are not invited here."

"Major Perkins, don't be silly." The governor's wife had smoothly and gracefully alighted next to the RAF Major. She annunciated his name with registered dislike. A striking woman even in her sixties, she had a regal manner and moved with the aplomb of a much younger woman.

"Of course they are invited," she said. "The Colonel and I are old friends. Do come in, gentlemen, and welcome to my home."

The disgruntled Major Perkins stepped aside.

As the pile of men untangled themselves and got to their feet, the governor's wife turned to J.T. and Charles Henry.

"Colonel, Major, please join me at the bar."

The foyer opened up into a grand ballroom. J.T. and Charles Henry, with Trey in tow, dutifully followed the governor's wife to a finely carved, oak portable bar. Trey was spellbound by the grandeur of the place. He had expected a governor's mansion like those he had seen in the States, not a palace from Europe. Crystal chandeliers, marble, tapestries, art, with silver and fine china – everything seemed to be gilded. He stood, mouth agape as he tried to soak it all in. J.T. tapped Charles Henry and smiled as he nodded at Trey.

"Hey sport, close your mouth," laughed Charles Henry.

J.T. turned his attention to the governor's wife.

"Sorry to intrude on your party, ma'am."

She smiled genuinely.

"No intrusion at all, Colonel, these back echelon bastards are a pain. It was quite a boring party. I do imagine your lads will liven it up a bit."

"Oh, you can bet on that!" quipped Charles Henry, quickly adding, "I mean yes, ma'am."

The Seven Alpha boys moved in on the nurses with the same fervor they had stormed the front door. Jon went directly to the band of Indian nationals, who were visibly as bored with the music selection as the Yanks, and whispered into the band-leader's ear as he slipped him a twenty-dollar bill.

The bandleader looked to the governor's wife, who almost imperceptibly granted permission with a tilt of her head. The bandleader acknowledged her with his own subtle nod, rattled off a sentence in his native tongue – the only words Jon under-stood were "Glenn" and "Miller" – and the band seamlessly shifted into American swing.

Jon stepped off the bandstand like a conquering hero. As he strutted across the dance floor, a brunette with stunning green eyes caught his attention. He stopped in front of her and held out his hand, beckoning her with his smile to join him. The tempo of the music enveloped the room and they danced across the floor, inducing the rest to join them. In a mere three minutes, the Americans had ignited the party.

Standing by the bar with Charles Henry and Trey, J.T. had seen the subtle exchange between the bandleader and the governor's wife. He looked back at the front entrance hall and saw that the broken bottles from their tumultuous entrance were already cleaned up. He was impressed.

"You run a tight ship, ma'am."

Her steel-grey eyes sparkled, perfect lips betraying the hint of a smile.

"Well, the governor is always charging off to the sound of cannon," she said. "I have to make do in his absence."

The party was in full swing. Trey kept peering over and around Charles Henry to see the action, but Charles Henry kept moving to block his view. Trey was so intent on seeing the dance floor that he didn't notice what his father was doing. Unable to contain his laughter anymore, Charles Henry took mercy and released him.

"Go ahead, boy," he said. "Go have some fun."

Trey hesitated a second.

"Okay…you coming? How about you, J.T.?"

"Nah, we sowed our oats in the last war, son," replied his father. "You go and have fun. Be at the field at 10:00."

"Yes, sir!" Trey exclaimed, scampering toward the crowd. Halfway across the floor he was intercepted by the blonde who had hailed their arrival.

"Hello, I'm Jean. What's your name?"

Before he could answer she pulled him onto the dance floor.

The governor's wife ordered three beers.

"I feel like a cold beer. Will you gentlemen join me?"

"Yes, ma'am," they responded in unison.

She passed a beer to each.

"So it's not your first war either, is it, gentlemen?"

"No, ma'am." Again, both responded.

Charles Henry added, "Your second, ma'am?" as he watched Trey dancing.

She shook her head.

"Third, actually – Boer War and all. I do hope it's my last." She followed his gaze. "That's a handsome lad."

"Thank you," beamed Charles Henry.

She raised a curious eyebrow.

Charles Henry clarified, "He's my eldest son."

A touch of alarm flickered in her eyes.

"You are serving with your son?"

J.T. inserted himself into the conversation. "It's a long story, ma'am – "

"It's okay, J.T.," Charles Henry interrupted.

"His boy volunteered first, ma'am," J.T. went on.

"I see," she responded, the look of concern still evident. Then she changed the subject. "Do call me Martha. We old vets must become friends."

By 10 p.m., the party began to reach a crescendo. The nurses had caught up – and the old Brits had lubed up – on fine, single malt scotch. The palace was hopping. Even the band seemed to be having a great time.

Charles Henry's prediction of ugliness came true at about 10:01. Thumper, a former naval aviator of the Marine Corps type, started "aircraft carrier qualifications". He cleared off a long table and splashed a beer on the smoothly polished top. A crowd gathered, curious as to what the Yank was up to. Clearing a path as he backed away to about 20 feet, he suddenly yelled, "Make a ready deck," ran at the table full tilt and dove onto the tabletop. As he slid toward the far end, he dropped his "hook" – actually, his right foot – and snagged a gilded drapery rope that Jon and Trey held across the table, like the arresting cable on an aircraft carrier. Thumper had performed a successful arrested landing.

The crowd went crazy and a line quickly formed, but the neophyte carrier aviators were not nearly as successful as Thumper. Almost all of them missed the cable (boltered in Navy lingo), ending up in a heap on the floor. Thumper acted as LSO (landing signal officer), guiding and cajoling the neophytes. He spied an athletic-looking nurse watching from vulture's row, the front row next to the table.

"Why don't you try, sweetie?" he asked.

She shook her head.

"C'mon, become a tail hooker!"

She put her hands on her hips.

"I already have a profession."

"I know," protested Thumper, "but tail hookin' is much more fun!"

She cocked her head looking into his eyes.

"I'm sure it is. All right, Yank – stand clear."

Thumper jumped with excitement.

"Outstanding! Make a ready deck!" He dumped a fresh beer on the table. "Man the arresting gear!"

Jon and Trey pulled the drapery rope tight.

"Stand by to recover aircraft!"

Thumper looked at the athletic nurse, who had got into position, and barked out, "Ready deck."

She started her run, reaching top speed just as she went airborne. Upon landing on the tabletop, she dropped her right foot and expertly caught the drapery rope. Again, the crowd went crazy.

Every man in the crowd now had his very manhood challenged. The line grew longer, and to make things worse, the LSO abandoned his post, rolling in on the athletic nurse.

Thumper held out a small bar towel.

"You got big balls for a girl, honey, what's your name?"

She was definitely amused by this Yank.

"I suppose I should take that as a compliment. My name is Brenda. What's your name?"

He smiled big. "They call me Thumper."

Brenda looked at him sideways.

"Thumper, huh? You must have had a cruel mother."

"My mom called me Sean."

"I like that better," said Brenda, pulling him onto the dance floor. "I'll call you Sean."

The dancing had become steamy while the carrier quals were going on. Fifty years later, it would be called dirty dancing.

With the LSO platform abandoned, bedlam followed, culminating in the collapse of the table when a rather large RAF colonel thudded on the makeshift flattop. The naval aviators in the crowd screamed in unison at the top of their lungs, "Ramp strike!"

It was funny, damn funny. Unfortunately, experience told J.T. and Charles Henry that the next guest to the party would be an ambulance – or the military police.

"We'd better get these guys out of here, J.T."

"Roger that, Charles Henry."

Neither wanted to leave. They had been enjoying the company of the governor's wife – and her ice-cold beer as well. J.T. pried himself from the bar.

"Martha, I'm afraid we must go."

"You gentlemen are welcome to spend the night," she said.

"Trust me, we would love to spend the night on clean sheets. But we'd better keep an eye on these knuckleheads. And we must definitely get them out of your house."

"I suppose you are right, J.T. Do be careful."

"Yes, ma'am," both men answered in unison again.

J.T. had buttonholed a butler an hour earlier, making it clear that if he wanted to save this house, he needed to find some transportation. The butler had successfully procured a bus that was waiting in the courtyard. One problem solved, but the next one would be a lot harder.

"How are we going to get these guys out of here without a fight, Charles Henry?"

"Free booze," his friend responded.

"They have free booze here."

"Trust me, J.T., we just need some place to rally. Any ideas, Martha?"

The governor's wife had a knowing look on her face.

"Yes, I hear the Calcutta Club is just what you need, and it is close to the base as well."

J.T. took her hand. "Your advice is perfect as always, Martha. We shall take our leave. Your hospitality has meant a great deal to us. I'm sure these men will never forget it. I know I won't."

She smiled a worried smile.

"You are quite welcome, Lieutenant Colonel."

Charles Henry had made his way to the bandstand, where he picked up the microphone and silenced the band.

"Ladies and gentlemen, let's hear it for our hostess."

Loud, rowdy applause broke out. He quieted the crowd again.

"We have some good news and bad news. The bad news is that we have run the good lady completely out of booze." Loud boos and cat calls broke out. "Hey, hey, wait for the good news.

There is a club called the Calcutta Club and it is serving up free booze for all of us." Cheers again filled the ball room. "We've got a bus out front. Let's thank our lovely hostess for her hospitality and load up."

The revelers formed a receiving line, filing out of the grand ball room and genuinely thanking Martha, some a little too vigorously, but she didn't seem to mind. As they filed out, J.T. kept a head count.

Charles Henry walked up. "What's the count?"

"Three short. Come to think of it, I haven't seen Irish, Quigs or the chief since we came through that door."

"Oh, that's not good," muttered Charles Henry. He looked around and noticed a set of French doors slightly ajar. "Come on, J.T."

They rushed through the French doors and found themselves on an ornate balcony; in the middle was a small table, on which a candelabra burned brightly. The candlelight reflected on evidence of a private party, yet there was no sign of any people – until Charles Henry heard giggles. He and J.T. stepped to the balcony rail. Below them was a Roman-style swimming pool surrounded by polished granite deck and a border of flower gardens and palm trees. Beyond the pool area, a lavish lawn stretched for acres. In the moonlit water cavorted Irish, Quigs, the chief and four lovely nurses – all seven of them skinny-dipping.

"Extra girl." Charles Henry elbowed J.T.

J.T. winked. "My money is on Irish."

Charles Henry thought for a second.

"No doubt." He leaned over the rail. "Ah, sorry to interrupt, gents, but we have to go."

J.T. added, "We will be out front in a bus – chop, chop, knuckleheads."

Martha walked up next to them.

"My, my," she said. "It appears they are having the most fun of all."

After pushing the soggy dippers out the door, J.T. thanked the governor's wife again.

"I hope you won't be too hard on the sergeant for not keeping us out," he said. "He put up a valiant resistance."

"I think thirty against one is a good fight," she laughed, "even when lost. By the way, J.T., I had the butler put a few cases of beer on the bus, enough to get your crew to the Calcutta."

"Nothing gets by you, does it, ma'am?" asked Charles Henry.

"Not a thing."

"Good night, Martha."

"Good night, lads, and do be careful."

She started to close the door, then paused. "Charles Henry," she called after him.

"Yes, ma'am."

"You are a good father. Take care."

"Thank you, Martha."

She waved goodbye and closed the door to the mansion.

The bus was a madhouse, an absolute madhouse. Thirty-three Shangri-La boys, twenty-plus nurses and ten or so Brit escorts, all in a thirty-man bus. The ride was definitely going to be interesting.

The driver, a local, was completely unfazed by the unfolding events – even when the men started climbing out the door and up onto the roof, then back in through the open windows in the rear. After the third rendition of "99 Bottles of Beer on the Wall," the bus finally pulled up in front of the Calcutta Club.

As J.T. and Charles Henry stepped off the bus, they were met by a meticulously manicured Frenchman, in an impeccably tailored white suit.

"Lieutenant Colonel Dobbs and Major Brennan?" he queried.

"Yeah, that's right," asked J.T. "Is there a problem?"

"Oh no, no, no, my friends! Allow me to introduce myself. I am Pierre Laclede. I have spoken to the governor's wife. She told me to expect you and requested that I show you my hospitality."

J.T. and Charles Henry looked at each other.

"That's one incredible woman, J.T."

"Man, that's a fact."

They all shook hands, and J.T. nodded to the bus.

"Well, Pierre, we brought you some business."

Pierre waved his hand.

"Oh no, my friends, you misunderstand. You are my guests. I

have set up a private room for you and your men. Oh, I see lovely young ladies as well." He turned to his assistant and quickly whispered into his ear. The assistant hurried back into the club. Pierre turned back to his guests.

"Please come in. Welcome, welcome!"

The Calcutta Club was an international establishment that opened into an authentic English pub: low ceiling, smoke filled, and lots of dark-stained wood. Once inside, you would swear you were in a pub in London's Piccadilly Circus. Pierre led them through the crowd of Brit expats, RAF, and Royal Navy.

At the rear of the pub, a door opened, revealing a balcony overlooking a brightly lit European-style casino straight out of Monaco. Formally decorated, there were bright chandeliers, gilded wood and deep red velvet. The balcony stood two full stories above the casino floor, with the ceiling another two stories overhead.

At least eighty gaming tables were neatly lined up on the casino floor: blackjack, craps, baccarat. The group stopped to take it all in. Even Jon was impressed. "Wow!" was all he could say.

Pierre led them down the balcony, which wrapped around the entire casino. On the outside walls, ten-foot tall double doors in French provincial style, opened to private rooms. Each time they passed a room, they went up three steps until they reached an end room. By the look of its entryway, it was more luxurious than any of the rooms they had passed.

Pierre swung open the perfectly balanced doors. The opulence of the room assaulted their senses; the nurses were now impressed. It was a large parlor, furnished with chaise longue, love seats, French arm chairs, and two leather-topped card tables at one end. The floors were covered with Persian carpets, the walls with tapestries of the French countryside and impressionist oil paintings.

A large bar was the central focus on the far wall; a barman stood already in position. In the center of the rectangular room sat a circular couch of red satin. On top of the central back of the couch, a silver fountain flowed with champagne. At the far end of the room, to their left, a wall of glass French doors opened to a large veranda.

The Frenchman pointed out the amenities, then led them to the veranda. By night, Calcutta was a nice city; it was a clear moonlit night, and the natural light glistened off the Hugli River down below them. They had entered on the street level, but through the series of short steps and the slightly sloping terrain, they were now four stories up on the veranda. They even had a view of the RAF Base.

When all the troops were on the veranda, J.T. pointed to RAF Dum Dum.

"Be there at 10:00 tomorrow morning," he said. "This room will be our admin; you will find Charles Henry and me either here or on the tables giving our host some business. Questions? Have fun, be safe."

Charles Henry leaned over and whispered into J.T.'s ear.

"Man, this place looks like a French cathouse."

"I believe that is exactly what it is," J.T. responded. "Pierre had his assistant shoo off the girls when he saw we had our own. Did you smell the perfume when we entered?"

The party restarted with the same vigor from all participants. Some of the men slipped away after a while, with a nurse escort, others hit the casino or English pub. J.T. and Charles Henry bellied up to the bar with Pierre.

"Nice place you've got here, my friend," said J.T.

"Thank you, Colonel, and I thank you for helping me to keep it. We have heard of your, how shall I say it, achievements at Shangri-La?"

"You are quite welcome, Pierre. Hopefully, it will help."

Charles Henry was intently watching Irish, who still held the attention of two red-headed nurses.

"J.T., look at Irish," he said. "What the hell does he have?"

"Hormones, Charles Henry, lots and lots of hormones."

Surprisingly, there were only two incidents. The first occurred shortly after 01:00 – a loud noise emanating from the balcony suddenly burst into the room as a military-issued BSA motorcycle flew past the bar, did a barrel turn around the champagne fountain and stopped in front of a young, shy-acting nurse.

The rider yelled over the revving engine, "Get on!"

The nurse hesitated at first, then mounted the machine behind him. The motorized couple sped off as quickly as the machine had appeared.

J.T. leaned over to Charles Henry.

"Was that Man-child?"

"Yes, sir, I believe it was."

"Huh. I think our little boy is all grown up."

Pierre was unruffled by the flyby, adding, "An interesting technique for picking up a woman. I shall have to remember it."

The three laughed and ordered another drink.

The other incident was allegedly a fight, but by the time J.T., Charles Henry and Pierre had reached the pub, the reported location, all they found was the chief singing an unrecognizable tune with his arm around a rather large Brit. Mysteriously, each had a fresh black eye.

Somewhere around dawn, most of the bubbas lay down on a couch, chaise longue, or the floor. Some partied all the way to takeoff the next morning. Others disappeared with nurses.

Charles Henry was trying to count heads; it was 10:00. The Seven Alpha Warriors were passed out in the Buff, on the Buff and under the Buff. The constant sound of vomiting played in the background. He rolled men over, checking faces as he counted.

"How goes the count, Major?" asked J.T.

"Thirty-three," was Charles Henry's response.

"Hey, that's great."

"Not really. There's at least a couple of Brits in there."

"You find your boy yet?"

"Nope."

As they stood on the hot, muggy tarmac, a red convertible pulled up to the DC-3. Trey opened the passenger door to get out, and the blonde nurse ten years his senior pulled him back in for one last kiss. J.T. smiled at Charles Henry.

"Think she taught him any new tricks?"

"I just hope she didn't hurt him."

Trey finally escaped and walked over to his dad and J.T.

"Just in time there, stud," said Charles Henry. Trey smiled sheepishly, and his father picked up on his discomfort. "Don't worry, boy. What goes on deployment stays on deployment."

"Okay, gentlemen," J.T. interrupted, "we better hi-yacca before the MPs get here."

The chief strolled up, his eye much blacker now.

"Hey, skipper – no Irish, two Brits."

"Okay, put the Brits in that idiot major's office. Make sure they outrank him first."

"What about Irish?"

No sooner had the words left the chief's mouth than a wailing ambulance screeched onto the tarmac, siren and engine going full blast. It squealed to a halt right in front of the group, and out stepped Irish.

"Sorry I'm late, lads."

The two redheads popped out of the driver's side window.

"Irish, give us a kiss goodbye," said one.

He turned and blew two exaggerated kisses, winking at Trey.

"Wonderful lasses, regular Florence Nightingales, they were."

J.T. stood, arms crossed on his chest.

"Hey, Irish, how 'bout you two loverboys fly us home?"

"No sweat, Lieutenant Colonel. C'mon kid," he said to Trey. "Let's get going."

"Irish, Irish!" yelled the redheads, "a picture first."

"Okay, lassies – line up, gents, the ladies want a Kodachrome to remember us."

They all lined up for a hasty photo.

"That's gonna be ugly," Trey added to no one in particular. Then he climbed into the Buff with Irish struggling in behind him. They had to step over ten of their passed-out comrades. Trey was about to slip into the copilot seat when Irish pushed him into the captain seat.

"You drive, kid."

While Chief was getting the drunken Brits out and the drunk Yanks in, Trey and Irish started the engines. With everyone loaded, they began to taxi. Just then, they saw the local MPs pulling up under the tower, jump out of their jeep and try to wave them back. Irish pushed up the power and fast-taxied straight to the runway.

"Don't slow down," he said. "Roll."

"We don't have clearance for takeoff," protested Trey.

"No, and we won't get it either. That major runs the tower."

They rounded the corner onto the runway. Irish reached below the console, locked the tail wheel for takeoff, pushed the mixtures to auto rich, and set 2,600 RPM on the props, then shoved the throttles up to 43 inches of manifold pressure. As they started the takeoff roll, Trey protested again.

"What about the checklist?"

"Do it amongst yourself, let me know later if we missed anything." Irish slid his seat back and pulled his hat down over his eyes.

"Don't screw it up, kid," he muttered, and was asleep before Trey got the DC-3 airborne.

Standing in the passageway, just out of sight, stood Charles Henry, looking over his son's shoulder.

* * *

Deep in the dark jungle of Burma, Gunny Paillou and Sergeant Major Menzies crouched under giant fronds, trying to escape from the rain. Already soaked to the skin, they wanted to keep the rain out of their meager rations, packaged in green tin cans. In the rain, the cans would fill rapidly with water, ruining the contents – which were already pretty nasty.

Gunny Paillou smiled through the rain.

"At least it keeps the mosquitoes away."

Menzies tipped his c-rat can.

"Cheers, Gunny."

"Cheers, Sergeant Major."

Date time group: 0340 ZULU 09 MAR 1942
From: COMMANDER AIR TRANSPORT COMMAND
To: COMMANDER SEVEN ALPHA
Subject: WESTPAC INTEL UPDATE
Classification: TOP SECRET SCI/EYES ONLY COM7ALPHA
Text: RANGOON HAS FALLEN. BURMA FORCES REELING. ALLIED COMMAND ATTEMPTING TO ESTABLISH NEW FRONT IN NORTHERN BURMA. LASHIO NEW FOCAL POINT. IF THEY CAN'T HOLD ENTIRE LENGTH OF BURMA ROAD LOST. IN THAT EVENT AIR ROUTE OVER HUMP WILL BE ONLY GAME IN TOWN. WYA.
C.R. SENDS

Chapter 29

The Grind, Part Two
9 March 1942

Three weeks after the crews showed signs of wear and tear, the aircraft began to show the same signs. The chief's crew worked around the clock to put up the maximum effort every day. They were beginning to lose the battle.

The chief walked into the operations office. It was after breakfast, so both J.T. and Charles Henry were present.

"Gentlemen," he said, "something has got to give."

J.T. looked up from C.R.'s message.

"What do you need, Chief?"

The chief leaned on J.T.'s desk.

"What I need," he said, "is to pull one ship out of the rotation per day to perform some preventive maintenance."

J.T. had known this was coming. It had been a maintenance miracle that they had been able to juggle the tired DC-3s for as long as they had. He glanced again at the message.

"Those guys need us pretty bad over the Hump, Chief. I know this bucket brigade is hard on the aircraft, but the Allies are getting some traction on the air war and we should move to the Assam soon."

The chief cut him off.

"It won't be long until these airplanes start falling out of the sky," he said.

Charles Henry chimed in from across the room.

"They seem to be holding up pretty well right now. Can't we stretch it a couple more weeks?"

"Major," said Chief, vigorously shaking his head, "I got three engines past time between recommended overhaul (TBO) now. I have my guys changing the oil every damn night. I run samples on the oil, looking for metallic bits just so I can sleep when I get the chance. I've got my small crew split. If we lose an engine at the depot, we're screwed. I don't have the men to cover it. If you lose one over the Hump with a full load – well, I don't have to tell you the result."

The chief stood erect and set his jaw.

"Look, the reason the Brits were out of aircraft is they ran them into the ground. Give me a ship a day now, or in two weeks it will be two or three. I will not put crap in the air, period. Your choice, skipper."

"What about the spare?" asked J.T.

"I use it every day," snapped the chief. "Both of its engines are past TBO."

"What about the Buff?" asked Charles Henry.

"Buff runs fuel and parts all day, every day. No logistics run, no fly. By the way, it has the other engine past TBO."

J.T. was still holding the message from Washington. The Allies were going to lose Lashio; he knew that was the message C.R. was sending him between the lines. He also knew that the chief was right. He could hand the chief the message, but that would be a chickenshit thing to do. It was his decision, a command decision; he would have to make it himself. The three men stood in silence.

Finally, J.T. responded.

"Okay, Chief, you win. Let Grumpy know which ship you are going to pull every day. We will start tomorrow. Is that good for you?"

The chief grunted a response and left to put together a maintenance schedule.

The Seven Alpha operation settled into the grind again, six on and one off. The crews welcomed the day off and the maintainers welcomed having a ship on which they could do some real maintenance. Still, J.T. was worried. They were starting their fourth month and already, half his pilots had over 1,000 hours in the air since leaving Dallas. The other half would have that much by the middle of the following week. They were each getting one day per week to rest, but there was no end in sight. He knew that many had already flown sick; they had not wanted someone else to pick up their load. The landing zones, or LZs, were getting hotter every day. He had a bad feeling that their luck would run out.

Every one of his guys had at least eighty combat missions. That meant they had earned four air medals per man, so far. The bomber guys being sent to the Eighth Air Force in England were being told they would rotate after twenty-five missions. That was a little tidbit of information he didn't even tell Charles Henry. Granted, the flak was thinner and the fighters few by comparison, but the Eighth didn't have to contend with the Hump.

They had been lucky. Even the loss of Bluto had been. They should have lost that entire crew, considering the circumstances and amount of damage the aircraft had sustained.

"Thumper bagging a Zero; figure the odds of that", he thought to himself. Getting Quigs and his crew out without a scratch? *"Lucky, damn lucky."* They were due. J.T. believed with all his heart that a pilot made his own luck. However, he made his luck by keeping his options list open, and long. Their options were becoming increasingly limited.

The crews were tired, the aircraft beat, their mobility tied to Shangri-La. Their routes and airfields were out of his control and getting repetitive. He felt his options slipping away – and with them, his unit's luck. He had sent C.R. a message three days ago detailing the flight time and mission count of his boys. The only reply he got was:

HEARD YOU HAD A GOOD TIME WITH THE GOVERNOR'S WIFE.

They were due. Bad shit happened in threes in aviation. J.T. knew it was a stupid superstition, but he'd be damned if it had not always played out according to script. Bluto was gone; he knew there would be more unless he could get them out of here.

As he sat in his dingy quarters, J.T. felt the mildewed walls closing in. He was sending these men up every day. They had become family – the young ones, the sons he never had. He had an overwhelming sense of doom, of cataclysmic calamity, and that it would be him, the Great Captain-turned-Lieutenant Colonel J.T. Dobbs, that sent his family to their ultimate fate.

Grumpy nudged him out of his self-imposed emotional exile.

"Skipper, I knocked but you didn't answer – I knew you would want to see this."

Grumpy stopped and looked at him.

"Are you okay? You look sick."

J.T. mumbled and took the message.

"It's good news, skipper, finally. I thought you would want it right away."

DATE TIME GROUP: 0800 ZULU 25 MAR 1942
FROM: COMMANDER AIR TRANSPORT COMMAND
TO: COMMANDER SEVEN ALPHA
SUBJECT: WESTPAC INTEL UPDATE
CLASSIFICATION: TOP SECRET SCI/EYES ONLY COM7ALPHA
TEXT: GOT YOUR LAST MESSAGE LOUD AND CLEAR.
LASHIO EXPECTED TO FALL. BURMA FORCES BEING
WITHDRAWN TO INDIA/CHINA BORDERS WITH BURMA.
THE MOUNTAINS WILL ASSIST ALLIES TO HOLD THE
LINE. HUMP NOW FRONT BURNER. FORCES FINALLY
SPOOLED UP. RELIEF ENROUTE OVER YOUR FAVORITE
PLACE. ETA 15 DAYS. RTB SAME. SHANGRI-LA TO BE
CLOSED WITH 7ALPHA DEPARTURE. WYA.
C.R. SENDS

J.T. smiled, for the first time in weeks.

"Sir," asked Grumpy, "where is your favorite place?"

"Alaska," he replied. "I always told C.R. Alaska was my favorite place in the world."

Grumpy still looked confused.

"I don't get it Colonel."

J.T. stood up, folding the message.

"It means they are coming over Alaska, then Russia. He is telling us to return the same way. Safer, plus shorter legs, no auxiliary tanks required so we can all fit in one DC-3. C.R. is still an operator at heart."

Grumpy couldn't control his glee; he cracked a smile.

"Shall I spread the good word?"

J.T. thought about it for a second.

"No, we still have a lot of flying between now and the Air Force's arrival. I want to keep everyone focused. Anyone else know?"

Grumpy fidgeted. At least one other person had been in the office and knew.

"No," he fibbed.

"Okay, thanks, Grumpy."

J.T. walked out in search of the one person he had to tell. Grumpy went in search of the one he had to tell to shut up.

J.T. saw the chief on the tarmac and walked over to him. Time to drop a little hint the size of an elephant.

"How are the machines holding up, Chief?"

"Terrible."

J.T. nodded. "Can you pick a winner?"

"When?"

"Fifteen days."

"Auxiliary tanks?" asked the chief.

"No."

"Route?"

"North," replied J.T. "Russia, then Alaska."

The chief rubbed his stubbly chin.

"It's early April, still cold..." he said. "We'll take the Buff."

"Really?" said J.T., surprised. "I thought we pieced that one together."

"We did," responded the chief. "It is just about new. Both engines are fresh, the anti-ice works, and it has a celestial bubble and a good HF radio."

But J.T. had stopped listening to the chief. He was looking down the Shangri-La valley to the hole. A DC-3 had just shot through it. J.T. looked at his watch: it was 10:45. This aircraft was off schedule; it should be headed to the depot. That could only mean trouble. As it flew closer, he could see one engine was shut down and trailing smoke.

The chief turned to see what had grabbed J.T.'s attention.

"Shit," he said and ran for a converted Willy's jeep that acted as a makeshift fire truck. J.T. was a step behind him. The chief fired up the engine as J.T. jumped in. They raced toward the end of the runway. The Indian medics were right behind them in their ambulance, also a converted jeep.

The DC-3 braked hard and shut down the operating engine as it rolled out. The jeeps caught it as the engine sputtered to a halt. J.T. and the chief each grabbed a CO_2 fire extinguisher, going straight to the smoldering engine and spraying it to ensure that it was out and would not re-flash. The medics went straight into the aircraft, not waiting to check that the fire was out.

They emerged with an unconscious Danny boy, who was bleeding from multiple wounds. Irish followed under his own weight, bleeding profusely from a gash over his left eye and a small caliber gunshot wound to his left shoulder.

"Russell and his men are jammed up bad," he blurted out. "Japs have them pinned down at B-5 near Lashio. Half of them are trapped in the hanger at mid-field. The other half are in the tree line to the northeast."

J.T. held pressure on Irish's head wound, trying to stop the flow of blood.

"We got the shit shot out of us on short final," Irish went on. "Had to go around. We tried kicking out the ammo boxes, but it just made a big mess. That's when Danny got it; I had to get him home. The number two burned but kept running until we cleared the Hump. Sorry, J.T., I made a mess of it."

"You did good, Irish," said J.T. "You did real good. Sit down here on this stretcher. Chief, get some ammo loaded in the Buff, enough for Russell's boys to hold on, and rig that popgun of yours."

"Aye aye, skipper," the chief snapped off and started for the Buff.

Charles Henry had run up behind the jeeps with Trey.

"Have my aircraft loaded with small arms ammo too," he yelled after the chief. "It sounds like they will need more than one load. Trey, go man up our bird and run a checklist down to engine start."

"Yes sir," Trey responded and ran to the flight line.

Irish was talking through spikes of adrenaline.

"Come in from the east, short field landing," he told Charles Henry. "The Japs are on the southern and western perimeter. The hanger is in the middle."

Another medic had relieved J.T. of holding pressure on Irish's wound. J.T. stood up and pulled Charles Henry by the shoulder.

"What do you think you are doing?" he said. "You don't need to come. I'll take care of this."

Irish continued his adrenaline-hyped orders.

"You'll have to walk out with Russell. Get clear and we will come get you tomorrow."

Charles Henry brushed off J.T.'s grip.

"Bullshit, J.T."

"Look Charles Henry," J.T. began to plead, "I didn't want to say anything but we are going home in fifteen days. The Air Force boys are en route as we speak. Let me do this."

"No, J.T. It will probably take two ships to get one load in there, and you know it."

The two lifelong friends stood toe to toe. J.T. was out of arguments and time. Charles Henry broke the silence.

"I'm not letting you go alone."

J.T. let the statement hang. Charles Henry started for the flight line.

"Okay, Charles Henry, but I'm the primary. You are backup only, got it?"

There was no response as Charles Henry moved for the flight line.

"That's an order, Major," J.T. called out.

Charles Henry snapped off a very military about-face, rendered a perfect salute, and winked.

"Oh yes, sir, I get it."

They both laughed and he continued for the flight line.

"They got triple A, you hear me, J.T., real triple A," Irish yelled, describing anti-aircraft artillery. The medic tried to lay him down on the stretcher.

"I hear you Irish," J.T. responded. "Lie down and listen to the doc. I'll see you tonight."

J.T. bumped into Man-child, who had been standing behind him, looking pale.

"Man-child, where is Jon?"

"He's pre-flighting your go bird, Colonel."

J.T. started for the flight line.

"Come on," he said. "You are going with me in the Buff."

"Yes, sir."

Charles Henry ran down the long flight line for his DC-3. As he ran past J.T.'s go bird, he saw Jon finishing his pre-flight.

"Jon, come with me," he called. "We have an emergency re-assignment."

Jon didn't respond; he just fell into step with Charles Henry.

They were lucky. The aircraft was already loaded for a mission for the next day, with exactly what they needed: small arms ammo, and a lot of it. As they scrambled into the cockpit, Trey looked over his shoulder.

"What's Jon doing here?" he asked.

Charles Henry pulled on his parachute and strapped in.

"You're not going."

"Like hell I'm not," said Trey. "I got you into this."

Charles Henry stopped and turned to his son.

"I would have come anyway. I hid behind you to shield me from your mother. Trey, we go home in fifteen days and – "

Trey raised his hand and stopped him, like his father had done to him so many times before. Charles Henry fell silent.

"I know," he said. "I saw the message. Dad, I have to go, and you know that."

The father looked into the son's eyes. The boy was gone. A man was staring back at him – a reflection of himself in many ways, enough to know that any more argument was wasting time. A stabbing pain filled his heart, a pain that could only be generated by love and the fear of loss. He nodded, a surrender that was much more than mission-specific. It was a relinquishing of influence and control of his son. Jon had remained uncomfortably quiet. He felt like an intruder in a very private conversation.

Finally, Charles Henry turned to him.

"We got it, Jon. Go with the skipper, he's manning up the Buff."

Jon welcomed the escape.

"Okay, Major," he said. "Good luck."

Jon ran at full speed for the Buff and got there just in time to see J.T. and Man-child taxi out of the chocks. The chief, who was manning the fifty in the open door, shrugged and half-waved a salute as they turned for the runway. Jon thought about going back to Charles Henry's bird, but they too were already underway. Trey waved as they taxied by and Jon popped off a perfect salute in return.

As Charles Henry turned onto the runway, J.T. was already roaring down it.

"All the important stuff is done," Trey yelled over the din. "Let's roll."

On the tarmac, Jon stood perfectly still until the second DC-3 disappeared into the hole. He noticed that he was at attention. The hair on the back of his neck stood up.

Chapter 30

Ambush
25 March 1942

Captain Russell had his troops hastily dig in on the perimeter of drop zone Bravo-5. They had been operating deep in the Burma Theater for three weeks, raiding the Japs in the back echelon and generally wreaking havoc. Obviously, they had stirred up the hornets' nest.

He and Cantrell had operated separately, hooking up for re-supply at Bravo-5 near Lashio, Burma. They had been out of radio contact for the three weeks and had not realized how thin the Allied lines had become recently. The Allies were obviously bugging out of Burma. Cantrell and Russell had decided to re-supply and beat feet to China until the dust settled.

At some point in their withdrawal, they had gone from hunter to hunted. The Japanese commander had been disciplined, trailing them patiently, and then striking when they were most vulnerable, during re-supply. To make things worse, the Japanese had disrupted the re-supply. They were low on ammunition, desperately low. By the amount of fire that the DC-3 had taken, Russell figured that at least a reinforced battalion was on the other side of this airfield.

Cantrell's troops had drawn the short straw and were going to offload the supplies. They were still in the hanger, waiting, when the Japanese attacked, driving off the DC-3. Cantrell had wisely ordered his men to hold their fire during the re-supply effort. His ammo was low and he did not want to give away his position.

The airfield at DZ Bravo-5 was a cleared circle, with two equal-length gravel runways running north-south and east-west. The runways intersected at their center; the affect from the air was to make a perfect cross, like those worn by the Knights Templar during the Crusades. The hanger was located in the northeast sector near the intersection.

Lieutenant Colonel Togo's plan had been to flank Cantrell's Raiders to the north and south in a classic pincer maneuver. His scouts reported a deep river to the north, preventing a northern thrust. His scouts also reported that the Raiders' entire force was on the eastern perimeter tree line. They had returned to the main force before Cantrell moved his company into the hanger.

The Japanese commander decided to split his force anyway, sending a southern pincer to remain under the jungle cover. The second force, he would send straight across the field to take the hanger.

Tactically, he decided to use the hanger as a blind; he would send his troops in a column and have them try to keep the hanger between the Raiders and themselves, to shield their movement. The southern force would attack if the northern one was seen and received fire from the Raiders. According to the scouts, the Raiders were not in tactical position. If they could be taken by surprise, it would be a short fight.

The Japanese commander was about to move when the DC-3 arrived, changing everything. He did not want the Raiders to be re-supplied, so he directed withering fire at the DC-3 to drive it off. With the element of surprise gone, he had to redeploy his troops immediately.

The scouts reported that only a road had to be crossed to attack the southern flank, and that the Raiders, thinking they were safe, had left the flank exposed. He sent a company to the south, at double-time, to cross the road before the Raiders could redeploy. Then he sent the northern company to take the hanger.

He ordered the simultaneous attack to begin immediately. The hanger company would uncover first and draw the attention of the Raiders, allowing the southern pincer to cover the ground. Once his men took the hanger, they could direct fire on the tree line. They would be his anvil; the southern company, sweeping from the Raiders rear, would be the hammer. They would also prevent the Raiders' escape. His main force, consisting of two infantry companies and an anti-aircraft company, would provide cover fire from the southwest perimeter.

Togo's plan would meet with total disaster for two reasons. First, the hanger was already occupied by Cantrell's men. Sergeant Major Menzies had positioned his men and maintained a watch on the tree line. The side of the hanger that faced the Japanese troops had ten windows. He had positioned four men at each window – two squatting below the window and one on each side. All forty of his men were well hidden.

The Japanese broke cover in a column, rushing the hanger at double-time. They were wonderfully disciplined, maintaining their formation perfectly.

Major Cantrell calmed his men by slowly, clearly repeating, "Hold your fire... hold your fire..."

Quickly, the entire Japanese company was exposed. Cantrell continued to let them close, unmolested. His men were visibly uncomfortable when the lead element reached 20 feet.

At 10 feet, Cantrell gave the order: "Fire!"

The Raiders opened fire with a virtual hail of lead.

The Japanese had been at a full run in their column formation, allowing the Raiders to concentrate their fire with a devastating effect. A third of the company fell in the first volley. Before they could reverse direction, another third fell as the Raiders emptied their magazines.

Togo was so shocked by the sudden carnage that he delayed the order for cover fire. When he finally gave it, his troops dutifully fired at Russell's men as they had been previously ordered. By the time Togo redirected fire to the hanger, Cantrell's men had reloaded and were picking off the survivors as they reversed and ran in full-fledged panic for the cover of the jungle.

The second reason for disaster was that Gunnery Sergeant Paillou had felt exposed on the southern flank even before the DC-3 had been shot up. He asked Captain Russell for permission to take a squad of five men, three armed with Browning Automatic Rifles, or BARs, and cover the southern flank. He had them positioned in the tree line, covering the road, when the shooting started.

Gunny issued one order to his men: "Hand grenades first, two per man, then fire for effect. Cue on me."

The Japanese southern unit was moving at a rapid pace. The company commander thought he was late, thanks to the firefight already under way, so he did not take normal precautions and pushed across the open road. Halfway across, he caught sight of something arcing out of the tree line, and five more following in close order. It was the last thing he would ever see.

The twelve fragmentation grenades tore into the hammer company. The troops that were not ripped by shrapnel were stunned by the concussion. They stood, flat-footed and disoriented, as the BARs raked them. Again, a panicked and unorganized retreat ensured maximum casualties.

The Japanese troops had been so surprised in both cases that they hardly got off a shot. Japanese society is highly structured, with its army being hyper structured, and thus does not flex well when the original plan comes apart. Had the Japanese set a fire line and re-attacked, they could have easily overwhelmed the six Marines.

While they wasted time establishing communications with Battalion, requesting further orders, Russell reinforced Paillou's squad with an additional twenty men. The second Japanese charge was repelled more ferociously than the first. After it failed, both sides dug in and the forward edge of the battle area stabilized.

The battalion commander became so enraged during a staff meeting that he had the Sergeant of the Scouts summoned. As the Sergeant stood stiffly at attention, Togo drew his Samauri sword and decapitated him. His spattered staff got the point.

Even though almost a third of his troops were casualties, Togo still outnumbered the Raiders at least two to one. Of that, he was certain. He squatted over a map of the tactical situation. He had lost the initiative; his surprise attack had only surprised him. Not only had Lieutenant Colonel Togo lost the initiative – he had also lost face.

The two DC-3s were approaching LZ Bravo-5 20 knots over redline airspeed.

J.T. picked up the microphone.

"LZ Bravo-Five, LZ Bravo-Five, American One in the clear, how copy? Over."

In the clear meant no code. J.T. knew the Raiders were coming out of the bush and wouldn't have any code books. Russell answered immediately.

"This is Raider One, American say posit?"

"Ten mikes until overhead, say your situation?"

"Hot, damn hot! I've got half my unit pinned down in the hanger. Ammo critical."

"Roger that, Raider, American is inbound with two."

"Copy, American, come in from the east, taxi straight into the hanger, we will provide cover. If we can surprise them, this might work."

Lieutenant Colonel Togo had to re-evaluate the tactical situation. He knew that they had to be low on ammunition; the DC-3 crew had tried very hard to get some to them, even after taking heavy fire. He also had half of the Raiders pinned down in the hanger.

It would be a moonless night. If the Raiders held on until darkness, they would melt into the jungle. He must draw the last of their fire and overrun them now. If they escaped, his humiliation would be complete.

As he contemplated and formulated a new plan, the presence of his communications officer broke Togo's concentration.

Without looking up, he grunted, "Speak."

Lieutenant Sachi Ishihiro, UCLA class of 1939, bowed deeply.

"Colonel-san, we have intercepted communications. Two more cargo planes are coming."

"Direction?"

"From the east at low altitude."

Togo nodded. "Set all available anti-aircraft guns and automatic weapons for barrage fire when they attempt to land."

J.T. got a tally on the field, then transmitted, "American One is in, Two orbit east."

Trey acknowledged, "Two."

American One dropped to the tree tops. J.T. called for the landing checks and was configured at a half-mile out.

He transmitted for Russell, "Half-mile out."

The Raiders put up what cover fire they could. Ominously, the Japanese didn't answer.

Instead, they waited. When Lieutenant Ishihiro heard the engines of the DC-3, he gave the order to open fire. Bullets slammed into the DC-3 as it cleared the tree line. There were so many tracers in the air that it looked like a snowstorm.

The heavy rounds hit all over the aircraft. The instrument panel exploded, the right front windscreen spider-webbed, J.T.'s side windscreen shattered. He jammed on full power, snapped on a hard turn to the right, and made for the tree line to the north.

He transmitted, "I'm off, I'm off."

Tracers continued to hit the Buff all over as J.T. fled. Charles Henry watched from 1,500 feet.

"Now's our chance, Trey," he said. "Gear down full flaps." He jammed the mixture knobs to auto rich and the props up to 2,600 RPM for landing, and pushed the nose over violently making a play for the deck.

"We'll sneak in while they're hammering J.T.," he said.

Then he transmitted, "Two's in."

The Japanese communication officer redirected the guns to the east.

J.T. was fighting to control the Buff and trying to get small.

"Get the gear! Man-child, raise the damn gear!"

He looked over at Man-child and saw him grasping at his neck. Dark red blood oozed between his fingers. A small caliber bullet had torn into his throat, piercing his carotid artery. Their eyes met for a soft moment. J.T. could see in that short glimpse, the young man's life draining away. Man-child struggled, weakening rapidly. He released the wound and raised the gear handle with both hands. As he did so, blood spurted as though from a parted hydraulic line. He sat back in his seat and died.

The Japanese anti-aircraft artillery gunner saw the second DC-3 diving for the runway. He swung his gun perfectly and began to fire. Lieutenant Ishihiro tried to get the other machine gunners directed to the diving DC-3. It wouldn't be necessary.

The expert gunner walked the heavy-caliber, high-explosive shells from the left engine down the nacelle and ripped into the wing root. The fuel cell ruptured by the shells was ignited by the disintegrating engine. The tank exploded. The wing spar, already weakened by the direct hits from the gunner, failed and the left wing shed. With the right wing producing normal lift and the left wing separated, the doomed DC-3 snap-rolled left. The centrifugal force threw Trey into his father's lap.

"Dad!"

"Sorry, son."

The DC-3 impacted the ground, 40 degrees nose down and inverted, erupting into a huge orange and black fireball.

J.T., now out of the fire zone, had begun a climb when Captain Russell's voice seared into his brain.

"American Two is down, American Two is down."

J.T. cranked on a hard left turn and saw the funeral pyre. He knew the answer, but asked anyway.

"Survivors?"

"No chance, American. Sorry."

J.T. hammered at what was left of the glare shield.

"Damn, damn, damn!"

Before his grief could even take hold, the spider-webbed right windscreen imploded, and again he was in a fight for survival. The aircraft shuddered and buffeted uncontrollably. With the windshield out, the aerodynamics of the aircraft, already compromised by the damage of multiple hits, just wouldn't keep the aircraft flying. They began a descent into the trees.

J.T. leveled the wings and went to emergency power. The chief, feeling the aircraft fighting for survival, went forward. Red fluid was swirling around the cockpit. He thought it was hydraulic fluid until he glanced right, and recoiled at the sight of Man-child's lifeless body. The noise was deafening.

"Jesus, skipper," he shouted. "What's going on?"

"We won't fly long with that windscreen out, Chief."

"Hang on, skipper."

The chief disappeared back into the cargo bay. He frantically searched for something, what he didn't know, and then he saw it. Ripping the flat metal lid off one of the ammo boxes, he rushed back into the cockpit.

"Get slow, skipper."

"We can't get much slower, Chief."

The chief struggled to get the lid sideways out the opening where the windscreen had been. He successfully got it out, then turned it flat and pulled it flush against the outside of the window frame, sealing the hole. He held on to the handles with all his might.

The buffeting stopped. J.T. regained control and started a climb.

"Hang on, Chief."

J.T. slipped out of his seat and kicked a slat out of the radio rack. He handed it to the chief, who slid it under the lid's handle, letting the ends grab the inside of the window frames to hold it in place. The chief kicked out another slat and slipped it into place to reinforce the first.

The radio came alive again.

"Abort, abort, abort, this is undoable American, return to base, I say again RTB."

J.T. responded in a guttural, primordial voice.

"Negative, we're not done yet by a long shot."

The voice unnerved Ishihiro, who was still listening in.

J.T. pulled the chief close, pointing out the window.

"You see that point right there?

"Yeah, I see it."

"Go rig that pop gun," he ordered.

"It's rigged, skipper. I'll go get on the intercom."

The chief set up the .50 caliber machine gun, loaded it, turned on the intercom system and got a check.

"ICS check."

"I got you loud and clear," J.T. responded.

"I got you the same, skipper," said the chief. "Give me a nice, 20-degree angle of bank turn directly over the top. I'll get them sons of bitches."

J.T. trimmed the aircraft as best he could, then set up for a low pass. He flew a crescent-shaped pass, approaching from behind the Japs. They didn't expect it.

"Standby, Chief. Ten seconds out."

"Standing by, skipper."

"Okay, let them have it."

The chief started hammering away with the fifty. His priority was the Jap AAA gun; he held a four-second steady stream on it when it began to fire. He won. His deadly fire killed the gunner and all his loaders, even resulting in some secondary explosions.

They set up and made multiple runs, the chief firing his fifty like a man possessed. With 100 knots of wind across the barrel, the gun stayed nice and cool. He ran four box magazines of ammunition through it before switching to grenades. J.T. got in on the payback too; with the aircraft trimmed up hands off and the side windscreen shot out, he simply pulled the pin and dropped grenades on the Jap position. Between the two of them, they tossed eighty grenades on top of the Japanese troops. They made multiple attacks, always from different directions.

The machine gunners kept guessing wrong but even so, the small arms found their mark occasionally.

The chief came forward.

"All right, skipper, we got a bunch of the bastards, but it is still damn hot down there. Now what?"

J.T. started wiggling out of his parachute.

"Here," he said, handing the parachute to him. "We are going to drop it in. Get Man-child's and yours off too. Put four big ammo boxes in a cargo net, then strap the parachute to it. I'll call the drop and roll up on a wing to help get it out the door."

"Aye, aye, skipper."

J.T. transmitted on the radio, "Raider, where do you need it the most?"

Captain Russell was still on the radio.

"We need it most in the hanger, but you won't make it. Recommend RTB."

"Tell your boys to get their heads down," replied J.T.

Ishihiro lay dead. The gunners, hearing the chatter, set up for the east again.

J.T. streaked out of the north, pointed straight at the open end of the hanger. The DC-3 was barely 50 feet off the ground and doing 180 knots. Flat on his back, the chief leaned against the fuselage on the opposite side of the door with his feet on the crates and his hand on the parachute's D-ring.

"Stand by for drop," J.T. called on the ICS. He rolled up on the left wing slightly. "Stand by... stand by... drop!"

The chief simultaneously kicked out the crates and pulled the D-ring to activate the parachute. The chute popped open, decelerating the ammo crates. It wasn't a soft landing, but the crates held together. The placement was perfect; the crates slid right into the hanger.

J.T. cranked on a hard turn, egressing over Russell's men. He was in and out before the Japs could focus their fire. He got back on the radio.

"Raider, we've got two more chutes. Where do you want them?"

"On me," transmitted Russell.

"Roger, get your heads down."

They dropped the last two with the same precision as the first. The chief's voice crackled over the ICS.

"Hey, skipper, I still have some firecrackers back here. What do you say we use them up?"

"Yeah," agreed J.T. "Let's use them all."

They made two more devastating runs, the chief's fifty spitting death along the tree line. As they made their last run, they could see the Raiders' guns coming back to life.

"Skipper, I'm Winchester (out of ammunition) back here." The chief's voice sounded metallic and distant. "Let's go home."

J.T. was looking at the funeral pyre of American Two. Small arms rounds were still cooking off, and billowing smoke climbed into the atmosphere.

"Cappy, you hear me?" the chief repeated. "Let's go home."

"Yeah," J.T. nodded to no one. "Home."

He turned the battered DC-3 west and started for the Hump.

"Raider, American is RTB."

"Outstanding job, American, Bravo Zulu (well done), you saved our butts."

J.T. was trying to assess the mess that used to be an aircraft. Most of his instruments were shot out, but he did have the airspeed indicator on his side and the altimeter on Man-child's panel. That would be enough to get them home.

It was a clear, pristine day, spoiled only by a black smear that was now behind them. He knew the way home; he didn't need a compass, but he could only nurse the DC-3 to 11,700 feet. They would have to fly through a pass in the Patkai Range. Fortunately, the weather and the relatively low height of the Patkais would allow their passage into the Assam. The Himalayas would not have been so generous.

His concern turned to the number one engine: it was starting to run rough. The chief popped his head into the cockpit.

"We got a rough runner, Gregg," J.T. said.

"I hear it."

The chief looked at J.T. closely. He never called him Gregg. Then he looked around the cockpit – it looked like a slaughter-house.

"Any of this blood yours, Cappy?"

J.T. looked around in a hypnotic state.

"I don't know."

The chief leaned into the cockpit, looking directly into J.T.'s eyes. He was not happy with what he saw; they seemed unfocused. Quickly, he began to examine J.T. and found fresh, bright red blood.

"Shit, I knew it."

He went back into the cargo bay and came back with a first aid kit, the portable oxygen bottle, and a mask; the cockpit oxygen had been shot up. He pulled out a dagger and cut J.T.'s khaki pants away from the wound in his right thigh. He applied a pressure bandage to stop the bleeding. Next, he put the oxygen mask on J.T. and turned the valve on full.

It wasn't too bad, but J.T. had lost a lot of blood and was showing signs of going into shock. That was the last thing they needed as they approached the pass in the Patkais. Chief disap-peared again into the back. He came forward with a blanket and a thermos of coffee that had miraculously survived the day. It was getting cold at altitude. To combat it, he put the blanket across J.T.'s lap and handed him a cup of coffee.

"Here, drink this."

In a few moments, the coffee and oxygen had revived J.T.'s senses. He pulled up the mask to yell to the chief.

"How did you know?"

"Because you were acting goofy, now put that mask back on."

As they entered the pass, the number one engine started running rougher, and their airspeed began to decay slightly.

"Chief, time to lighten the load."

"Aye, aye."

The chief went back and threw out everything that he could. Guns, ammo cans, tie-down chains, food, water, spare parts and tools, everything not nailed down. He went back forward.

"I stripped everything I could," he said, looking over at Manchild and hesitated. "What about him, skipper?"

"No! We bring him home."

They continued into the pass. The ridgeline was in sight.

"Come on, baby," J.T. muttered. "Hold together ten more minutes."

Just before the ridge, the number one engine sputtered and died.

"We gonna make it skipper?" yelled the chief over the wind noise.

"We have to, Chief!"

"I know we have to, but are we gonna?"

"It's going to be close, Gregg."

The DC-3 began to mush toward the ridge.

"We ain't gonna make it, Cappy!"

J.T. pulled up his oxygen mask.

"Stand by the flaps, I'm going to try and pop us over the ridge."

J.T. flew straight at the lip of the ridge; they were getting way too close for comfort. Just before an assured impact, he yelled.

"Full flaps, now!"

Chief threw down the flap handle, praying they would work, while J.T. pulled hard on the yoke.

"Ho-ly-y-y-y sh-i-i-t-t-t," screamed the chief as they hopped over the ridge.

His relief was short-lived. They had cleared the ridge but were too slow to maintain level flight. The DC-3's nose fell through the horizon; the aircraft was in heavy stall buffet. Fortunately, the back side of the ridge dropped off steeply into the Assam. J.T. relaxed pressure on the yoke and let the nose plummet into the valley. As the airspeed built up again, he regained control.

"Put the flaps back up," he told the chief.

They accelerated as they continued a now-controlled descent into the Assam Valley. Passing below 10,000 feet, J.T. handed the chief the oxygen mask to stow.

"When are we really going home, skipper?" asked the chief. "I've about had enough fun for one war."

J.T. looked over at Man-child, his young face spattered with dry blood. It had transformed after drying on his cherub face, dark and crusty now. He looked more like a boy who had played in the mud than a man who had died in combat.

"Some of us won't be going home at all," he muttered, barely audible.

J.T. looked out at the shutdown engine to hide his emotion and began to weep. The chief squeezed his shoulder, then slipped into the back to let him grieve in private.

That night, the Raiders made their escape by turning the tables on their Japanese foe. After holding off several futile Samurai charges during the day, the Raiders counter-attacked as soon as it got dark.

Cantrell's men crept unnoticed out of the hanger and rendezvoused with Russell's company. After making preparations for a rapid withdrawal, Gunny Paillou led an attack across the road on the depleted southern Japanese flank.

Again, the Japanese didn't anticipate. Gunny crossed, undetected, with two squads of twenty men. They performed a wheeling maneuver and attacked the unprotected flank of the Japanese, even getting five of their men behind their firing line. The Japs, thinking they were in danger of being surrounded, withdrew again in disarray.

Lieutenant Colonel Togo redeployed his troops and counter-attacked the hanger. A fierce firefight erupted across the airfield. His troops took the hanger and reported it empty. He suddenly realized that all return fire had stopped. He ordered a ceasefire, and the airfield fell totally silent.

After crushing the southern flank, the Raiders had reversed and immediately withdrawn, forging the river to the north again, doing the opposite of what Togo had expected. He'd thought that he had them contained and would finish them off at first light.

Togo deployed his scouts but already knew what they would find: nothing. He had failed; the Raiders had beaten him. His disgrace was complete. Saying nothing to his staff he retired to his tent, drew the sword that was still stained with the blood of his own man, and committed hara-kiri

Date time group: 0300 ZULU 8 MAY 1942
From: COMMANDER IN CHIEF
To: COMMANDER SEVEN ALPHA
Subject: BRAVO ZULU
Classification: TOP SECRET SCI/EYES ONLY COM7ALPHA
Text: THE 7ALPHA CREW OF SHANGRI-LA ARE TRUE HEROES. YOU DID MORE TO WIN THE WAR THAN YOU CAN IMAGINE. IT ALLOWED US TO HANG ON. ADMITTEDLY BY OUR FINGERNAILS. YESTERDAY U.S. NAVY ENGAGED PORT MORESBY INVASION FORCE IN CORAL SEA. STOPPED THEM IN THEIR TRACKS. TACTICALLY A DRAW. STRATEGICALLY A HUGE VICTORY. JAPS STOPPED FOR THE FIRST TIME. TIDE HAS TURNED. YOUR COMMANDS SACRIFICES HAVE ALLOWED USA TO REGROUP. WE WILL WIN. JOB WELL DONE.
F.D.R. SENDS

Chapter 31

Homecoming
8 May 1942

J.T. awoke from a sleep so deep that he was disoriented. The number one engine was shut down. Where was he – the Assam, China, still in Burma? As the fog of unconsciousness lifted, he saw Guadalupe Peak float by in the background. "Texas. Almost home."

He got up and limped forward to the cockpit. Jon was acting as captain with the chief riding shotgun.

"It's a little quiet out there, Jon."

"Yep," replied Jon. "You want it?"

"Nope."

Jon shifted in his seat to face J.T.

"Chief and I decided to press on to Dallas. Do you want to divert into El Paso? We are abeam Guadalupe."

"Your ship, your call." J.T. looked Jon square in the eyes. "But if you're asking my opinion, I vote with the chief. Let's go home."

The chief vigorously nodded his agreement. "Yeah, home."

The DC-3 flew a perfect single-engine approach to Dallas Love Field.

"Love Field", thought J.T. The irony was sickening to him now. That is, until they rolled out on the runway and he saw all the families gathered and waiting. *"Maybe it's appropriate after all"*, he thought. There were no banners of celebration, just a single American Flag fluttering over the group.

The worn-out DC-3 pulled up to the subdued gathering. Jon shut down the number two engine as twenty-nine gaunt, Seven

Alpha men and one ugly dog emerged. They were thinner, older, and sadder after the five long months – five calendar months, a short duration in measured time that held the experience and sorrow of 1,000 years.

J.T. sat transfixed by the fluttering flag, thinking of Charles Henry, Trey, Man-child and Bluto, wondering: was it worth it? The guilt consumed him. It sat on his shoulders with the weight of the Himalayas, holding him, crushing him into his seat.

He felt a hand touch his shoulder.

"Cappy."

He looked up to see, as always, the chief.

"Yeah, Gregg?" he answered feebly.

"Let's get out of here. It's getting hot."

Gregg held his hand out and J.T. took it, letting the chief pull him out of his self-imposed purgatory. He steadied J.T. and guided him out the door. J.T. winced with embarrassment as the chief helped him onto the tarmac. The Doc had said he would probably never walk normally again, but his wounds were nothing in comparison to what he'd seen. And his physical wounds were nothing in comparison to the anguish he would feel for the rest of his life.

The families had gathered at the door in a similar mood of collective guilt, one that they had to admit to themselves. They were glad that it had not been their loved ones who had not returned. Their tears were tears of relief, not joy or celebration.

The crowd instinctively opened, parting to reveal Charles Henry's family: Laura, David, Kaitlyn and little William. The crushing weight sat back on J.T.'s shoulders and his knees began to buckle. The chief subtly held him steady with one arm, while he hugged his own wife and six kids with the other.

J.T. made eye contact with his wife Kate, who was standing with the Brennans. Her eyes buoyed him like a line thrown to a drowning man. He walked toward them, holding her eyes.

Kate saw his deep pain and wanted to cry, but knew she had to be strong for him. She also knew that the dreams would return, and this time they would be much worse. She would be there for him, and he was strong; he would be back, but she could sense that he would never be the same. J.T. broke eye contact with his wife and, with a twinge of shame, met Laura's.

"Laura, I ah…I'm … we, all of us will take care of – "

Laura touched her finger to his lips.

"I know, J.T., I know."

There was a long silence while Laura gathered herself. She looked down for a few moments, then raised her head to him with a tear rolling down her cheek.

"Were you there?"

J.T. nodded, unable to speak.

After another short pause she asked, "Was it quick?"

"Yes," was all J.T. could manage to croak out.

It was the last time she would ever speak of it again, to anyone. She gently nodded and slowly turned to go back to the car. Her one question, a question that had burned in her heart and raged through her dreams, had been answered.

David stood fast and broke the silence.

"Captain Dobbs?"

"Yes, son."

"Will you teach me to fly?"

Laura looked at her seventeen-year-old son briefly and resumed her walk to the car. Jon, Irish and Thumper had walked up; Irish spoke first.

"I'll teach you, kid."

"Me too," added Jon.

J.T. glanced at both men, then met David's dark brown eyes.

"We all will, David."

David's brown eyes held J.T.'s, riveted with determination.

The same brown eyes, brimming with tears, now gazed upon pictures in a scrapbook as David Brennan sat in the captain seat of an American Airlines DC-10. It had been forty-three years.

The scrapbook held a lifetime of tears, tears of joy and pain: his father and brother at Shangri-La; his own winging as a naval aviator at NAS Pensacola; a grizzled Gunny Paillou at his commissioning, hero pictures of himself standing in front of an F-6 Hell Cat during WWII, on board the USS *Suwannee*. David stopped at a wedding picture of himself and his bride under an arch of swords. The arch was formed by eight squadron mates in dress whites, holding their swords aloft. Five would not survive that war; two more would fall in Korea.

The First Officer pointed to the wedding picture.

"Geez, Dad – how old were you and Mom?"

"Nineteen. We had to grow up fast, especially after you showed up."

Corey flipped another page. "That's you and Uncle William – where was that?"

David looked at the picture. "On board *Boxer*, off the North Korean coast, 1952. We were flying Able Dogs."

The young Flight Engineer was looking over their shoulders.

"What's an Able Dog, Grandpa – I mean, Captain?"

"It's an AD-One Sky Raider, Willie-Boy, a flying dump truck and attack aircraft extraordinaire."

David flipped through some American Airlines pictures. There was Jon as a brand new captain, standing with him in front of a DC-6. Next was his own brand-new captain photo, standing with his brother William in front of a Lockheed Electra. Then, a group shot in front of a Boeing 707, Irish's last flight, and the same group standing in front of another Boeing 707 for J.T.'s last flight.

David flipped another page.

"Well, well, well. Look who's here," he said, smiling.

It was a picture of Corey, kneeling in front of a McDonnell F-4B Phantom II.

"Ooh Rah, Semper Fi!" Corey rasped out like a drill instructor.

"Yeah, yeah," muttered David. "How the hell did the son and nephew of real naval aviators end up in the corps?"

"Thumper," smiled Corey.

"Thumper?"

"Yep, he told me at a barbecue at our house, after slipping me a beer: why go second class when you can be the best?"

David shook his head. "I should have known."

"Dad, seriously. Tell me, how did you get my knucklehead," Corey pointed aft to the FE with his thumb, "hired at 19 years old?"

David had flipped to the last page of the scrapbook, which held one eight-by-ten-inch picture: his father and brother standing, arms around each other, in front of a DC-3 in Shangri-La. His response was far away and melancholy.

"C.R. owed me a favor."

He stared at the photo for a long time, then closed the book. He stared out into the stars, replaying the last forty-three years like a silent movie in his mind. It had been an amazing ride, a glorious life. And now here he was, not only with his son but his grandson. How could a man ask for more?

But even with his family around him, he felt hollow, unbalanced. A part of him had been taken forty-three years earlier. A part, no matter how he tried, that could not be filled. He had tried vengeance; it had burned with ferocity. He had tried love through his family; it had and still burned with intensity. But the emptiness was always there, just below the surface.

The feel-good fools of the day urged acceptance. Acceptance! David scoffed at these New Age morons. What did they know? They had never risked anything; how could they possibly lecture on life? For him there had been a single solace: flight.

David felt whole in the air, complete. He didn't really understand why. Perhaps the mental demands kept him focused on the present, temporarily suspending the past.

The flashing of a yellow, master caution light on the instrument panel brought him back from his thoughts to the task at hand. First Officer Charles Henry Brennan IV, also known as Corey, reached up and pressed the light to extinguish it. He looked over at Captain David B. Brennan; his father was calmly winding the clock. Corey smiled as David turned to Flight Engineer William G. Brennan II.

"What do you have back there, Mr Engineer?"

Willy had been tapping his fingers, again lost in the new wave rock and roll of The Police. He saw his grandfather turn around and figured something was up. As he pulled the Walkman headset off, he pivoted his seat to face the FE panel and was startled out of his nonchalance.

"Shit, Grandpa – I mean Captain – we've got a problem here!"

The oil pressure gauge for engine number two was at zero. With no oil pressure on the main bearings of the GE-CF6-50C jet engine, they would heat up, then lose their shape until the axial flow internal compressor and turbine sections locked up. When they did, the force of all that mass going from 11,000 revolutions per minute to zero would shatter the engine. A catastrophic engine failure was like a bomb going off, scattering engine parts like shrapnel. It could easily bring down a jumbo jet.

Willy searched frantically for his DC-10 operating manual in his kit bag.

"We've got no oil pressure in engine number two, he yelled. "I'm getting out the engine shutdown checklist!"

David looked at the oil temperature gauge on his center panel. It was normal. He slid his captain's seat aft on its track.

"Hang on there, Junior," he said and turned to his son. "You've got the aircraft, Corey."

"I got it, boss," Corey responded.

David stood up and leaned over behind his grandson to better see his panel. Willy was rapidly flipping through the pages of the "Abnormal" section of his DC-10 operating manual, looking for the correct checklist.

David gave him a little pinch on the shoulder to get his attention, then reached over him and tapped the oil pressure gauge. The needle instantly jumped from zero to the green band.

"AC lies, DC dies," he said, straightening up.

Willy looked confused. "What?"

David stretched and put his hand on the young FE's shoulder.

"AC-powered gauges stick at their last position when power is interrupted. DC-powered gauges go to zero. There is a loose connection in the gauge."

"Oh. Sorry, sir." Willy nodded, feeling stupid, his cockiness having sustained a temporary setback.

David patted him on the shoulder.

"No need to be. Write up the gauge as intermittent in the aircraft log book."

"Yes sir," the deflated flight engineer responded.

"One more thing, Mr FE, and this is important: first, do no harm!" David winked at Corey, who watched with a large smirk. He had been there, as he knew his father had.

Captain Brennan slipped back into his seat and put his left

foot up on the frame of the bottom edge of his instrument panel. Willy excused himself and went aft to the lavatory.

Corey leaned over.

"Could you imagine him, married with kids, charging off to war?"

David laughed.

"He'd do fine if he had to. We did our job so he could be a kid a little longer."

Corey looked out the forward windscreen at the stars.

"Do you envy him?"

"Me?" said David. "No. No way! I was never more alive than when I was jousting with Zeros or MiGs. I was never more fulfilled then when my babies were born. Willy-Boy is still just cruising. His life is before him; he just doesn't know it yet."

Corey nodded.

"Yeah, I know. Even he has some surprises in him," he said, as if thinking aloud.

"How's that?" asked David.

"I got a call from the commanding officer of the guard unit in Saint Louis. Willy has applied for a pilot slot."

"Lindbergh's own flying F-4 Phantom II's?"

"That's a fact, Dad. The CO is an old American Airlines bubba; he knows our family history. Said we've done enough and asked if I wanted it pulled."

"What did you tell him?" David asked, trying to hide a slight hint of concern in his voice.

"I told him every generation has to pull their weight. If Willy has chosen fighters, and he is qualified, so be it."

David looked out to the stars. Their infinity drew him as much now as the first time he gazed upon them from a cockpit. The light of the first day of the rest of his life began to creep from the horizon. It was a trite, irritating phrase that he just could not shake from his mind, like hearing a dumb song on the radio early in the day and playing it over and over again in your mind. Lost in contemplation, he finally spoke.

"That was the right thing to do, son."

The shimmering DC-10 rolled onto Runway One Seven Center at the DFW Metroplex in the early morning sun. David thought back to that day forty-three years earlier and how much things had changed and yet, stayed the same.

"You still got it," said Corey as David eased the nose gear onto the runway and deployed the thrust reverses, "for an old dude."

"Well, maybe," he replied, "but I don't need it anymore. It's your turn now. Don't get too comfy, though, because Junior back there is breathing down your neck."

The tower controller broke the conversation.

"American One, you are clear to cross Runway One Seven Right, switch to ground on one two one point six five."

"Clear to cross the right, point six five," answered Corey.

The majestic aircraft crossed the inboard runway, turning onto the taxiway as the cockpit conversation continued.

"Are you going to bid captain now, Corey?"

"I start school on the Super Eighty next month," he replied as he switched radio frequencies.

"Good," replied his father. "I always liked Douglas best."

Again the radio crackled to life.

"American One, you are clear to taxi to Two Echo via Kilo."

"Kilo," Corey responded, again picking up the cockpit conversation. "You mean McDonnell Douglas."

"Still Douglas to me, Boy."

Willy interrupted from the FE seat.

"Hey, look at that."

Two fire trucks had formed an arch of water in front of them. As they passed under the liquid arch, their gate came into view. Both sides of the parking area were lined with maintainers and ground personnel, standing at attention.

At the head of the line on the captain's side was an ancient mechanic in an obviously dated uniform, rendering a salute. He was legendary to the men on the tarmac. He was the chief, an icon. Both young and old mechs had heard the WWII stories of how he had kept battle-damaged aircraft in the air as if by magic. But more than that, they knew to a man that he had climbed into those same aircraft and fought the Japanese like a pit bull.

David returned the old man's salute and the DC-10 glided to a stop, its engines shutting down as the brakes brought the giant aircraft to a final halt.

"After-parking checklist," called out David for the last time.

Willy called off each item as the captain and first officer responded while gathering up their personal gear.

He then added, "That's it, Captain."

"Now it's Grandpa, Willy-Boy."

David slid back his seat and released his harness, then stood up. He leaned over his seat, pulling a well-worn and oft-repaired kit bag holding his manuals from the left side. He turned to Corey and dropped the heavy bag in his lap.

"Here," he said. "I won't be needing this anymore."

Corey rubbed his hand over the black leather as David left the cockpit. Stamped in gold on top of the well-oiled and preserved bag were the words, "Captain C.H. Brennan, Jr., American Airlines."

"That thing sure is old," quipped Willy.

Corey didn't look up. "It was my grandfather's."

After the last of the passengers had filed out, the three American Airlines pilots walked up the jet bridge. A large group of family and friends was waiting in the terminal. Kids, grandkids, nieces, nephews, and old friends had gathered. David hugged his wife of forty-three years; she still made his heart pound. He looked up and saw his brother William and sister Kaitlyn. Off to the side, standing together, were Jon and Irish.

Corey and Willy had stopped at the doorway. Willy spied Irish standing with Jon and an incredible blonde about thirty-five years old.

"How does that old goat Irish stay alive?" he laughed. "What is he, 100?"

"Nope," said his father. "A spry 89, we think."

"Wow, that wife of his is a babe," said Willy. "Is it true he's a bazillionaire? How did he do it?"

"Stock market. He bought low and sold high. He also took financial care of your grandpa's family after 1942."

"Man, life sure is a crapshoot."

"That," said Corey, "is the smartest thing you've said since we left Hawaii. Let's join your Grandpa."

As they joined David, the crowd separated to reveal an elderly woman sitting patiently in a wheelchair on the perimeter. Kate was with her; they lived together, now that J.T. was gone.

David thought of J.T. as he walked toward his mother. He had never gotten over what happened at Shangri-La; he was always a little sad – it was something that they had shared through life.

David knelt in front of the strongest woman he had ever met, the 84-year-old matriarch of the family, Laura.

"Forty-three years," she said. "Any regrets, David?"

"Just one," he said as his eyes misted over. "I wish I had flown with Dad and Trey."

She touched his cheek gently, like only a mother can.

"You did, Davy, every day."

Epilogue

Project Seven Alpha is a novel about a historical event. It is set during the early setbacks of World War II. The novel honors the men and women who stood the line, facing overwhelming odds. While the characters' names are fabricated, the sacrifices they represent are not – except for Ding, a real dog who actually made that very uncomfortable flight by vulture. I came across her story in a newsletter from the Hump Pilots' Association. Ding made it all the way to the USA; unfortunately, her owner perished over the Hump. The term "Screaming American Steel" was borrowed from friend and squadron mate Lieutenant Doug Hora's last letter home. He and the crew of Iron Claw 606 were lost at sea, off the coast of India in 1987.

Acknowledgments

Thank you to my friends, who reviewed the initial manuscript, for insight and guidance.

A special thank you to Peter Coles; also Pen and Sword Books, for taking a chance on a new author and genre.

A very special thank you to my writing mentor, LaVonne Ellis, and editor Susan Econicoff. My parents, Lee and Hertzie, who raised me to believe you could accomplish anything; and my brother, Gregg, and sister, Bunni, for their support.